HORSE
SCENTS

HORSE
SCENTS

Thirteen Short Stories in Search of a Novel

MARC D. HASBROUCK

HORSE SCENTS
THIRTEEN SHORT STORIES IN SEARCH OF A NOVEL

iUniverse books may be ordered through booksellers or by contacting:

*iUniverse
1663 Liberty Drive
Bloomington, IN 47403
www.iuniverse.com
1-800-Authors (1-800-288-4677)*

*ISBN: 978-1-5320-6705-1 (sc)
ISBN: 978-1-5320-6727-3 (e)*

Library of Congress Control Number: 2019901532

Print information available on the last page.

iUniverse rev. date: 02/08/2019

And Allah took a handful of southerly wind, blew His breath over it, and created the horse...

Bedouin Legend

INTRODUCTION

I have been working and reworking, tinkering and tweaking this piece of fiction for years. At least ten or fifteen years, truthfully. As I said, it's fiction. Yes, I made this stuff up. Most of it, anyway. I've made alterations as the years went by to reflect the times, attitudes (mine) and personalities. Sometimes my characters would "speak" to me in the middle of the night. "Hey," one of them might say, "maybe you should have me say this...or that, etc., etc. Or maybe I should do do this." And I listened to them. Granted, I have taken some liberties with reality. Well, actually I took a *lot* of liberties with reality and, perhaps, logic. I repeat, it's fiction...go with the flow. I think it's fair to say, however, that many of you...maybe even *all* of you, my dear readers, have experienced at least one of the types of scenarios and/or characters I've depicted here. People and their quirks, foibles and peccadillos fascinate me. And scare me to death.

In our daily lives, we encounter friends, family, co-workers and neighbors, all with stories to be told. There are those people who want to share everything with the world, hence the popularity of social media; there are those who wish to share nothing at all...the ones who disdain social media. Those people might have the most interesting and intriguing stories of all. They are keeping secrets. There are so many unwritten chapters waiting to be lived. How many truths? How many deceptions?

And don't even get me started on politics. That's a whole other ball of dirty wax.

I have created a series of stories, some intertwine with others, and some stand alone. The threads will all come together at the end. The time frame consists of one year. The stories involve several disparate characters with one common bond: horses. There will be horse scents, horse sense and nonsense in abundance. Pay attention. Look closely. Keep an open mind. You just might see yourself here.

JANUARY

Grade A Gray Day

"The only time you really live fully is from thirty to sixty. The young are slaves to dreams; the old servants of regrets. Only the middle-aged have all their five senses in the keeping of their wits."

Theodore Roosevelt

It was late in the afternoon and the horses were getting restless. The sky, that had been a milky white earlier in the day, was turning a darker gray, becoming heavy with the threat of rain. The horses could sense that it was nearing feeding time. They jostled for position at the battered metal gate leading from the pasture to the stable and their awaiting stalls. Their only instincts now were hunger and impatience, with neither a thought about yesterday nor a care about tomorrow.

Seriously in need of repair, the old stable had a tin roof with corners loosened by years of storms, wind and neglect. A dusty tack room was at one end of the building, nearest the parking area. Its squeaking screen door flapped in the afternoon breeze. The window panes on the main, locked door to the tack room were frosted from the cold and the mist that hung in the air. A wide metal gate, attached to the side of the riding ring nearest the parking area stretched towards the tack room end of the stable and barely made it. A walk-through space, just wide enough for a person but too narrow for horses, enabled boarders to access the stalls without having to open the large gate. The stable had been turned over from one owner to the next for so many years that no one remembered how old the place actually was. It was not a fancy place, for fancy horses or snooty riders. It was a simple stable for people whose hobby happened to be to own a horse or two. "Expensive pets" as many of the boarders laughingly referred to their equine charges and riding them became a once-in-a-while event for most of them. The place was located on the outskirts of a quiet little town more or less thirty miles to the east of Atlanta, as the proverbial crow flies. For that matter, a flock of crows lived in the surrounding woods and could often be heard angrily cawing at each other as they flew in large dark circles over the treetops. Two horse trailers were parked off to the side, nestled in between a cluster of poplars. One trailer had been moved so infrequently that weeds and vines were growing up around its wheels. The short dirt road leading up to the stable's driveway was quietly residential, with six weathered houses, most of which dated back to the 1940s and were in need of repair as much as the stable. The one exception was a well-kept little house directly across from the stable's entrance with a perpetually manicured lawn and perfectly trimmed hedges. Crepe Myrtles, their bare limbs looking even more forlorn on this gray day, lined the driveway. A rustic, wooden sign, "CedarView Stables", was nailed to a fence post at the head of the entry although there was nary a cedar on the entire thirty-five acres. Of the thirty stalls, all but three were occupied. The tall Georgia pines surrounding the pasture leaned and swayed gently in the increasing wind, their creaks and groans adding a sorrowful sound to the already dreary afternoon. Let's set the mood. Cue the soundtrack. Jazz. Always cool, melancholy jazz. And throw in Chris Botti with a plaintive trumpet solo.

It was early January but there were still remnants of holiday decorations hanging on some stall doors: Christmas stockings with their carrots and peppermints long since eaten and forgotten. A hand-scribbled note of season's greetings was still visible tacked on the crude cork bulletin board hanging just outside the tack room door. Another note requesting that someone please feed Flapjack on New Year's Day morning still hung and flapped in the breeze. A very large notice hung dead center on the bulletin board: YOU CAN NEVER CLOSE A GATE TOO MANY TIMES. This note was taken seriously following several occasions of horses getting out due to careless boarders and improperly latched gates. For some reason, whenever a horse or horses *did* manage to get out, they ended up in the front yard of Mrs. Critchley, the widow who lived across the street. She prized her lawn and despised the horses.

The sound of car tires coming down the gentle slope of the gravel driveway alerted the horses to the first arrival in several hours. A Cadillac slowed to a halt in the parking area at one end of the vast riding ring. Jeremy Major paused to listen to one more item on the radio before turning off the engine. Zipping up his jacket, he braced himself for the frigid air, opened his door and stepped out. His breath was visible as he cursed the cold. He pulled his hat further down on his head and slid his hands into very warm gloves. Remy, to everyone who knew him, was co-owner of the stables along with his wife of thirty-five years, Zara. But he was not a horse lover. He had bought the stable to keep Zara occupied and to give her some sense of responsibility. She seriously needed that. His only task was to maintain the facility and, on rare occasion, help feed the horses. During the winter months, and especially on days such as this one, Zara and Remy would bring in all the horses from the pasture and dump their feed. The boarders appreciated this and, unless they notified Zara otherwise, the horses would be put back out again after they had finished eating. A couple of the horses had not seen their owners for weeks.

Remy stood there, surveying the surroundings, as he did almost every day. A large old oak tree bent over the weathered deck that was built into the end of the riding ring, closest to the parking area. A long thin dead limb extended over his head and he made a mental note to have the limb cut and removed before it fell and hurt someone. It was a mental note that he had made several times during the past couple of months and still the limb remained.

Remy was a joyless man. In his early 60s, his craggy face and dour expression made him appear older. He rarely smiled, was rarely friendly, yet always polite. He cared nothing for the horses and even less for most of his boarders. It was rumored amongst the boarders, albeit humorously, that he must suffer from chronic constipation, hence his demeanor and pained expression. Although he *had* been slightly over six feet tall, he was shrinking. At each of the last two of his annual physicals he had been measured close to an inch shorter. Hell, he thought, at this rate in another ten years I'll be a midget. When he stood up straight, one could see that his right shoulder was definitely lower than the other. He had just noticed it one morning while standing in front of the mirror shaving. He worried about that. Well, just damn, he thought to himself. This kinda shit happens when you get old, doesn't it? Well, doesn't it? But what can you do? He thought to himself a lot. He was slender but with just a slight paunch. He didn't like that either, so he did the plank for two minutes every night in the privacy of his home office to tighten those core muscles. His hair had remained shiny black except for a little graying at the temples and, when he was younger…much younger…he had been considered handsome. His once-tight jawline had given way to a dewlap that irritated the hell out of him. Exercises didn't seem to help that. He had been a successful salesman, then promoted to sales manager at an electronics company in Pennsylvania. After being transferred to the Atlanta area eight years ago, Zara began "collecting" horses, as she called it. Considering his almost-constant disposition, the boarders could never understand how he could have been a successful salesman. Being a successful salesman…hmm. Didn't that require a modicum of pleasantness along with a substantial amount of bullshit? After receiving a sizeable inheritance from his now-deceased parents, Remy decided to take an early retirement. There were times when he regretted that decision. Today was one of them.

Zara had unimaginable patience, both with Remy and her horses, all of which took up a dozen of the stalls. Horses were her passion, now that their two daughters were grown and out on their own. Every wall in their home was covered with horse paintings. Horse-themed wall coverings and borders were in the kitchen and in every bathroom. Horse statues, large and small, were on every shelf. Her cell phone ring tone was "Assembly of Buglers", sometimes also called "First Call", the tune played on a bugle prior to practically every horse race. Zara had been a beautiful young lady and aged well. Her long blonde hair was always tightly wrapped as a bun at the back of her head, held by colorful scarves. She had long forgotten the natural color of her hair although she imagined that now it would be gray. At 56, she was 8 years younger that Remy. She had had hopes of becoming a veterinarian and was early in her college years when she became pregnant with her first daughter, thanks to an over amorous Remy and a careless night of wine and marijuana. She elected to put her education and her career on hold. They were still holding.

Remy took a deep breath, sighed and looked around once more. "I'm going to sell this frickin' place," he thought to himself. "Some developer just might be waiting to turn this shit hole into a hundred over-priced houses". This thought had entered his mind at least once a week over the past few years. He never followed through with it, any more than he had followed through having the dead limb cut down.

The sound of another vehicle coming down the driveway awakened him from his private reverie. It was not his wife. Zara and Remy rarely spoke to each other. When they did, it was usually argumentative in nature. Their respective daily calendars kept them apart. Remy was definitely a day person and Zara was a night owl. Each one had forgotten the last time they had been intimate or even had the desire. Zara was very popular at the stable. Remy, not so much. Well, that wasn't totally accurate…or fair. Yes, he was a grump at times. Most times. Yes, he marched around looking as though someone walking directly in front of him had just cut a monstrous fart. Many of the boarders felt there was more to Remy than they could see or hear. There was more to his sourness than he wished to share. And they would be correct.

An old Ford pickup came to a grinding halt next to Remy's Cadillac, throwing up a small cloud of dust which quickly dissipated in the breeze. Amber Givings hopped out, slammed the truck door and called out for her horse. Flapjack was with the group huddling around the pasture gate and he let out a low nicker. Amber was just about the only boarder Remy liked, although he wasn't fond of her boyfriend-du-jour. She always seemed to make such poor choices. Often. She was in her early 20s, a bit overweight by a mere five pounds, neither really attractive nor unattractive, but she was perky and always ready with a cheerful smile. She attended college, hoping to become the vet that Zara had dreamed of but never achieved. Her schedule allowed her to get to the stable to see her beloved palomino, Flapjack, occasionally during the school year and on her off-hours from her job. She found the time to enter local horse shows during the warmer months.

Pulling her knitted ski hat down over her ears and tucking in a few loose strands of her hair, she ran hurriedly to the tack room. Remy had started the small space heater to get the chill out of the air. Amber backed up to it, folding her arms over her chest, hugging herself to get warm. Through the side door to the tack room, she saw Remy working his way down the aisle between the stalls.

"Hey, Remy!" she called out. "How ya been, man? Haven't seen you in ages. Ya got horse duty tonight, eh?"

"Yeah," Remy responded flatly. "Zara's still sleeping so I thought I'd check the place out and go ahead and feed the horses."

Zara, without fail or change in schedule, napped every afternoon from 2 until 5.

"Oh, cool," answered Amber as she turned to get her horse's feed and some grooming equipment.

Spook and Shadow, the two barn cats who had been sleeping on a bale of hay in the center aisle between the stalls, stirred at the sounds of activity. They yawned, stretched and hopped down in hopes of getting some attention. Shadow was slick, shorthaired and pitch black, hence his name. Spook, a very fluffy puffball, would be by one's side one minute and then, in a flash, the next second would vanish. Content with occasionally catching a mouse or chipmunk, and always-generous handouts, they had become fat and somewhat lazy, but nevertheless loving stable mates to the horses. A colorful rooster strutted around, looking for kernels of horse feed that may have dropped here and there. Oedipus Pex, so named for his irritating habit of pecking at the backs of one's legs when they least expected it. The rooster was smart enough, however, to keep away from Remy. Even roosters can learn from experience. Mother Clucker, an old hen, would scamper around, often laying her eggs on bales of hay. Remy had just finished dumping the feed in all the appropriate stalls when he saw Zara's pickup truck drive in and park. Almost before it came to a complete stop she quickly jumped out and headed to the stable. She was dressed in her usual tight jeans, high riding boots and layers of sweaters under her winter jacket. She pulled on her gloves as she walked. On her head was a very smart Irish wool newsboy's cap.

"You ever gonna learn to buckle up when you drive?" Remy asked tersely.

"Nope," Zara answered succinctly. "Too confining. Too tight. You know I'm claustrophobic".

"That's stupid. And dangerous. And it's illegal," he scolded.

Zara shrugged her shoulders, shook her head, rolled her eyes and went about her business. They had reached that particular stage in their marriage where it didn't take much to antagonize each other with the simplest of words or a gesture. Zara couldn't care less when that happened, but Remy would let it fester.

"You've dumped already, I see," she said to Remy. "You ready for me to let them in, then?"

"Sure," was his simple and sullen reply.

All the stall doors were standing open. She went to the pasture gate, unlatched the chain and stood back as she opened the gate wide. There were thundering hooves, a few nickers, a few nips on the butt from one horse to another but they all managed to head into their proper stalls. One horse backed out, got confused and entered his neighbor's stall causing some loud snorts, whinnying and a scuffle.

"Get outta there, ya son of a bitch!" Remy yelled at the unruly horse. He grabbed a whip and was about to use it when the horse decided he needed to return to his own stall. The rooster, who had been pecking around in that stall came flying out squawking, almost hitting Remy in the face. The horse nearly knocked Remy over in the rush, which caused him to utter even worse profanity. Amber pretended not to hear it. It only solidified her opinion that Remy was an asshole.

"Good horses!" Zara called to them as, one by one, she closed their stall doors. "Eat up, kids," she said to them as she latched the stalls. "Your suppers will help keep you warm tonight."

A slow, cold, drizzly rain had begun. With the temperature noticeably dropping, Zara hoped that it didn't become a freezing rain. There was the sound of feed being hungrily munched coming from up and down the aisles. A side door to the tack room opened directly into the long aisle that split the front stalls from the back. Large barrels holding the horse feed for each horse stood in this hallway along with stacks of hay bales. Zara went along, dropping flakes of hay into each stall to keep the horses busy. By the time all the stall doors were closed and horses fed, another car had arrived and parked. Zara looked up to see another boarder, Julia Constance, heading towards the tack room, a cell phone pressed to her ear.

"I don't care, Rance!" Julia said angrily, almost through clenched teeth. "I. Don't. Care! Period."

Zara didn't *really* want to eavesdrop (yes, she did) but, as an avid lover of soap operas, she enjoyed hearing about the real-life woes and joys of her boarders.

"Why do you have to be such a prick?" Julia continued, loudly this time. Zara's interest increased on hearing that. She reached for flakes of hay to put into the horses' stalls, moving quietly and ever so slowly, closer and closer to the tack room door. Julia's voice was fading in and out as she gathered up her grooming utensils, making it difficult for Zara to make out all the dialogue. She cautiously leaned a little closer to the tack room door, trying her best not to be noticed.

"Your selfish antics have the kids all upset. Don't be such a goddamn bastard. Can you do that, at least for them if not for me?"

There was silence. Leaning even closer, cocking her head, Zara almost stopped breathing so she could hear something. Anything.

"Zara?" came a voice directly behind her.

"Jesus!" Zara jumped and dropped the hay she was carrying.

"Oh, I'm sorry. Didn't mean to startle you, Zara," said Amber sheepishly.

Zara caught her breath. "That's OK, sweetie. I was off in la-la-land thinking about something else," she lied.

"I was wondering if I could get your advice about something?" asked the naïve young boarder.

"Sure thing, sweetie, what is it?" Zara answered, with a backward glance towards the tack room.

Amber was having boyfriend problems. Again. Zara didn't always have the right answers to everyone's problems but she was a good sounding board. She had problems and secrets of her own but those were never discussed with the boarders. And, although she didn't always follow Zara's advice, Amber enjoyed just being able to vent at times.

She followed Zara from stall to stall as the hay was being deposited for the horses. The two of them chatted at length, with Zara keeping an eye out for Julia. Julia had gathered up her grooming kit and headed towards the stalls of her two horses. She got to the first stall but not before Zara heard her say "Fuck you!" as she finished her phone call.

Julia saw the two ladies chatting and called out to them. "Hey, ladies, how y'all tonight? Weather sucks, doesn't it?"

"Oh, hi, Julia," Zara called back. "I didn't know you were here too. Must not have heard you drive up. Yeah, this weather is awful. Just glad it's not icy. Sure wish summer would hurry up and get here. Ha! Seems like I say that every year at this time."

"Sorry to say, Zara, but I think it'll probably get colder before it gets hotter. When the summer gets here we'll all be pissin' and moanin' because it's too damn hot. We're never satisfied, are we?" And then Julia said softly to herself so no one could hear, "Nope, nobody is ever satisfied...especially me". She wiped away a tear that had started to roll down her cheek.

"Well," Zara continued, "I really do prefer the heat over the cold. I think it's a lot easier to try to cool off than it is to warm up. The heat is just on the surface but the cold...damn, the cold goes right through to your bones. And, frankly, I'd rather contend with hot flesh than cold bones."

"I hear ya, Zara. I hear ya," answered Julia.

"Hey, I have a class tonight." Amber said. "Gotta go. Thanks for your opinion, Zara. I really appreciate it. You're really cool".

Zara gave Amber a big, motherly hug and sent her on her way.

"Don't worry," Zara called. "I'll let Flapjack out for you". The two waved goodbye.

"I don't know why I'm grooming these big plugs," Julia called to Zara. "It's such a pissy night. I'm just gonna put 'em back out when they're finished eating and be done with it for the night".

"I'll be happy to put them out with all the others if you don't want to wait around," offered Zara.

"You wouldn't mind?"

"Aw, hell, no. Gotta wait 'til mine are all done anyway. What's a couple more? Go on. Don't worry about it. They're good."

"Hey, thanks, Zara. I really, really appreciate it. You're a sweetheart."

Julia's cell phone started chirping. She glanced at caller ID and muttered under her breath "Drop dead, you big shithead!"

Zara's interest was piqued but pretended not to hear. Julia's husband, Zara assumed, had been the caller and, like her own husband, Julia's was no prize.

"Drive carefully!" Zara called out as Julia hurried away. There was no return response.

Julia Constance kept her maiden name. She was in her early forties, slender, extremely attractive, an exceptional rider and as foul-mouthed as any longshoreman. She was a highly successful salesperson for a pharmaceutical company, which required out-of-town travel on occasion. She took advantage of that situation. Often. The corporate headquarters for her company were located in California. She flew out there several times a year. Several. Her husband, Rance Hurakon, was an obnoxious little weasel of a man who must have been attractive enough at one time to have enticed and seduced Julia. He was the most sarcastic, hateful person anyone at the stable had ever encountered. He had opinions about absolutely everything and thought he was above absolutely everyone. Rance considered himself a good rider. Actually, Rance considered himself exceptional in all he endeavored. He fooled only himself.

Zara stood in the hallway between the stalls watching as Julia drove away and wondered about that call. She was imagining all kinds of scenarios when Remy, having finished his chores, came up behind her.

"Don't you just wish you could be that proverbial fly on that proverbial wall sometimes to see what's going on in other people's lives?"

Don't we all, at times? Honestly…don't we?

"Nope. Don't give a shit," Remy responded. "They don't give a rat's ass about us and I sure as hell don't give a rat's ass about them either. Everybody has his or her own problems, just like you and me. Everybody has his or her own damn story. I don't want to hear their bitchin' and moanin' any more than they want to hear us. As long as they take good care of their horses, keep their stalls clean and pay their board on time, I don't give a flyin' fuck if they're axe murderers."

"Damn! Somebody's in a blacker mood than normal on this gray day, aren't we?" Zara exclaimed.

"So what else is new?" Remy muttered as he headed towards the pasture gate to open it. The horses had finished eating and it seemed apparent that none of the other boarders were going to show up tonight.

Zara shot him the bird as he walked away, unseeing, and stuck out her tongue. "You old grump," she said under her breath.

"You ready?" she called to Remy as he stood by the gate.

"Yeah, let 'em run!" he called back as he swung the gate wide.

Zara went to every stall, opened the doors and shook a horsewhip with a large plastic bag taped to the end. The rustling sound of the bag always startled the horses no matter how often they heard it and, one by one, they all bolted from their stalls heading towards the open gate. They were familiar with this routine.

"Shoo…shoo!" she called loudly, chasing a few stragglers towards the gate. The last horse to leave his stall was a large sorrel gelding. Closing his stall door, she stopped. "Aw, Joe-Joe, you big turkey," she muttered. "You couldn't have waited until you got back out in the pasture to do that?" She mucked out the stall, then closed the door and called out to Remy. "That's all of them. Finally."

He closed the gate and securely latched it. He watched as the herd bucked and kicked at each other as they meandered out into the cold, now-wet pasture. He went back to his car as Zara locked the tack room, turned out all the lights and headed back to her truck.

"Another day closer," Remy thought to himself. He felt the next big event in his life was death. He started his engine, followed Zara's truck up and out of the driveway and drove home.

"Now what the hell is *that* supposed to mean?" Mary Anne, one of the boarders, asked herself out loud. Arriving at the stable an hour after Remy and Zara had left, she was staring at a note hanging on the bulletin board. It had obviously been created on a computer, using bold type and printed on an 8½ X 11" sheet of bright yellow paper. She looked at it for a few moments, trying to make sense of it. Was this a message for someone at the stable? A crazy weather report? She scanned the other notes on the board quickly to see if this note referred to any of them.

THE LAST IS FIRST,
THE FIRST IS LAST.

A CLOUDY FUTURE,
AND A STORMY PAST.

She shook her head, shrugged her shoulders and unlocked the tack room door. Until recently, the tack room door had always remained open. But several saddles and leather bridles were stolen one night, so Zara and Remy had issued keys to all the boarders. The police had been notified but, with no evidence of a break-in, nothing could be done. The boarders whose gear was stolen were very angry and disappointed in human nature these days, but nobody held it against Zara or Remy. There was a mix of western and English riders at the stable and, strangely, it was only the English gear that had been taken. They were all concerned that an unknown someone had made an unwelcome visit.

Mary Anne had arrived at the stable later than usual because of her schedule. She discovered that, apparently, her horse had been fed and put back out into the pasture already. She knew that Zara or Remy often did this. Sometimes she appreciated the gesture, sometimes it annoyed her. She checked her horse's stall to see if it needed mucking out, which it did. She hurriedly cleaned out the stall, locked the tack room, turning out all the lights and headed back to her car. She was eager to get home for a cup of hot chocolate. She drove away, listening to a song on the radio about a rainy night in Georgia.

She was unaware that she had been watched.

"God, Remy," Zara started as they shared one of their rare dinners together. "Why have you become *so* impatient with everybody and everything? You didn't used to be this way. You used to be fun."

Remy took a bite of his pork chop before answering.

"I don't know. When I got old maybe. When things stopped working."

"Well, you're *not* old…and there's a pill for that now, you know."

"Pills don't work for everything," he answered with an edge to his voice. "And that wasn't what I was referring to." Zara knew what he had meant. Some things are best left in the past. Some things can never *stay* in the past.

"But your attitude about other people," she continued. "Especially our friends, is deplorable. Sometimes your surliness even embarrasses me, really it does. And it take a lot to embarrass me, as you know."

"Friends, HA!" he shot back. "How many of your so-called friends, the ones you've known for years, remember what your favorite drink is? What your favorite color is? I know, sure as hell, they don't know *everything* about you…about the girls or us. And I'd sure as hell like to keep it that way. Nobody's damn business. Folks just want to poke and pry…and spill their guts and air their dirty laundry on every kind of social media that they can get a hold of. Not me. Out of habit or courtesy, they might ask you how you're doing. Do they *really* care? Do they *really* listen to your reply?"

"I don't drink," Zara answered matter-of-factly. "Not any more anyway. Isn't it about time we moved past all that now?"

"I think you get my point, Zara. And, deep down, I think you might agree. For Chrissake, come on, Zara. We've had this same damn conversation over and over again. Nothing changes. Nothing will ever change."

"Every day with you," Zara continued, "it's just criticize and complain. Don't you…every once in a while…just wake up and say Wow! Let's have some fun today. Let's just do something fun. Don't you?"

"No," was the simple and only reply.

Zara thought to herself, "Well, you sure as hell will never see *our* story on the Hallmark Channel".

They continued the rest of the meal in silence. When they were finished, Zara put the dirty dishes into the dishwasher, tidied up the kitchen, and then they both went their separate ways for the remainder of the evening. Zara buried her face in the latest monthly horse magazine and Remy buried his mood in a book. Remy enjoyed reading thrillers and espionage spy novels. Not that he *really* fantasized himself as the next, older James Bond, but he often pictured himself as a heroic character of some sort in every book he read. Nobody, not even Zara, had a clue about *that*. Some secrets were silly, harmless flights of fancy. Even for an old grump like Remy.

Who really knows what happens when the sun goes down, the doors close behind us and the lights come on…or go out? How often has every one of us overheard just a tidbit of conversation and, in our mind, created a scenario to complete the story? A tone of voice, a hushed whisper or an arched eyebrow can change the complexion of truth. Rampant rumors have killed relationships, formed alliances and sold more tabloid gossip-rags than there are grains of sand in the Sahara. Our public personas can be quite different from our private ones, even though we might share similar thoughts, ideals, dreams, frustrations…regrets. Regrets. Remy had a few of those.

So why did Remy stay around? He asked himself that question often. He loved Zara, in his own way. But he hadn't liked her. For years. He still felt he had to protect her…watch out for her. Certain bad habits have a tendency to return. Why did he stay around? Simple answer: he had nowhere else to go.

Nightly, following a mostly silent dinner, Remy would disappear into his home office and lose himself for a couple hours on the computer or another book. He rarely watched television. Could barely tolerate most of the stuff on it. It wasn't unusual for him to be in bed by 10 P.M. After dinner, Zara would recline on the large, comfortable sofa in their family room, watch the recorded soap operas of the day and drift off to sleep, waking up somewhere around 2 or 3 A.M.

Their two daughters, Kristine and Taylor, had long since moved out. Taylor, the eldest, was married with two children of her own, two boys, who idolized both Remy and Zara. The only time Remy was halfway decent was when his two little grandsons were around. But something had happened between Zara, Kristine and Taylor a few years before and they rarely spoke or saw each other, even though they lived just a few miles apart. Taylor was dark-haired, like her father, and had a tendency towards overweight. She could be abrupt with people and seemed to lack certain social skills. Kristine, blonde, slender and good-looking, was extremely quiet and reserved on the rare…extremely rare, occasions when she visited the stable. Periodically, Zara proudly showed off photos of her grandsons to the boarders but her daughters' names never seemed to come up in the conversations.

However, many at the stable silently suspected Kristine of being gay, although, of course, the topic was never even hinted to Zara or Remy. Kristine was in her mid twenties and, apparently, had never had a serious… or *any* relationship with a boy. She never dated any boys at all. When she *did* stop by the stable for a short visit, she would have a girl friend or two with her. Every once in a while, curiosity would get to a boarder.

"How's that sweet Kristine doing, Zara?" someone might ask. "Any husband in the near future?" if they were feeling a bit more brazen.

"Nah, not that I know of," would be the usual response. "She has pretty high standards, I guess…not like me," and then she'd laugh.

Zara knew what they might be thinking. And it pissed her off.

The mysterious note stayed on the bulletin board for a week. Neither Remy nor Zara knew if it might be some cryptic message from one boarder to another. But, as it turned out, nobody knew anything about it and nobody declared his or her guilt for putting it there.

"It must be a prank of some sort," thought Mary Pat, another boarder. "Kinda stupid though, if nobody knows what the hell it means."

The sun rarely shone for the remaining days in the month. Gray, gloomy days and below average temperatures made it unpleasant to be outside too long. Zara realized that she was letting all of the horses in and feeding them more often this month than usual. A few of the boarders would show up now and then to muck out the stalls, drop off bags of feed or simply tack their rent checks on the bulletin board. Zara also realized that with warmer springtime weather, the boarders would be more attentive and present.

During the night, exactly three weeks after the appearance of the first mysterious note, another piece of bright yellow paper was tacked up.

THE FIRST IS LAST,
THE LAST IS FIRST;
A THOUSAND TEARS
CAN'T QUENCH A THIRST.

These mysterious notes angered Remy. What purpose did they serve if nobody could decipher them? For whom were they intended? But he also had the nagging suspicion that someone, perhaps a sick or dangerous person, was encroaching upon his privacy. Zara had her suspicions as well, but kept silent about them.

Although neither Zara nor Remy could possibly know at this point, but a couple more of those strange notes would appear on the bulletin board within the coming weeks, before their motivation could be resolved.

FEBRUARY

Haunted Howce

"We suffer primarily not from our vices or our weaknesses, but from our illusions. We are haunted, not by reality, but by those images we have put in their place."

Daniel J. Boorstin

Marty Howce was afraid of snakes. And toilets. His father had forged this improbable combination of phobias years ago. Carson Howce smoked too much, drank too much, cursed too much and, above all, told the most outlandish stories that were believable only to naïve little boys.

"I tell ya, boys," Carson bellowed one drunken Saturday night when Marty was eight years old, "ya gotta watch it when you sit on the crapper."

Marty and his brother, Garret, were seated at Carson's feet in the living room. Garret was two years older than Marty and knew that their dad told the wildest, never-to-be-believed stories. Marty, on the other hand, took everything his father said as gospel. At that time, anyway.

"There I was, tending to my business, sittin' on the can reading a Sports Illustrated. I heard a quiet splash of water under me but I knew that I hadn't done anything yet. And guess what? A big ol' snake had somehow gotten into the pipes and slithered all the way up into that damn toilet. Well, he saw my boys just hangin' there and, God only knows what he thought, but he reached up and grabbed hold and bit in. Oh, man, I thought the world was comin' to an end! I jumped up off a that pot, with that friggin' snake just hangin' on to my nuts and I let out a holler!"

Garret was laughing so hard he thought he might wet himself. Marty trembled in fear.

"I don't know what that little ol' snake had in his mind, but he let go and dropped to the floor. I grabbed that fucker by the tail, swung him around my head a couple a times and smashed him down onto the marble floor. Oh, God…snake guts all over the place. Your Momma was gonna be pissed, I tell ya, so I just cleaned it all up and flushed him back down the toilet again. She never knew and I never told her. But my nuts were sore for days."

Marty had not considered the fact that this story was way too outlandish to be anywhere near the truth. It stuck with him throughout the years. He could never bring himself to completely sit down on a toilet. He was always poised to jump up at the slightest sound. Consequently, he had very strong thigh muscles. He always slowly, cautiously opened any toilet lid before attempting to do anything. The only place where he felt somewhat safe was in a high-rise office building or hotel. Snakes could never slither up dozens of stories in the pipes. Could they? He was only slightly less apprehensive on airplanes.

Over the years, Marty would repeat his father's outrageous tale to friends and shake his head in disbelief that he had actually fallen for it. His two sons, especially, wanted to hear it over and over, laughing harder each time. It was the equivalent of telling ghosts stories around a campfire, albeit a silly, humorous one. But then, Marty loved ghost stories and could conjure up some creepy scenarios to throw chills into his own little boys. More often than not, his stories would involve time travel and reincarnation…with ghosts from another time zone returning to terrorize poor innocents in *this* time. Time travel intrigued him and he fantasized about it often.

Even at an early age, Marty was creative. He loved to draw and his talent amazed his mother, teachers and classmates. His dad, however, would insult him and be derisive of his "sissy talent". Any chance he got, it seemed, his dad just criticized or contradicted anything he did or said. Marty tried to ignore it. Marty was wise enough to write it off as his dad's ignorance and…well, possibly jealousy. Marty was a scrawny kid and he grew into a tall, lanky teenager. Carson teased him about that also. "Hell, kid, if you get any thinner, you'll slip through your asshole and hang yourself!" Marty thought the image of that was actually pretty funny, although he didn't let Carson know that. He was growing up… growing more intelligent…growing more independent. When Marty was 15 and a sophomore in high school, the English teacher gave the class an assignment to write a short story. Any topic, he had said, just keep it clean. His classmates wrote about their puppies, their horses, fantasies about their futures, a favorite sport, cars, imaginary kingdoms and creatures…or going to visit their grandparents in the mountains. A black kid had written about the Civil War with an alternate ending. *That was interesting!* Mostly trite, mundane, trivial, but innocent, stories. But not Marty. No, not Marty. He delved into his extremely creative imagination and conjured up an allegory. "The Seashell Sound":

By the time the man arrived at the middle of the bridge he was winded and puffing heavily; it had been a long and steep climb. He turned around to see where he had been, but was blinded for the sun shone fiercely into his eyes. He then turned and looked forward, to see where he was going, but it was dark on the other side of the bridge and he saw only the stars.

The bridge, a massive mixture of mortar and muscle, was suspended over a deep chasm that was divided by a wide, murky river. Wind thrust up at the bridge, pushing it, making it sway. Occasionally on his journey the man had lost his balance and had clung to the railing, for fear of falling off. Winded now, he rested, leaning on the railing that had, in the past, saved him. He viewed the great expanse of nothingness below him. The rocky ridges were lonely and dark, and constantly changing; the wind would play games with their dusty mantle, lifting the dry cloth, peeking lustfully underneath and then replacing it on another ridge. The river watched with a million brilliant eyes, blinking teasingly, but always watching; it was an intruder…it was a cesspool.

The man's eyes ached from the sight and he closed them. The pain was absorbed, pulled in, wretched by his body. He could feel the infliction race through his body, race through his veins, and surge down his arms and veritably pull his fingers from his hands. The anguish flowed down his back; it was a knife severing the flesh which was then pulled back to reveal his insides. Nothing. He wept.

The man stood watching the flight of a great white bird when he caught sight of something coming towards him. He could not tell what it was for the sun still shone into his eyes, but the silhouetted shape was approaching from the once-visited, never-returnable place on the bridge. The shadowy shape was holding something, long and pointed. The swaying of the bridge did not affect the progress of this creature. As the thing came closer, the sunlight let its fingers creep around it, filling in the vacant areas of darkness. The thing smiled. It was a little boy. He looked up at the man and asked where he was going.

"I'm lost," said the man.

"I know," answered the boy, toying with the large paper airplane that he held in his hand. "Did you come here alone?"

"What?" asked the man, shielding his eyes and squinting, for he had to look into the sun to see the boy.

"Did you come here alone?" the boy asked again, as if he was already bored with this question.

"Yes," answered the man, confused.

"I know", was the boy's response.

The man shook his head, tried to ignore the boy and wished him gone. Children…any human contact for that matter, disturbed him. He sighed into the wind, only to have it echoed.

"Do you have a father?" the little boy suddenly asked after a few moments of silence.

"Yes, of course I do!" answered the man, quite startled by the odd question, but realizing the fact that children can ask the stupidest things.

"I know," was the boy's simple reply.

"How __do__ you know? And why do you always say 'I know'?" The man's irritation was showing on his face like a rash; his face was red and his eyes filled with water.

"I don't know," the boy shrugged and smiled. "What does he look like?"

"Who?"

"Your father."

"He's dead. What does he look like? He looks like an empty seashell that lays on a beach bleached white by a cold sun. He lies cracked, splintered, open, hollow, and shallow. Just like I will someday. Like you, too. He can do nothing about the dogs that come and sniff at his bones and lick at his brains. He can do nothing about the men who kick at his bones and step in his brains. He can do nothing. He was murdered. He was in a building five miles high and he was on the top floor. The elevator doors opened but there was no elevator. A black, hairy hand touched my father on his shoulder and pushed him into the pit; the wind, as he fell, split open his body. Did you ever hold a seashell up to your ear and listen? That's not the sound of the sea. It's the sound of someone dying. My father is dead. He is dressed in black now. He wears black well; on him it looks good."

"You're wearing black," said the boy as he wrinkled up his face.

"Well, so I am," answered the man as he looked down at himself. "But this suit doesn't fit. See? The coat is too large and the trousers are too small. Besides, I don't look good in black; on me it looks bad. Blue is my color. Blue as the sky on a hot summer day. Blue, like today."

The boy looked up into the sky, squinting. "But the sky is green today," he corrected.

The man looked up into the sky. "So it is. Well, I look good in green as well.

"I know," responded the boy.

"Will you stop saying that!" the man scolded. "Why don't you leave me alone?"

The boy scratched his nose with his very pale hand and smiled, looking up into the man's face. "Your teeth are yellow."

"What?" snapped the man.

"I said, your teeth are yellow," and the boy smiled broadly revealing his own milky white teeth.

"That is none of your business," the man said, turning away from the boy. "They could be black, for all I care."

"Some are," said the boy, standing on his toes, trying to see further into the man's mouth.

"What's the matter with you?" asked the now-exasperated man, trying to control himself. He could get into serious trouble for hitting a little boy. "Don't you have anyplace else to play?"

"I came here to play," said the boy, holding up his paper airplane for the man to see. "I'm going to wait until it's real windy, then I'll throw the plane into the sky."

"You can throw it only once," said the man, "then it will be lost."

"I know", answered the boy nonchalantly, "then I'll make another one and come back to throw that one off the bridge too. I do it all the time. But sometimes it doesn't get windy enough and I have to keep the airplane until another day. I don't know if that makes me happy or sad. Sometimes I think the ones that I take off of the bridge should be saved, but I always bring them back and eventually throw them off the bridge anyway. I like to see them fall; they look like little birdies flying through the forest. It's fun to watch them fall into the river. If the sun is shining, all the eyes on the water splash and laugh and wink at me. I don't like it, really, when the planes hit the rocks; the dust flies up into the air and is caught by the wind. Then it just disappears and there's nothing more to see. You can watch when I throw this airplane today. Then you'll see how much fun it is."

"Why don't you throw it off now…and go home?" the man asked, wanting more than ever to be left alone.

"Oh, no," answered the boy, "it isn't time yet."

"Oh, Christ!" blurted the man.

"Why are you on the bridge?" asked the boy.

"I really don't know," answered the man, shaking his head. "I just found myself walking along…alone. I don't know where the bridge started; I can't see because of the sun in my eyes when I turn back to look. My life is the sun. Yes. On…on a cloudy day. My life is the sun on a cloudy day. I shine brightly but something, someone always gets in my way. Where is the sun on a cloudy day? People know I'm there, they just can't see me. They can't hear me, either. I guess maybe it's because I never say anything. My life is a street gutter on a rainy day. Full of everyone's drops but none of my own. And I just lie there along the street, going nowhere, full of other people's garbage. I don't even have my own garbage."

"You don't sound like a very happy man," said the boy, frowning.

"You show me a happy man today, my little, annoying friend, and I'll show you an insane man. There are no more happy men. They are all dead."

The bridge began to sway gently in a new gust of wind. The man grabbed the railing for safety. The boy held up his airplane and smiled. "I think it's time now," he said.

He pulled back his little arms and let the airplane sail with the wind. It was caught by the breeze and soared up like a bird in flight. The wind suddenly stopped and the plane dropped like a silver coin from the clouds. The boy jumped up and down gleefully. "I think it's going to hit the water!" he squealed as he clapped his hands.

But the airplane split down the middle before it hit the water, and turned from white, to red and then to black. The parts creased the water; the glimmering eyes laughed and the little boy waved.

"That was a good one!" exclaimed the boy, now exhausted by the ordeal. "Now I have to make another one. They don't last very long. Bye!"

And he skipped into the darkness, losing his image in the stars.

The man watched until the boy had disappeared. As he turned to look at the river once again, a strong wind picked up a handful of dirt, dust and stones and smashed them into his face, scraping the flesh from his bones. The man let go of the railing to cover the raw wounds; his right eye was bleeding, he was choking on his blood. The bridge was moving. No, the bridge was still; he was moving. He was falling. He reached for the railing that was not there. He heard a little boy laughing. The seashell sound.

And then the shit hit the fan.

At first, Marty's imagination and talent for writing flabbergasted the teacher. He was very impressed, and then he wondered if the story was truly original or if Marty had copied it…or parts of it…from some other book or TV show. He leaned back and thought about it for a while. He reread it. And read it one more time. Wait, he thought, am I missing some signals here? What, exactly, is this young man telling us? This could be, simply, a very clever metaphor for life and then death. Or. Or it *could* be a way to call for help. Does Marty have serious father issues? Is he being abused…emotionally or physically? The teacher decided to discuss the issue with the school counselor. Marty had seemed like the perfect student. He got good grades…even did things for extra credit, noted all his teachers. He was, basically, a nerd. A seemingly quiet chatterbox, as one teacher laughed. Although it was a difficult decision, Marty's parents were eventually called to the school for a conference. They were given Marty's story to read. This was the first either of them had seen it or even heard about it. Carson Howce was silent but exploded inwardly. His face reddened. He took it personally. Marty, obviously, wished him dead…his bleached bones sniffed at by a pack of dogs. Marty's mother was confused. She wondered who that little boy was and why would his mother let him play in such a dangerous environment.

His parents waited, his father in particular, almost in ambush, for him to return home from school. Marty had not been told about the conference beforehand, so it took him totally by surprise when his father went bat-shit crazy as he launched into his tirade about the story. There was yelling, there was screaming, there was stomping of feet, there was pounding of fists and slamming of doors and there were tears. When his father finally stopped to take a breath, Marty *finally* had a chance to speak.

"Oh, for shit's sake!" Marty blurted. "It was just a damn story. I wanted to experiment with some silly ideas and not write about the same old stupid stuff that I knew the rest of the class would. I wanted to do something different. You, yourself, tell outlandish stories, Dad. Good grief, Herman Melville once said he just wrote a story about a whale, nothing more. That's what I did. It was just a story. Nothing more. Maybe it was a bit too artsy-fartsy or obscure but, damn…I didn't mean to get everyone's panties in a freakin' wad!"

His father was not totally satisfied but kept silent about it. Their relationship had not been all love and kisses up to that point anyway, but it had just turned worse. He remained at loggerheads with Marty for the rest of his life. Marty's mom was *still* confused. She didn't remember a whale being in Marty's story at all.

Marty went to his room, furious that the situation had escalated to the level he never intended or imagined. No, he didn't need therapy. No, he wasn't being abused. No, he wasn't suicidal. No, he didn't wish his father dead. Well, maybe that one needed some rethinking. A further discussion with his teacher was necessary, he decided, to assuage the fears at school. He booted up his computer, pulled up the file with his story and deleted it. He also tore up the only hard copy that he had. End of story. Pun intended.

Fast-forward twenty-five years.

Marty grew up to be a handsome, well-built guy, losing his lankiness behind in high school and eventually art school. He was now an Art Director, working for Compton Paperboard Packaging Company. Compton, an international corporation, was based in Chicago and had fifteen facilities within the United States. Marty worked at one of the two locations in the Atlanta area. His office, within the sprawling complex, was located adjacent to the large pressroom. The door leading to the massive offset and gravure presses, the cutters and the gluers was right across the hall from the door to Marty's office. Whenever people went out through that door to the presses Marty could hear the sounds, could smell the inks and solvents…he loved that aroma. As often as he could, especially if one of his designs was on the press, he'd go and watch with pride. On rare occasion, he would work from home in his studio. He still liked to piddle around with magic markers (he loved that aroma, too) and layout pads although all of his real design work was done on the computer. His love, as far as graphic design was concerned, was packaging design. He had won numerous awards for his work, which he proudly displayed in his office. Food packaging was his forte and directing food shoots was a major pleasure for him. He was, as his clients referred to him, a "rock star". One wall of his large kitchen was covered with framed enlargements of his favorite food shoots, created in conjunction with the best food stylists and taken by the best food photographers from both coasts.

And then, one day, Marty began hearing sounds and sensing a presence.

It was while he was working on the computer, at home, one bright afternoon when he first heard the sounds. He was alone in the house. His wife, Jessica, was taking advantage of the beautiful day and had headed out to CedarView Stable to join Zara in a trail ride. Their two horses, Dan, a coal-black Tennessee Walker, and Gemini, a chestnut American Saddlebred, hadn't been ridden for a few weeks. Marty was hoping that Zara could shed some light on those mysterious notes being left on the bulletin board. Their two sons were in school.

There was the sound of breaking glass coming from the kitchen. Baillie, their dog, was sleeping at Marty's feet while he was working. She didn't react in any way.

"Shit, those damn cats knocked over that fucking vase," he said aloud. Jessica had a bouquet of fresh flowers on their kitchen table, a Valentine's

Day gift from Marty. Trinket was a beautiful 3-year-old Calico and Pagan was a frisky 5-year-old Siamese. He ran from his studio into the kitchen, nearly tripping over Baillie as he got up. Obviously annoyed at being awakened, Baillie got up, shook her body from head to tail, ears flapping. She turned around in circles three times trying to find that perfect spot again, then plopped down, laid her head on her outstretched front paws and went back to sleep. The cats were nowhere to be seen and the vase sat, undisturbed, in the middle of the table with all the flowers as perfect as when they were placed there earlier in the day.

"What the hell?"

He looked around. Nothing broken. Anywhere. Nothing out of place. He walked from room to room, seeking the source of the breaking glass. He found nothing unusual anyplace.

"Damn. Okay, so maybe I'm hearing things," he thought. He returned to his office, a bit confused, but he *had* been putting in a lot of hours on his latest projects and perhaps, just perhaps, his overactive imagination was getting the best of him. He decided he would not share this incident with anyone. For one thing, he didn't want to frighten his young sons. It was nothing. Probably just a noise from outside that sounded like breaking glass. Maybe.

There had been times, too, that Marty thought he heard footsteps coming down the hall toward his studio, only to find no one there. Sometimes, if he turned his head very quickly, he thought he glanced a shadowy figure disappearing into another room. He might walk into the little bathroom next to his studio to discover the water running, but not remembering ever turning it on.

After seeking out the breaking glass that wasn't there, he returned to his computer and became engrossed, once again, in his latest project. He was very pleased with his progress. Another award-winner, he thought. He was staring at the monitor, with the room behind him in the reflection. There was a sudden movement behind him and the feeling of hot breath on his neck. He spun around quickly in his chair to discover…nothing.

"I'm losing it," he thought to himself. "I need a vacation!"

Marty and his parents had been distant for years. They rarely saw each other and spoke occasionally on the telephone, usually on birthdays, anniversaries or Christmas. Marty was well read and well spoken. His parents were not. They actually felt intimidated by his intelligence and his talent. His father, Carson, neither fully understood nor appreciated his chosen profession, deriding it as "fluff stuff". Marty could talk, at length, about countless topics, esoteric or otherwise and had a very quick wit. Marty's dad could talk of nothing other than sports, rant about politics or concoct foolish stories. Marty's mom was befuddled by just about everything and considered Marty a snob. Marty's brother was the favored son. He knew it and played it for all its worth. He was boastful, had a tendency towards being a racist and homophobe and as much of a storyteller as their dad. He was also highly jealous of Marty.

Recently, Marty's two young sons had asked him why he was always hugging and kissing them, and telling them that he loved them. Marty didn't even have to think about how to answer that.

"Boys," he said with a slight catch in his voice, "when I was growing up, not once did my Dad ever tell me he loved me. Not once. Frankly, I don't even recall him telling my brother or my Mom, your grandma, that he loved them. Never. So I vowed that if and when I ever had kids, boys or girls, I would make sure that they knew every single day that I loved them. I will continue to do so until the day I die. Whenever I see even a silly sit-com or a movie where a dad hugs his son…I cry. Because I never had that. I wanted that. I needed that. So…you'll have to bear with me. I'll hug and kiss you even when you're grown up. And I'll always be telling you that I love you." At that point, both boys gave Marty a great big hug. He squeezed his eyes tightly shut to keep the tears from flowing down his cheeks.

Lately Baillie, their beautiful collie, would wake up Marty at precisely 5:02 A.M. She would go to his side of the bed, poke him with her long nose and start breathing heavily.

"Jessie, I can't believe that she never, ever comes to wake you up," Marty moaned one tired morning.

"Well, she knows that I won't give in to her and that I won't budge," Jessica responded. "She probably doesn't even have to go out. She knows that you'll give in and get up. She's ready to play or explore, that's all. Right?"

"But at the exact same time every damn morning? Every. Damn. Morning."

"What time did you say?"

"It's always 5:02, like clockwork. No pun intended. I can't miss those damn big red numerals on the alarm clock".

"Hmm," Jessica thought aloud. "That's a bit odd, isn't it?"

"It's a pain in the ass, that's what. Same damn time, every damn day. Wait. What? What's odd about it?"

"Well, not that it really means anything. Just strangely coincidental I guess. But, isn't that the exact time of day your dad died?"

"Oh, for Chrissake, Jess. What the hell are you insinuating? It's really his ghost waking me up…or prodding Baillie?"

"No, no…no. I wasn't insinuating anything," Jessica responded, shaking her head. "It just seems like an odd coincidence, that's all".

Marty chuckled, shaking his head as well. "You've been watching *way* too many horror flicks, lady! There's nothing paranormal going on around here". Except strange noises, he thought, that nobody could hear but him.

Marty thought about his father while driving to the office that morning. Obviously it had not been a good father-son relationship at all. But, Marty thought, perhaps some of the blame was *his*. Did he ever give his dad a chance? True, they seemed to have nothing in common except their last name. Was Marty a good son or a bad son? Should he feel guilty now for not even trying? But it was a moot point.

Flashback: A couple years before, his dad, who had never been sick a day in his life, called to his wife for help shortly after midnight. He bolted upright in bed and was disoriented. All of a sudden he couldn't breathe. An ambulance was called. He died on the way to the hospital but was revived. Marty's Mom, Seranda, called her two sons from the hospital, alerting them to the situation. It would be too late for any reconciliation. Marty lived a 4-hour drive from his parents; Garret lived a 3-hour plane trip away. By the time both sons arrived, Carson, who had not been able to be revived after his second seizure, had been dead for several hours…his death was called at 5:02 A.M., never regaining consciousness. The cause was given as septic shock.

Marty's parents had not been religious people and did not believe in the "barbaric ritual" of funerals, with all the pomp, circumstance, crying and moaning that accompanies them. In that respect, Marty agreed completely with his parents. Neither parent wanted a service of any kind. Again Marty concurred. Closure was something for other folks, but not the Howce family.

"Just cremate me and throw my fuckin' ashes to the wind," Carson had said at one time. "Hopefully it will be during the summertime so I can blend in with all the other hot air," and he laughed raucously.

Carson was cremated within a reasonable amount of time following his death. His cremains were placed in a clear plastic bag, sealed with a twist-tie, placed in a plain brown corrugated box and handed, unceremoniously, to his wife. Seranda wasn't sure when or where she would scatter her husband's ashes so, when she brought them back home, she placed the box in the center of her dining room table. It looked so forlorn and depressing there so, considering that it was one month before Christmas, she placed a big red bow on top. To make it look more festive, she thought.

Marty, Jessica and Garret stayed with Seranda for several days following Carson's death. Carson had always been the one to do everything, make every decision and voiced every opinion. The two brothers were concerned about their Mom being able to function on her own. Five days following the death, Seranda called the boys into the dining room and asked them to sit around the table. The corrugated box with a big red bow still sat dead center. No pun intended. She had gotten Carson's will out of the safe and had it lying on the table.

"Read it out loud, Marty," his mother requested. "I haven't looked at it since we both wrote our wills together years ago. I can't really remember everything, but I know that everything will come to me. It's really very simple. I also want to make sure, though, that you two get something to remember your Dad by."

A lawyer who had been a friend of Carson's had drawn up the will officially, legally. It was dated seven years earlier.

Seranda's old cat wandered into the room and jumped up into her lap, purring softly. Garret tried unsuccessfully to hold back his emotions and sniffed loudly. It was at that exact moment that Marty suddenly realized that his mother had not shed even one tear.

Marty opened the will and started to read it aloud. It was, as his mother had stated, very simple…very basic. If Seranda survived him, all of Carson's possessions went to her. If she predeceased him…and this is where Marty reacted ever so slightly…two thirds of Carson's material wealth would go to Garret and one third would go to Marty. He kept reading as though his heart had not been wounded, his brother never catching the slight arched eyebrow as he read that sentence. His mother caught it, however, and put her hand to her mouth. Jessica had also caught it. The will concluded with the usual verbiage. No more surprises. No mention of his grandchildren…neither Marty's nor Garrett's kids. Marty was positive that he noted a very slight gloat to Garret's face but perhaps that was just his imagination.

"Marty, can I talk to you in the kitchen for a minute?" asked his Mom.

Seranda had a sheepish look on her face. She was several pounds overweight and often suffered shortness of breath as a result. It was obvious that she was now distraught, but not because of her recent widowhood. She was breathing heavily when Marty approached her.

"Marty, I know your feelings were hurt in there. I am so, so sorry about that. I know you and your dad had issues over the years, and could never really figure out why. I know we haven't been as close as families should be. Oh, well, that's over now as far as Carson is concerned. He wasn't an easy man to live with, as you well know. I know that it should have been fair. Your dad should have made it 50-50. I tried to reason with him but he wouldn't listen. I hate that. I know that you always knew Carson had an eye out for Garrett. You were always the smarter one, though. The more successful one. But it still wasn't fair. I hate it. I'm sorry, dear".

"Don't worry about it, Mom. I understand. It doesn't bother me a bit… really," Marty lied.

"Well," said his Mom with a catch in her throat, "that's not all. Your dad convinced me to write my will the exact same way. With the same split. I didn't want to. I wanted to be fair, but you know how persuasive your father is…was. So that's how it stands. I am so sorry, again, dear. As soon as I can, though, I'll look into rewriting my will."

Marty concealed his hurt. He convinced his mother that he understood and that he was fine with it. It had nothing to do with his dad's money or property. His parents had lived very conservative lives. His dad had lost a small fortune in the stock market years ago, but had gained it all back and more since then. Their home was totally paid for and they had no debts. No, it really wasn't the material things that mattered. It was simply the realization that his arrogant dad had, indeed, thought less of him than of his brother. But then, Marty thought, his dad probably realized that Marty was not all that fond of *him* either.

Later that day, when everyone was in different parts of the house doing whatever needed to be done, Marty approached that corrugated box with the big red bow sitting dead center on the dining room table.

"You fucker," Marty whispered through clenched teeth, leaning close to the box. "You goddamn fucker. You even had to make sure you jabbed me in the ribs after you were gone. You were a bastard alive and one even now. Wherever the hell you are."

Although he would regret it years later, Marty grabbed the box and took it into the kitchen. When he had first seen the bag containing the cremains, he was surprised to discover that they didn't look like ashes at all. Of course, he had never seen anything of that nature before. He had assumed that…well, if they are called ashes, they must look like ashes, right? They looked more like dried bone fragments that had been pulverized and bleached by the sun. What remained was something sandy gray in color and had a very course-looking texture. As a matter of fact, they reminded Marty of something else. The bag weighed about six pounds, surprisingly light, he thought. He looked around, spotted what he was looking for and then opened the bag. He poured a third of his dad's cremated remains into the old cat's litter box, and mixed it in with a scoop he found nearby. The litter box had not been cleaned out for at least a day. Several cat turds got mixed in with what remained of Carson Howce. Marty smiled.

"Ha! I know you hated that poor old cat as much as you obviously hated me, you old bastard. Rest in peace, you big shit."

Marty resealed the bag with the remaining cremains, put it back into the corrugated box dead center on the dining room table, replaced the big red bow…and fixed himself a gin and tonic.

Marty and Jessica were both 40, had been the proverbial high school sweethearts and married at 22, soon after graduating from college. Five years later, their first son, Duane, was born and two years following that along came Jason, their second son. Jessica had to admit that she had something in common with Remy Major, not that she was at all proud of that fact. They both were, basically, unhappy people. She joked that she had been born with the "Unhappy Gene". She knew that she really had nothing to be unhappy about. Her marriage was strong, they were extremely comfortable money-wise, and she loved her two sons dearly, enjoyed their two horses and had a satisfying career as a supervisor of the clinical toxicology department at a local laboratory. She didn't know why, but that wasn't enough. She knew, too, that she let the smallest things get under her skin. Simple, silly things, at times, annoyed her. Marty would razz her about it…and that annoyed her even more. One morning, after returning from grocery shopping, she was noisily banging shut kitchen cabinet doors and muttering to herself as she put the groceries away in the pantry. Marty heard the commotion and simply asked what was wrong. "Nothing. Not a damn thing." She replied. "Well…" Marty started. "Something has you pissed off. Did Kroger raise their prices again? What happened?" "Nothing. Don't worry about it, alright?" was her terse response, as she slammed down a can of stewed tomatoes on the counter. "Okay, okay!" Marty replied, throwing up his hands as if to surrender. He asked no further and retreated back to his studio, shaking his head. Jessie did reassure herself that, unlike Remy, she enjoyed being with people. At least, up to a point. She actually preferred the company of animals to humans.

Marty was annoyed by one of her irritating habits. She might start but never complete sentences at times. "Could you please hand me the…", "What do you think about…", You know, that really…".

"Finish the damn sentence!" Marty would protest, rolling his eyes. That only irritated Jessica, which consequently led her to muttering "Never mind," as she dropped whatever subject had been on her mind. Marty was amused…and, at times, annoyed by another of Jessie's quirks. Not only did she hate to shop but also she hated to spend money. Marty might suggest something to buy and Jessie's first question was always "How much?" This question would often be followed by "Do you really need it?" "Would you die if we didn't get it?" "Wait until next month, we're at the top of our budget already for this month." Her budget was an arbitrary number she felt was livable...doable. Marty scoffed at the need for such silliness. Budget? Really? With our respective salaries, he thought, it was nonsense. A five-dollar whatnot wouldn't send then into bankruptcy.

And, in turn, Marty had a habit, or quirk, that annoyed Jessie. Since he was a packaging designer, every packaged product in their house, whether it was in the refrigerator, on a kitchen shelf or in the pantry, had to have its front, principle display panel facing forward. He wanted to be able to see the graphics (well-designed or otherwise) and read each label immediately. Jessica purposely turned jars and boxes askew whenever she could, just for the hell of it. Marty would shake his head, grumble something under his breath and realign the package.

They had traveled around the world and he kept a "shrine", as Jessica mockingly called it, on his dresser top. There were framed photos of Jessica taken at his favorite places: walking on the Great Wall of China, riding a camel at the Pyramids in Cairo, on horseback on a trek in Australia, on top of a hill overlooking the Acropolis and half a dozen more. They were his "memories under glass".

"Memories can be funny and elusive things," Marty commented at one time. "Sometimes they can play tricks on us. We can distort and contort our memories to suit our needs. We can convert bad memories into good memories if we so desire."

"You know where I keep all of my memories?" Jessica asked. "Right here", she said as she tapped her head.

Marty was silent for a moment. "Sometimes we don't...or can't retain that luxury of memories. Sometimes they get lost."

Marty pulled into the parking lot at Compton and headed into his assigned spot. He listened to the final few minutes of an intriguing news item on the radio before stepping out into the windy, cold February day. Although the deadlines, at times, were killers and customers would call with constant revisions, this was his favorite job ever. Not only was he an excellent designer, he was also a sought-after speaker at various organizational functions. He also lectured quarterly at a small design school in Atlanta. A frustrated actor, Marty came alive in front of an audience and always had them in the palm of his hand after his first sentence. Standing at a slim, trim, toned 6' 5", with sandy brown hair and a youthful face, he presented a commanding figure. Having a fantastic, deep speaking voice helped also. Without fail, he was placed on the agenda of every sales meeting held by the local management. As often as not, salesmen would grouse if placed on the agenda immediately following Marty.

"Shit! How did I get so fuckin' lucky? How come I have to follow Howce?" was the usual response. Marty would always leave his audiences gasping for breath, either from dazzling concepts, intriguing marketing strategy or his rapid-fire humor.

He reported to the local sales manager, but he pretty much ran his own show. Marty was a one-man in-house design studio until things began to get more frantic, business-wise, then he might call upon a freelancer for assistance. A design student had cautiously approached Marty after one of his lectures at the school and asked about either free-lancing or being an apprentice. Marty laughed, because he hadn't heard that term in ages. The young man, Peter Scott, "The guy with two first names," as Marty would joke after Peter became a little more familiar with his dry wit, impressed Marty, even if the poor guy seemed nervous all the time. The design profession required nerves of steel…and a very thick skin.

He had seen terrific potential when looking at Peter's portfolio during their first interview at the school. His computer skills were outstanding. Peter was very reluctant to open up and talk at length…not the best way to look for a job…so Marty had to pull information out of him. Peter's portfolio was expertly put together. Printed examples of his computer-generated designs were laminated on colorful illustration board and were also on Peter's iPad that Marty scrolled through. He included a thick sketchbook as well, that Marty flipped through. He stopped at one page that had a beautifully rendered pencil sketch of what looked like a plaster cast. It was a male nude, appeared to be a life-sized statue, the torso was twisted slightly, the arms were missing from below the shoulders and the man's head was turned slightly, almost looking at the viewer. Marty looked confused. Peter blushed.

"Ah, actually that's one of my favorite drawings." Peter said with a slight giggle. "In life drawing class, obviously we had real live models… naked and everything, but that statue I found fascinating from all angles.

So I drew it a lot." He blushed again and giggled shyly. "I dubbed him the Penis de Milo."

Marty couldn't help but laugh until tears came down his cheeks. He liked what he saw in this young man's work. So he hired him, from time to time, as a freelancer with the thought that it might lead to a full-time position. Peter fit in well, albeit quietly, within the company, impressing everyone with his design skills if not his verbal skills. In short order, Marty had a well-oiled machine with the two of them. In other words, a perfect design department.

When the amount of projects became almost overwhelming, Peter would be called to come in and work until things calmed down again. Marty doled out the projects to either himself or Peter, depending upon the nature of the business…or the temperament of the client. He kept the projects dealing with the most hard-nosed and annoying clients to himself. There were only a few really problematical customers, but they required babying and schmoozing, which Marty handled with aplomb.

Peter would begin every project tentatively, so Marty seemed to spend more time helping and guiding him, at first, but it didn't take too long for the young guy to start to come out of his shell.

"Why whisper when you can shout?" Marty would offer if a concept was headed in too conservative a direction. "Be bold…daring…take chances. It's so much better to cast your line waaaay out there and reel it back in if necessary. Don't *inch* your way out to a solution. Remember, there are no rules in graphic design. If something different, unusual works…great! If it doesn't work…don't do it again."

Marty had wondered why those mysterious sounds were never at the office…or in the car while driving…or when he was out with the horses. Of course, he never mentioned the sounds or his brief "sighting" with anyone, especially Jessica and not to his young, impressionable sons. He went to GOOGLE and typed in "hearing sounds that aren't there", "seeing things that aren't there". After scrolling through several items that had popped up, he hit upon an interesting term that was completely unfamiliar: Hypnogogic hallucinations. He also read about auditory hallucinations. Fascinating stuff, he thought. But more often than not, those would happen when one is either just falling asleep or waking up. Could he actually have been nodding off at his computer when he heard or saw what he thought? Quite often, as he just read, these hallucinations are caused by stress or anxiety. Well, he had been stressed at work when these happened. Damn deadlines! Well, he thought, maybe there's nothing to worry about after all. No big deal. "I'm not haunted after all!"

His phone rang. Glancing at caller ID, he saw that it was Max Holliday, his counterpart in Compton's Corrugated Container Division, on the other side of town. He liked Max a lot; they had been friends ever since joining the company and often met for lunch or socialized with their respective wives.

"Hey, Max!" Marty said with a big grin on his face, "How ya been? I know that Jess probably sent a note off to you guys, but I want to thank you and Camellia for another spectacular New Year's party. Have you recovered yet?"

Max chuckled. His wife, Camellia, was an incredible hostess, always planning almost a year in advance for one of her themed New Year's functions.

"Yeah, yeah…hangover's just about gone," Max joked…being that it was the second week in February. "Glad you both could come. You and I need to do lunch sometime soon. The reason I called…have you been hearing any of the rumors out in the field lately?"

"Rumors? Rumors about what, exactly?"

"Oh, I don't know where they're coming from. One of our sales guys just mentioned something to me he had heard from God knows where. Says our company is up for sale."

"Whaaaaat? No way. Haven't heard a frigging thing about this. Selling Compton? Why? To whom?" Marty asked incredulously.

Max shrugged his shoulders, then realized he was on the phone and answered, "Haven't a clue. Just thought you may have heard something, that's all I can tell you. Hell, I'm getting close to retirement. I better not lose my pension!"

"I'll ask around here and see what I can sniff out. Damn. I don't like the sounds of that. You know how even the *hint* of change can throw people into a tizzy!"

They chatted for several more minutes before they said their good-byes.

"Shit," Marty said out loud. "Something else to worry about."

A month had gone by without any further unusual sounds in the house. He had been putting in extra hours at the office with a couple really critical projects with unreal deadlines and trying to help guide Peter through this rough patch. No further mention of the rumors about Compton had been heard. Jessica held dinner for him and the four of them enjoyed a chatty meal. He and the boys joked and laughed about silly stuff but Marty could hardly keep his eyes open at the table.

"No further info from either Zara or Remy about those cryptic notes over at the stable?" he asked Jessica between yawns.

"Nope. Nada, zip. Marty, finish up and, for God's sake, go to bed. You're gonna fall face first into the dessert."

Marty smiled sheepishly and offered an apology for being such a poor dinner companion. The boys had finished their homework before dinner, pushed back their chairs and headed off to their respective rooms to watch television or play video games before bedtime. Marty, also, pushed back from the table and groggily got to his feet.

"Thanks, I'm sorry. I *am* beat," he said as he kissed her on the cheek, apologized for not helping her clean up and headed upstairs to the awaiting soft, warm, comfortable bed. After closing the bedroom door, he stripped naked, pulled back the covers and slowly slid under the warmth and into a relaxed slumber.

The room was pitch black. He didn't know how long he had been asleep. He didn't know if he was even awake but he felt a presence. He rolled over to the empty side of the bed…Jess's side. He felt the bed give as someone sat down on the edge.

"Jessie, what time is it? How long have I been asleep? Are you just coming to bed now?"

There was no response. The bed moved as though someone had just stood up from sitting on it. A floorboard creaked. Marty reached over to his nightstand and switched on the light. He blinked and looked around. The door was closed and he was alone in the room.

"Oh, for shit's sake!" he said as he plopped back down onto the pillow.

MARCH – FIVE YEARS AGO

A Tick Attack

"In every walk with nature one receives far more than he seeks."

John Muir

Ticks are annoying, sneaky and dangerous little parasites. They can be found on one's body without warning, long after they have started their work. People or animals walking through the woods, playing or working in the yard are fair game. These blood-sucking demons will wait for a host and then silently attach themselves, head first, into a warm body. Ticks can neither fly nor jump. They either have to drop down onto their prey from above or crawl onto their next meal. They will move, unnoticed, up a pants leg, down a shirtsleeve or under a hat. Ticks can easily detect the heat and body odor from a potential nearby host. Some people believe that ticks climb up into trees limbs and wait until they sense the vibration of a living creature walking below. Then they drop from above and slowly crawl over the body until they can find just the right spot to dig in and latch on. If ticks can't find a host, they may die. Sometimes merely brushing up against a tree is all it takes. In less than thirty seconds a tick may have found its food supply.

The young hiker had been walking the mountain trails for days. It was familiar territory to him as he had hiked this way since childhood when he and his father had vacationed in the area. The two of them had hiked a variety of trails from coast to coast, but this area always remained his favorite and he returned to it as often as he could. He loved anything about the outdoors and could identify every tree, every birdcall and every little animal footprint in the dirt. It was getting late in the day. He was tired and hungry so he stopped, pitched his tent and carefully built a small campfire. The days were pleasantly mild and nights were still chilly in the north Georgia mountains. He traveled alone so he had no need to bathe or change his attire while on his trek. He had a five-day growth of beard on his youthful face, but he carried no mirror to see how he looked. He plopped down hard under a large tree, sending a signal to the branches above.

The young man ate a sandwich he had purchased from a convenience store earlier in the day and drank some bottled water that he had carried in his backpack. He took out a sketchbook from his pack and began drawing the trees around him. He liked the way certain branches interacted with others to create interesting patterns. He had soon sketched the entire landscape around him. He was very good. Several sketchbooks were filled with his drawings and some of them would eventually become paintings.

The sun was gone, his campfire had been allowed to die down and the hiker was tired. He slid into his tent, curled up in his sleeping bag and, within minutes, was asleep.

The tick liked this warm body. It had dropped down from the tree under which the hiker had been sitting and had landed, unnoticed, on the young man's neck. It slowly crawled down inside the hiker's t-shirt. It tried to find the right place to attach itself, slowly crawling across the man's smooth chest and finally came to rest under the man's right nipple. There was a bit of perspiration and it liked the moisture combined with the heat. There is no pain when a tick attaches itself. No sensation at all… for a while, that is. The tick had found its meal. It effortlessly inserted its chelicerae, then its hypostome and began to feed.

It was a few days before the hiker began to notice an irritating itching feeling on his chest. He hadn't removed any clothing since beginning his hike, so he had not been able to see his attacker. He was nearly back to the spot where he had begun his journey and where he had parked his car. When he got there, he threw his backpack into the trunk, and then lifted his shirt to see what was itching him so badly.

It was then that he saw the blood-engorged tick, still firmly attached to his chest. He knew exactly what it was and he knew exactly what he *shouldn't* do to remove it…but he did it anyway. He grabbed the tick's body and pulled. Although it was not easy, the hiker pulled the tick until the body separated from the head, which remained embedded in his flesh.

"You creepy little bastard," said the young man as he smashed the tick with a rock. He saw his own blood ooze out onto the rock, and he was mad. Mad at the tick and mad at himself for not checking his body periodically on his journey. He had encountered ticks before and knew that this was a common hazard on such trips.

It is very dangerous to leave the head of a tick embedded. Aside from disease, infections can set in. And this is exactly what happened to this hiker. Whether it was an allergic reaction or just a very nasty infection, his nipple was swollen and itchy for weeks afterwards. Never bothering to seek medical advice, he simply put hydrocortisone on it daily but the damage was done. It left the hiker's right nipple permanently and noticeably larger than the left.

It was soon thereafter, however, that the hiker noticed a benefit to this bite. His right nipple had become extremely sensitive. Just a slight touch of it would get him aroused. Whenever he entertained a female companion in a sexual romp, should she brush against that nipple…or stroke it…or, better yet, flick it with the tip of her tongue, his erection would instantly become rock-hard and ramrod-straight. He was well endowed anyway, but this added attraction brought joy to many girlfriends. If the lady should happen to manipulate his nipple during penetration, the most violent and intensely pleasurable ejaculation would immediately follow. He had no control at that point. Nor did he want any.

This is not the end to this young man's story. It is just the beginning. We shall cross paths again with this hiker further on down the road. Be patient.

APRIL

3 Hale Marys

"If you find confident women intimidating, then grow some confidence yourself"

Kailin Gow

Marty was going to work from home today. There had been too many distractions at the office the past couple of days and several critical deadlines were looming. Peter was handling the smaller jobs just fine and Marty felt confident that things were going smoothly at the office.

Peter was holding down the fort and had even picked up a lot more gumption over the past several weeks. "Might have to take him on full-time," Marty thought to himself. A bit of his ego allowed him to think that it was because of his mentoring which, of course, it was.

His sons were already awake, getting ready for school, and Jessie was preparing breakfast. Coffee wasn't quite ready yet so Marty, still groggy, padded down the hall towards his studio. In these early mornings, he preferred to use his little "private" bathroom, just outside his studio door.

He took the latest Design Direction Magazine in with him and closed the door.

As he had done for years, out of habit, Marty slowly raised the toilet seat to peek inside, just checking. But today was different. As he lifted the lid, he saw it. A long black snake was in the water.

He dropped the toilet seat with a bang, screamed like a girl, and leaped straight up into the air. As he did so, he struck his knee against a towel rack, sending a shooting pain down his leg. He dropped to the floor, letting out a very loud and resounding, "Fuck!"

It was then that he heard the giggles coming from outside the door.

"April Fools, Daddy," said one of his sons.

"Shit!" he muttered to himself. Still sitting on the floor, he swiveled around, opened the door to face his happy and laughing boys.

He arched one eyebrow and gave them a squinty look, which made them laugh even more. "Very funny, you little twits! Now get your asses in here and get that fu…er…darn snake outta there."

The boys grabbed their rubber snake out of the toilet and ran up to the kitchen to tell their Mom about their success.

Mary Anne Forde dropped two ice cubes into a tall glass, set the glass on her kitchen table and took a seat. She popped open a can of Diet Coke, poured it too quickly and stopped too late as she watched it foam up in the glass and overflow onto the table.

"Well, just damn," she said out loud. This happened more times than she could remember but she still did it, time after time.

Mary Anne was somewhere in her middle thirties, although she kept her actual age to herself. She was short, just barely over 5 feet, trim and perky with sandy blonde hair. Married and divorced twice, she never had children although she loved them. She had started college with the hopes of becoming an English teacher but, after just the first semester, grew tired of school. She was sorry that she had wasted so much time and money. She floundered around for a while, traveled throughout Europe for a couple months, and then bought herself a horse. She was exceptionally organized and loved to give parties. So an idea was born. She started her own little business,

Cater-Tots, an event planning service dedicated to children. She drove a large white van with a colorful logo on both sides that Marty Howce had designed for her. Below the logo, in dancing letters, was her tag line: *"From Birth 'Til 8, Their Parties Will Be Great!"* Marty thought it was a terrible line and tried to talk her out of it, but she prevailed. Below the tag line, in bold type, was her website address. She liked the freedom of setting her own schedules. She truly enjoyed showing kids how to have a great time at parties. Quite often the parties would end up at CedarView Stables, with permission from the parents and safety precautions always in mind. Most of her parties were for little girls and several of them rode. This was, after all, horse country.

She got a sponge and soaked up the spilt soda, then poured the rest of the can slowly into her glass without incident. When her cell phone rang, she knew that it was going to be her best friend and riding partner, Mary Pat Phillips. It was nearly noontime and the crisp early spring day was perfect for riding.

"Hey, Mary Anne," said the chipper voice on the other end of the line, "You ready to saddle up?"

"Yeah. No parties to do today and I'm bored shitless. Let's go. I'll meet ya in 30."

"Okey Dokey...Hey, did Jessie call you about the prank her kids pulled on Marty this morning with a rubber snake? Ha! She called first thing this morning to tell me. I'll tell you when we're riding. Poor Marty! See ya soon," said Mary Pat and the conversation was done.

Forty-five minutes later, they both pulled down the driveway at the same time. Getting out of their cars, pointing at each other, they said simultaneously "You're late!" then they both laughed.

Mary Pat was a bit taller than her friend, with wavy brown hair and packed a bit more weight on her bones than she would have liked. Not that she was considered overweight, but she was solid. She, too, was somewhere in that undetermined age-range between thirty and forty. She and Mary Anne had been friends for fifteen years, having met when they each got their first horse and were taking riding lessons together. They loved each other like sisters despite each other's quirks and foibles. Mary Anne had a habit, silently, in her head, of correcting the pronunciation and grammar of virtually everyone at one time or another.

"You're doing it again, aren't you?" asked Mary Pat once.

"What? What do you mean?" responded Mary Anne, surprised.

"I just mentioned apricots…and I know you are judging or correcting my pronunciation somehow. I can see it in your face," she laughed.

"Oh, I love apricots," Mary Anne answered, using a long *a*, "and I know you say apricots," using a hard *a*, "I looked it up. They're both correct."

They laughed, too, at Mary Anne's "cake incident" within this past year. Electing to not make one of her own, she had ordered a very special cake for one of her events from a new bakery she had never tried. When the clerk brought the finished cake out for Mary Anne's approval before boxing it, she took one look at it and winced.

"Ooh, you forgot the comma." She commented shaking her head.

"Comma? *What* comma?" asked the clerk, dumbfounded? "What do you mean?"

"Wait. You mean that you *don't* know there should be a comma in the greeting?" Mary Anne was incredulous. She let out a loud, exasperated sigh, shaking her head again. "It should read Happy Birthday, *comma*, Beth!"

The clerk just stared at her. "I don't know nothin' 'bout no comma."

Evidently *someone's* grammar had gone with the wind.

"Well. There you go. You just learned something today, didn't you?" And Mary Anne smiled politely, hands on hips. "Go ahead, get your little frosting thingy and squiggle a comma in there. There's room. I'll wait."

The comma was added, although it *did* look somewhat out of place because of the spacing. Mary Anne didn't like the cake after all was said and done following the party in question, so she never returned to that particular bakery. Under her breath, the clerk had called Mary Anne a very profane word as she left the building, but she never heard it. Nor would she have approved of its pronunciation.

Mary Pat's little quirk was endearing…to some…annoying to others. She was originally from New Jersey but she would feign a southern accent at times and lay it on really thick. One of the other boarders had actually dubbed her Miss Magnolia Mouth before realizing the accent was a fake. Mary Anne, who *was* from the south and had a soft accent to prove it, thought that her friend was mocking her.

"You dip-shits from Joisey just don't know how to tawk proper." She joked.

They would banter back and forth before eventually bursting into laughter.

The chilly, windy winter had melted into a mild spring. The sweet fragrance of honeysuckle filled the air. The vines grew all along the fence bordering the long, sloping driveway down to the parking area. Remy was at the stable, walking the fence line, doing his normal grousing to himself about life in general and the current administration in Washington in particular. He, again, made a mental note to cut down that damn dead tree limb before it falls and hurts someone.

Mary Anne and Mary Pat had gotten their horses in from the pasture, tethered them to the fence around the riding ring and brought out their saddles from the tack room. The sound of another vehicle slowly coming down the gravel driveway made them turn to see if anyone else might be riding today. An unfamiliar dark blue pickup was pulling a large horse trailer.

"Oh," said Remy, coming up behind the two ladies, "I forgot to tell everyone that we're getting a new boarder. Evidently, she's here!"

Although there were a couple of vacant stalls, the pasture was so over-grazed that there shouldn't be any additional horses. The two Marys just glanced at each other and shrugged.

The truck came to a halt and a horse could be heard nervously stomping and shifting in the trailer. The driver's door opened and out stepped a very tall, strikingly beautiful raven-haired woman.

"Damn!" Mary Pat muttered almost to herself, as the new arrival walked towards them.

"Hey, Remy…and hi, ladies," said the stranger with a broad, beautiful smile and nodding her head. Nothing shy about *this* one. She stretched out her hand to the closest, Mary Pat. "I'm Myrina Gordon, but I go by Mary."

"Oh, good lord," said Mary Anne, laughing. "Another Mary!"

The new Mary looked quizzical.

"Mary Pat and Mary Anne," Mary Pat said, as she pointed her finger back and forth between the two of them.

"Ha!" laughed the new arrival. "Well, I'm just plain Mary, then."

While there was nothing plain about her, an instant friendship was born, right there, between the three of them.

Just plain Mary was a couple inches over six feet tall, with short-cropped jet-black hair. Her smooth skin was tan from the sun, which made her sparkling green eyes even more pronounced. Being very slender and wearing tight jeans made her appear even taller, especially to the two shorter Marys. Most of the boarders, with a couple of exceptions, rode western style. Mary rode English. There were jumps in the riding ring, used just for fun by all the riders. Mary had won countless ribbons throughout her riding years, primarily in the Hunter-Jumper classes. She loved the exhilaration of leaping over jumps, the higher the better. Her horse, Welcome Thunder, loved jumping as well. She had also shown in Dressage although she found it, basically, boring.

The stable where she had been boarding, a few miles away, had recently been sold to developers and would soon be demolished, making way for a new subdivision. The owners gave Remy's phone number to Mary, although they warned her about his temperament. She contacted him, met him, along with Zara, at CedarView one evening. None of the other boarders had been around at the time. Although it was definitely a comedown from the stable she was leaving, it seemed to be the only available place around. Mary had the feeling that it might just a temporary situation anyway. She had liked Zara right away but she realized it would take more than a little work to warm up to Remy. No big deal, she thought. She had dealt with assholes in the past.

Mary Pat and Mary Anne offered their help to Mary in getting Thunder off the trailer and unloading her tack. But Mary politely declined, not wanting to interfere with their riding.

"Saddle up, ladies," she said, "Don't waste this terrific afternoon. I'll find my way around the mess in my trailer and get my tack situated. I may join you later, but I want to get Thunder acclimated to the place and his stall. By the way, Remy, which stall did you say is ours?"

Remy had been taking down all the old and weathered notes that had been left on the tack room bulletin board. He had not really been paying too much attention to the three ladies chatting after Mary had arrived. The bulletin board was another of his gripes…and concerns. There hadn't been any more of those strange, cryptic notes, but neither had there been any solution to their meaning.

"I'm sorry. What did you just ask me?" Remy asked when he finally realized that Mary had spoken to him.

Mary cocked her head to one side. "Stall? Which stall is mine?"

"Oh," Remy sort of grunted. "It's one of the back ones. Come on, this way."

There was a small aisle in the middle of the front stalls, dividing the fourteen stalls, leading to the long hallway and the back sixteen stalls. Mary followed Remy as he walked through the entry and made a left turn down the aisle to the back stalls. A rooster was scrounging around, scratching in the dusty dirt, looking for bits of feed. He fluttered his wings and hastily got out of their way, protesting loudly.

"Watch out for him," Remy cautioned Mary. "He likes to peck at people's back sides. He'd be somebody's dinner by now if we didn't think he'd be too tough."

They arrived at the assigned stall. "I think…I *hope* this one suits your needs. It's actually larger than all the others for some reason." Remy said as he pointed to the stall.

She opened the door, checking to see if it needed cleaning and to make sure it was large enough. When they had met at the stable prior to her deciding to board there, it was late and it was dark and she hadn't bothered to check out the stalls but she had asked if there was a large one available.

"This'll be just fine, Remy. Thanks. You'll see why I made my request about a large stall in just a few minutes. I probably should have come out here to check out the size beforehand, but I trusted you. And my instincts were correct." She flashed another large smile at Remy, and then she went to get Thunder off the trailer.

Mary Anne and Mary Pat, by this time, had their horses saddled. Riding in the ring, they slowly trotted side-by-side chatting. For as long as they had known each other, they had never been without things (or people) to talk about. The story about Marty and the toilet snake earlier in the day was told and laughed about. They turned to watch as the clattering sounds of a horse trailer being opened up caught their attention. Then came the stomping sound of hooves as an impatient horse wanted to be out in the open air.

"Holy crap!" exclaimed Mary Pat, as she saw Thunder back out of the trailer. Mary Anne followed with a "Jesus, Mary and Joseph!"

Welcome Thunder, from muzzle to tail, was jet black He stood almost 17 hands and was solid muscle. His coat glistened in the afternoon sun. He was so black that, at times, he looked dark blue depending upon the light. Mary had his lead line firmly in hand as he nervously pranced around, snorting and sniffing the air. Mary walked him around the area, getting him familiar with the various horse scents of his new home. She gently stroked his neck from time to time, calming him down. More snorts. More sniffs. His nostrils flared and eyes were wide, taking in the strangeness.

"Bring him out here," shouted Mary Pat. "Let him meet our babies."

Mary Pat and Mary Anne both slid down from their horses and led them to the gate, opening it for Mary and Thunder. The three horses sniffed each other's noses, squealed and pranced, as strange horses do. The ladies held firmly to their horses' lead lines as this routine played out. Thunder towered over the two other horses.

"Damn, Mary," exclaimed Mary Pat, "do you need a freakin' ladder to get up on him? Did you say his name is Welcome Thunder? Unusual name. Did you pick that or was he named when you got him?"

"Oh, I named him," answered Mary. "I can't really remember where I read this…or if someone told me once…or if it's even true. But I seem to recall that *welcome thunder* may have been used as a password during World War Two. In case any spies infiltrated the troops. Two words that the Germans would have had trouble pronouncing, you know? It would come out as *velcome tunder.* I just liked the sound of welcome thunder and thought that it would be a great name for an imposing horse. So, when I saw him as a young colt, I knew that I had met my Thunder…and welcomed him into my heart. It was love at first sight, I guess."

"Wow, that is so cool!" exclaimed Mary Anne, as she gently stroked the large horse's muzzle.

For all his size, Thunder was a very gentle horse Mary had trained him well and he was, as horse people say, a push-button horse. Once everyone got over his size and striking appearance, they couldn't help but fall in love with him too.

In the weeks that followed, Thunder became very acclimated to his new home and the three Marys rode together daily, as long as the weather permitted. It may be short 30-minute workouts or longer rides that taxed both horse and rider. There were several trails in the area around the stable that took them out of the confines of the riding ring. The women shared their lives with each other and the bonds grew stronger.

"Well," Mary asked on one of their first rides together, "Mary Anne, you alluded to the fact that you've been unlucky in love, eh? Did you say that you've been married, what, twice?"

"Yeah, well…," sighed Mary Anne. "My first husband seemed to have a thing for nineteen-year-old girls. And then my second husband was… hmmm…bipolar".

"Bipolar?" responded Mary. "Was he on medication for that?"

"Nah, it wasn't that kind. He was bisexual and treated me cold as ice."

All three ladies laughed, although Mary Pat had heard this line several times. She just rolled her eyes.

"Yeah, I wasn't feeling well one day," Mary Anne continued, "so I left work around noon, which I never do as a rule. There was a strange car in my driveway when I got home. My husband didn't hear me when I came in. He was in the shower. He wasn't alone. Surprise, surprise, surprise!" she said, jazz hands in motion. "Turned out *he* had a thing for nineteen-year-old *guys*." She sighed, shrugged and slowly shook her head. "I hate teenagers!" she laughed.

Mary Pat told about her husband, Derrick, who also rode but on very rare occasions and their three young sons. As was the case with so many families, all three boys were involved in every sport imaginable and constantly busy with either practices or games. One season of sports melded into the following one. Basketball, softball, soccer, cross county and lacrosse. During each season, the boys and Derrick, who coached as well, were gone most evenings and Saturdays. Although she didn't enjoy it, sometimes she would be team mother for one boy's team or another.

"I swear," she said, "if those boys don't hurry and grow up and move out we'll be bankrupt. We deserve Frequent Buyer status at the sporting goods store. My home life consists of smelly socks, smelly shorts and smelly jock straps. Lordy! And little Jake, our rising lacrosse star, actually sleeps with a lacrosse stick in bed with him. Seriously!"

She didn't like the time away from the stable or her horse. CedarView was her "second home".

"And you, Mary?" asked Mary Pat.

"Ah, well…I guess I could use that old cliché about myself. I'm between relationships at the moment. I was married for a while, years ago. I have a son. He's an architect up in Chicago."

"Wait," said Mary Pat with an incredulous look, "You have a son who's an architect? How the hell old is he?"

"He's twenty-six, why?"

"Well, how old are *you*? You look like you're no older than thirty!"

Mary laughed a hearty laugh. "Well, thanks. A lot! Ha! I appreciate that, really I do. But I guess I'm a bit older than you think. I take great care of myself, for sure, but, in all honesty, I did have Greg when I was quite young. Oh, I was of age, mind you…but I was young, nonetheless." And she smiled.

Frank Gordon, Mary's husband, had loved everything about the military and made it his career. He had given his family a good life financially and they all had traveled around the world. The last time she had kissed him good-bye he was boarding a plane for his second tour of duty in the Middle East. The next time they were together he was in a flag-draped coffin.

Zara and the three Marys had a date to go on a long trail ride. As Zara pulled down the driveway into the parking area, she could see that there was a large piece of bright yellow paper tacked to the bulletin board. She was beginning to have her suspicions but did not mention it to anyone, nor would she until she was absolutely certain. She was the first to arrive, and glad because of it. She wanted to remove that note as quickly as possible.

THE LAST IS FIRST,
THE FIRST IS LAST.
A TINY LIE
GROWS LARGE SO FAST.

She yanked the note from its pin, stared at it for a brief moment, then crumpled it up and threw it into the trashcan. She suppressed the tears, but she was angry as hell. She thought about making a phone call but decided against it. She didn't want to make any accusations she might later regret.

She would ride Dare Devil today, a frisky liver-chestnut Saddlebred. He loved being out on the trails and was very familiar with the route that Zara would normally take. She called him DeeDee. She went and got him in from the pasture, hitched him to the fence to get her tack and turned to see that Mary Pat was coming down the driveway. Mary's truck was not far behind.

"Hey, ladies!" Zara called out as they both walked towards her. "Beautiful spring day, isn't it? It's about time." The two others agreed.

Oedipus Pex, the old rooster, was slowly approaching Zara from behind, quietly pecking at bits of dropped horse kibble as he went. Zara caught a glimpse of him out of the corner of her eye, turned around abruptly, pointing her finger at him. "Don't you dare!" she scolded, knowing what was in that bird's mind. "Git, you sorry sack of feathers!" The rooster squawked, jumped back, flapped his wings and sauntered away, trying to look as nonchalant as a rooster could.

"Mary Anne is running a bit late," Mary Pat informed them. "She just called me. She's getting her hair cut or something. Evidently there must be a mad rush at the salon for some reason. She should be here shortly, though."

Ten minutes later all three of them had their horses groomed, saddled and ready to ride. Mary Anne's car slowly pulled down the driveway and came to a stop. She excitedly hopped out.

"Jesus, Mary and Joseph," Mary Pat exclaimed as she saw Mary Anne. "What the *hell* has she done?"

Mary Anne's hair was, indeed, shorter than the last time they had all seen her. And it was now a color that would have made Lucille Ball envious.

"You like it?" she asked, as she struck a pose and patted the back of her hair with her hand. "I just had them put a little rinse in it."

"Really?" asked Mary Pat. "What did they use, Orange Kool-Aid?"

Mary Anne waved her off. "Silly," she said and smiled. "Give me a couple minutes and I'll be ready too".

As she left to get her horse, Shasta, out of the pasture, Mary, Mary Pat and Zara looked at one another, arching their eyebrows, shook their heads and stifled a big laugh.

"I guess she won't have to hire a clown for her next party," Zara said in a loud whisper.

"Hush, you. Stop it. She's heading back this way. Fine friend *you* are!" Mary Pat said…and they all laughed.

Mary just shook her head.

"Let's head to that little pond, okay?" Zara suggested. "It's getting warmer so the horses might like to go for a swim."

It wasn't really a swim, more like a deep wading that the horses would do around the shallow edge of the pond.

"Let's do it," agreed Mary. "I haven't been there yet and Thunder loves the water."

They rode single file through parts of the thickly wooded area on the way to the pond, then side-by-side when the space allowed. They chatted and laughed as they rode, laughing and joking about some of the other boarders, each other or the current events.

"Zara, have you figured out yet what all those weird notes mean?" asked Mary Anne.

"Haven't a clue. Sure like to sneak down to the stable some night and catch the creep doing it, though".

What she *really* wanted to do was change the subject. "Hey, I chatted on the phone with Jessie for a while yesterday. She may come out to ride with us over the weekend. She says to tell y'all hi".

"She and Marty are such love-birds," chirped Mary Anne. "They are *so* romantic."

"Ha!" blurted Zara. "Wait. That'll go. Romance doesn't last."

"Cynic!" exclaimed Mary.

"Realist," shot back Zara.

Marty and Jessica had the kind of loving, fun relationship that Zara and Remy had had. Once upon a long time ago. Too long ago.

They came to a clearing in the woods, rode out into the open, and there was a beautiful pond reflecting the clear blue sky.

"Oh, how nice!" exclaimed Mary. "Look, Thunder. We'll go swimming here during the summer."

Her horse snorted as he sniffed the air and all the ladies laughed.

"Did he really understand you, Mary?" asked Zara.

Mary laughed. "His response was sheer coincidence. He might be smart but not *that* smart! Hmm, I *love* the smell of springtime, don't you?" and she inhaled deeply, filling her nostrils with the woodsy, marshy aroma.

They walked their horses single-file around the edge of the pond, through areas of tall grasses, sending dragonflies and smaller insects buzzing. Georgia was in the second year of a severe drought and what had been a large pond a few years earlier had shrunk in size, leaving a wide ring of exposed muck, mud and soft dirt.

Mary Pat trotted her horse out in front of the rest and picked up the pace. All of a sudden her horse, Ginger, hit a very soft, muddy patch of the shore and began to sink up to her knees. The horse reacted with agitation.

"Oh, shit!" Mary Pat exclaimed. "Let's calm down, Ginger."

The horse was frightened and tried to move faster...to get out of the watery mud. But the more she moved, the deeper she sank. Ginger was now up to her belly in the mud. Mary Pat jumped off, into the water, holding onto Ginger's reins. The other ladies looked on in horror as they thought the horse would surely disappear beneath the water, but Ginger sank no further. But she appeared wedged in. Mary hopped off of Thunder.

"Take his reins, will ya, please?" she hollered to Zara, as she rushed into the water to help Mary Pat. "Don't panic," she called out, "and remain calm. We don't want either of you hurt. We'll get you outta this."

Ginger tried to lift her legs, now heavy with soggy mud and uprooted weeds. The mud made a loud sucking sound with each lift of her legs. She was struggling and getting more nervous but not yet panicky, although her eyes and nostrils were wide and she snorted loudly as she tossed her head.

Mary Pat pulled on the reins, straining the bridle, while Mary got behind Ginger, leaned into her and pushed on her rump. Mary had to make sure that Ginger wouldn't step on her in the muck. At this point, both ladies were almost hip-deep in the muddy water. It was very slippery and cold, but they seemed to be making headway. Mary Pat kept pulling, directing her horse towards the shallower edge of the water, while Mary kept pushing as hard as she could. Ginger's legs were straining against the weight of the mud and Mary Pat hoped that she wasn't hurting herself in some way. Mary had stopped for a moment to catch her breath and to regain some strength. Turning her back into Ginger's rump once again, she pushed and pushed even harder, digging her boots into the soft bottom of the pond. She felt that the horse was finally getting out of this mess.

Mary Anne and Zara were now off their horses, with Zara holding Thunder's reins tightly. Their horses had gotten nervous and pranced around, sensing Ginger's plight, but they weren't unmanageable.

Ginger was now able to lift her hooves without getting bogged down any further. Mary Pat felt the ground under her feet becoming more solid and she stepped out of the water, with Ginger close behind. "Good girl, Ginger…good girl" she murmured calmly.

The horse stepped onto the shore and shook like a dog shaking off rainwater. Mud and water splashed all over Mary Pat and she was finally able to laugh a nervous and relieved laugh.

"Ma word," she said, using her very best faux-southern drawl, fluttering her eyes and fanning her face with both hands. "Ma po' l'ill ol' haht is skitterin' like a June bug!"

At first the other three were silent. Then they all burst into laughter. Things could have really turned tragic in this beautiful setting.

"Damn!" Mary Pat exclaimed as she felt the mud that had hit her face. "I must look like a fright. My face is a mess!"

"Aw, hell," Zara chuckled, also relieved that their ordeal was over. "A blind man would be happy to see it!"

Mary still stood practically hip-deep in the water, exhausted but pleased with their efforts and the happy result. "Whew! Wasn't *that* fun?" she said as she slowly worked her way out of the muddy water and onto the shore.

Mary and Mary Pat, thick with mud and dripping wet, walked their horses back to the stable, while Zara and Mary Anne rode their horses several paces behind them. The conversation was not as animated on the return trip although they remarked that they would laugh at this incident someday. But not today. Too soon.

When they got back to the stable, Mary Pat slowly took the saddle off Ginger, now caked in dried mud. The one clean area on the horse is where the saddle had been. "Lordy, we're both a sight, aren't we, my girl?" she said. "Get ready, young lady, you're getting hosed off. And then when I'm done with you, you can hose *me* off!"

A still-wet Mary made sure that Thunder was okay, released him back into the pasture, and then bade them all a farewell as she headed towards her truck. "*Loved* the day, girls," she said sarcastically, "we *must* do this again sometime. Remind me to bring my bathing suit next time, though."

She waved to them over her shoulder as she got into her truck and left for home...and a hot shower.

Zara put DeeDee back into the pasture as well and watched as the horse galloped away, probably relieved to be back home and safe. She chatted, then, with Mary Pat as she was hosing off Ginger. "You know, Mary Pat," Zara said, shaking her head. "Nobody likes a good adventure more than I do but I think if I had my druthers, I'd start today all over again...and stay home!"

Mary Anne, who wasn't ready to call it a day even after all the excitement, opened the gate to the riding ring and led Shasta in, closing the gate behind her.

"Be careful down there," called Zara. "Shasta seems a little jittery after that fiasco at the pond."

"Yep...thanks. I'm just going to trot him around a bit to get his mind off things. I need a little stress relief, too...although, God knows, I didn't do a freakin' thing but sit on my ass during the whole ordeal."

Neither Zara nor Mary Pat were watching as Mary Anne picked up her pace with Shasta, got into a slow lope, then a faster canter. Mary Anne had watched as Mary had taken Thunder over the jumps in the ring with ease. She had tried a few of the low jumps with Shasta but nothing like Thunder could do. The jumps were set at a moderate height and Mary Anne was feeling adventuresome, adrenaline still pumping from the thrill at the pond. She pointed Shasta towards a jump, urged him on with a swift kick in the ribs, leaned forward as the horse took flight and felt exhilarated when Shasta's hooves hit the ground, clearing the jump beautifully.

"Wow! That was awesome! Good boy!" she exclaimed, almost to herself.

"Hey!" called Zara, who suddenly noticed the activity in the ring. "If you're going to do that put on your damn riding helmet. We don't need any more excitement today."

"Don't worry," Mary Anne responded, "No big deal. I'll be careful. I didn't see anybody wearing *their* helmets earlier today out on the trail. What's the difference, eh?"

They knew that, at times, they were cavalier about wearing their helmets. It was a precaution that they had all been taught years ago, but they had gotten sloppy on occasion.

Zara returned to chatting with Mary Pat, who was now using the sweat scraper on Ginger to get the water off. But she kept glancing towards the ring, just to make sure.

Mary Anne trotted around the ring a few more times, then urged Shasta towards the jump again as he picked up his gait. He was at a full gallop as he approached the jump when suddenly, Spook chasing Shadow, the two barn cats, ran from the woods and directly across Shasta's path. Spooked, he stopped abruptly, throwing his rider out of the saddle and headfirst into the vertical post. Her head hit the post with a loud thud and she fell to the ground with a resounding plop. She lay there, motionless.

"Jesus H. Christ! Oh, no...oh, no...oh, no!" yelled Zara in a panic when she saw Mary Anne fall. She ran to the gate, calling back to Mary Pat, "Call 911...call 911!"

Grabbing her cell phone, she did so and excitedly told the operator what had just happened. She quickly put Ginger back out into the pasture even though she hadn't finished grooming her. She started running towards the gate into the riding ring when she heard the sirens already approaching and she was grateful that the response was so amazingly fast. A fire engine slowed at the top of the driveway, then turned in and headed down the slope.

"A fire truck?" she said out loud to herself. "What the hell? I said she *fell* from a horse, she didn't set it ablaze!"

A heavy-set man hopped out of the truck and ran towards Mary Pat. He quickly explained that both a fire engine and ambulance were always alerted in calls involving accidents. Mary Pat hurriedly explained the situation; the man grabbed some equipment and ran into the ring, leaning down by Mary Anne. Zara was frantic, pacing back and forth a short distance from them, wringing her hands and near tears. Mary Anne started to move and let out a pathetic little groan.

"Thank God!" Zara sobbed. "I thought she was dead."

Mary Anne slowly opened her eyes to discover that she was in the shadow of a large, smiling man. A stranger.

"What the…where…?" she tried to speak but her head hurt and the ground was reeling.

The man examined her and tried to reassure Zara that it didn't appear to be anything serious, just a very nasty bump on the head. He wondered, though, if she shouldn't be transported to a hospital for better observation, considering that it was a head trauma. There could be swelling of the brain. Or bleeding. Another siren sounded as though it was getting closer and, within a few moments, an ambulance headed down the driveway, coming to an abrupt halt. The EMTs conversed, and then they all looked at and spoke with Mary Anne for a few moments.

"Follow my finger with your eyes," said the man kneeling by her side, moving his hand slowly from left to right.

"Why do you bite your fingernails?" admonished Mary Anne.

"Count to five," he said, quickly pulling his hand back.

"Five what?" she answered, a bit confused. "Oh, wait…I know what you're doing. 1, 2, 5, 7. The year is 1937 and Julius Caesar is the president." She tried to sit up. "Ooo…oow…whoa! Why is the ground spinning so fast?"

They all agreed that a trip to the hospital was, indeed, in order. A thorough exam, including x-rays was necessary in a situation such as this. The EMTs got her onto the stretcher, loaded her into the ambulance and told Zara where they were headed. Zara said that she would follow them to be with Mary Anne.

"I'll call you as soon as I know anything," she said to Mary Pat before running to her truck. "Could this day possibly get *any* worse?"

"Don't even go there with that thought," answered Mary Pat.

Two hours later, relaxing in their hot tub, wine glass in hand and her husband by her side, Mary Pat answered her ringing cell phone. She saw that it was Zara.

"Okay, what's the word? How is she? Anything broken? A concussion?" she stammered all at once.

"Oh, I guess she's fine. She's telling everyone over here how to pronounce things correctly. They *were* going to keep her here overnight for observation, but I think they are seriously reconsidering that decision."

Mary Pat laughed a nervous laugh. "Well, that's our girl, isn't it?"

"Really, I think they *will* be releasing her pretty soon. I'll get her home and settled, then I'll head back to the stable to take care of the horses." Zara said in a very tired-sounding voice.

"Already taken care of, Zara. Don't worry about a thing tonight. Remy and a few other of the boarders were here and we all fed the babies and put them back out."

"Oh, hey. Thanks *so* much, Mary Pat. You are a gem…and I love you! I am so tired that I just might be in bed by eight. Honestly, this has been one hell of a day, hasn't it?"

Mary Pat could tell that her friend was beyond exhausted.

"Rest up, sweetie," she reassured Zara. "Nothing more to worry about today. Enough is enough. Actually, enough is too much!"

Much later that night, another slip of bright yellow paper was tacked to the bulletin board.

**THE FIRST IS LAST,
THE LAST IS FIRST.
HOPES ARE LOST,
DREAMS ARE BURST.**

MAY

Miss Givings and Snapp Judgment

"Judgment comes from experience, and experience comes from bad judgment".

Simon Bolivar

Amber Givings had serious doubts about the long-term success of her relationship with Raymond Futtz, the latest in a succession of boyfriends. She was also in a quandary because, this year, two of her favorite annual events happened to fall on the same day: Mary Anne's Derby Day Party and the first horseshow of the season at Double D Farm. Double D, owned by Doreen and Devon Lockridge (hence, the name), was a very popular venue both for novices and seasoned riders hoping to add ribbons and trophies to their respective collections. In years past, Double D would schedule their first show either the week before or the week after Derby Day but, obviously, not this year. She had been showing at the Double D since she was nine years old. She and Flapjack had taken ribbons on a regular basis and she enjoyed the competition. It was a good learning show as well. The 4-H kids could hone their skills from the judge's remarks, guidance and critiques. Amber had been competing with many of the same young riders for years and she looked forward to seeing them again. But she hated the coincidence of the two events ending up on the same day. It was usually a long day at the show and she would be exhausted when she got back to the stable, took care of Flapjack and went home. Although Mary Anne's party wasn't until late in the afternoon, Amber thought she'd be too tired to enjoy the festivities.

Then there was the concern about Raymond. She liked being with him. But he hadn't really opened up to her. Not that he was shy. He was obviously smitten by her but there was something missing. The young man seemed pleasant enough, just a tad dense. Whenever the topic of horses came up, Raymond quickly changed the subject. They had gone out to dinner a couple times. Well, if McDonald's could really be considered dinner. And they had gone to one movie. It had been a loud comic-book type of action flick…Amber hated it…Raymond raved about it for days afterwards. Amber had spent several long conversations about him with Zara at the stable. Although she was always willing to listen and perhaps offer a bit of advice now and then, Zara knew that whatever she said to Amber went in one ear and…well, it went unheeded, suffice to say. Although she had not even met Raymond yet, based upon what Amber had been telling her, Zara thought that Amber could do…*should* do much better.

Amber was hoping that Raymond would go to the horse show with her, but she wasn't so sure how he would fit in with Mary Anne's crowd if she invited him to attend the party with her afterwards.

Raymond was working at Cousins Feed & Seed when she first met him. She had pulled her dusty, rusty pickup truck into the loading area to get horse feed. He had just moved up from South Georgia to work at his uncle's store and had just started to work on that very day. She thought he looked like a big, cuddly teddy bear, with scruffy sandy blond hair and dimples. She found that endearing. He was tall, had an early tan from being outdoors a lot and, with his rolled up sleeves, she could tell he was well muscled. He easily loaded six fifty-pound bags of feed into the bed of her truck, hoisting two at a time over his shoulder, and gave her a nice smile. She couldn't keep her eyes off of him.

"Yer good ta go, m'am," he hollered as he slammed the tailgate shut.

She caught his eye in the side view mirror and waved a coy little wave as she drove away.

She thought about him that night as she ate dinner. She was twenty-two, worked part-time as a waitress at a tiny barbecue restaurant, attended a community college in hopes of becoming a veterinarian and lived with her parents. Any spare time she could arrange was spent at CedarView Stables with her beloved horse Flapjack and conversing with Zara.

"There's a new kid working at Cousin's, Daddy," she casually mentioned during dinner. "He's cute in a sorta dopey, dorky way. He seems nice, though."

Roger Givings and his wife, Lacey, had heard their daughter mention one boy after another over the past few years. Poor Amber, they thought, falls in and out of love with every shift of wind direction. She was not particularly an attractive young woman if one analyzed her individual features, but she had a pleasant, perky personality and, when the mood was right, she could actually appear sultry. She was a virgin and expected to stay that way until marriage. She had seen too many of her high school friends end up pregnant without any prospect of marriage. She watched as her friends changed from sweet little "mommies" playing with their real-life baby dolls into haggard, tired, complaining bitches. That scared Amber to death.

She had "forgotten" to get something at the feed store and returned the next day, hoping that the cute teddy bear who had loaded her truck yesterday would be there. He was. She quickly found what she had forgotten and then browsed through the store, looking at this and that, until she was certain that he had seen her. He did. She looked up, in mock surprise, to see him watching her.

"Oh! Hey," she said, sweetness dripping from her lips and a sparkle in her eye. "I forgot something yesterday and I had to come back. Wasn't that silly?" She fluttered her eyes. She could do coy very well, especially for a virgin. "I guess you're new here, huh?"

"Yeah," answered the teddy bear, with a big smile. "Came up here to see if jobs were any better than down south. My uncle and aunt own this place so they gave me a job right off."

"Well, that was awfully nice of them, wasn't it? My name is Amber, by the way. Amber Givings."

"Hey, Miss Givings," he answered, tipping his baseball cap politely. "Amber's a pretty name. I like it." He repeated her name again. "Amber," except, with his clipped accent, her name came out as Ember. Oh, she thought, that was *so* cute. "I'm Raymond but all my friends call me Ray-Ray." Oh, she thought, that's *not* so cute. So juvenile. From that point on, she never called him anything other than Raymond.

Raymond Futtz, an only child, was raised by overindulgent and doting parents on St. Simons, a small island off the coast of south Georgia. He loved the ocean and everything about it. His dietary habits were deplorable. Aside from seafood (fried, of course), if sugar, cheese or gravy were not involved in some way, then he was not interested in any way. His eyes had a droopy, sleepy look, which, for some inexplicable reason, Amber thought was adorable. No one would actually call him handsome although he had a certain soft-edged but rugged look that many girls found attractive. He was twenty-three years old and had absolutely no idea what he wanted to be when he grew up. Which, of course, was the problem: he hadn't grown up. His main pleasures were video games, swimming and NASCAR. He didn't swear… "dang" was the strongest word he used and he didn't drink alcohol. Strangely, he was petrified of horses, a fact that Amber would soon discover.

The big day dawned with clear blue skies and the promise of plentiful sun. Amber awoke excited…and nervous. She was going to try something totally new at the show that morning. In the past years, she and Flapjack showed in the western events. Mary, the beautiful, newest arrival at CedarView Stable had been instructing her in English riding and Amber absolutely loved this new discipline. And, to her delight, so did Flapjack. He was, apparently, a natural at jumping. Who knew? Mary was an excellent teacher, had a lot of patience and was very encouraging. For that matter, it was Mary who had suggested that Amber show in a jumping class at the Double D show. She was that confident in the young rider's new ability. They practiced every day, for several hours, until both horse and rider were near exhaustion. But it looked like it might pay off. Mary had taken Amber to the Tack Shack to help her get outfitted properly. Amber practically fainted at the cost of everything…jodhpurs, belt, helmet, boots, jacket, shirt…but when she saw her reflection in the dressing room mirror, she squealed with delight. Okay, so it will take working some overtime to pay for it, but it was worth it, she thought to herself. "Day-um, I look *good*!" Amber was ready to blaze new trails.

She would still show in a couple of western events, then switch tack and attire for one English class: Hunter-Jumper. The thought of that made her heart skip a beat. She hitched up the horse trailer she kept in her parent's back yard to her pickup truck, loaded up her change of clothes and her packed picnic-style lunch. Raymond was going to meet her at the stable, so off she drove, eager for a new adventure.

She was surprised to see that Raymond had arrived before she did at CedarView, although he was remaining in his car. She thought he might have been out looking at or talking with the horses. A few other boarders were there, grooming their horses and getting ready to ride on this beautiful morning. Most of them were also going to be at Mary Anne's party later in the day. If he had noticed Amber's arrival he didn't react in any way. He stared straight ahead, almost in a daze. She walked up to his pickup truck and tapped on the driver's side window, which was rolled up. He jumped as though he had just been stung on his ass by a bee.

"Dang, Ember! Didn't see ya come up," he blurted out, as he rolled down the window.

"Well, come on out, silly, and help me get my stuff and Flapjack. I gotta get him pretty for the show."

Raymond winced and, if Amber was seeing correctly, he almost turned pale as a ghost, losing his nice tan. He slowly shook his head.

"Ember, perhaps I shoulda said somethin' before now. Horses sorta scare the you-know-what outta me."

"What? No, way. You big lug…what are you afraid of? Did you get hurt by one or something? You never mentioned this before. Why didn't you tell me when I invited you to join me today?"

"My grandpa had a nasty ol' mare when I was a kid. It bit me by surprise one day, then turned her rump and kicked the tar outta me. I was in the hospital for a few weeks…had nightmares every night…woke up screamin' that a horse was gettin' ready to jump onto my bed on top of me. Never saw that bitchy mare again. Don't know what grandpa did to her but I didn't care. Hope she became a nice bottle of glue somewhere. Kinda dumb, isn't it? Me working in a feed store, selling to horse folks and getting to know you, all horsey and stuff. I was scared to tell ya…scared to say I'd come with ya…and, dang, I'm scared right now!" Raymond chewed on his lower lip.

"Well, damn," Amber thought to herself "what a day *this* is turning out to be. Riding in an event I've never tried before and with a Nervous Nelly as a boy friend. Obviously Ray-Ray ain't gonna be worth jack shit today!"

She talked him into stepping out of his truck. There were no horses anywhere around to bite him by surprise or kick the tar outta him. What tar he might have left. She had things to do, time was wasting, but she talked gently and assured him that she would be there by his side, not to worry, and perhaps he'd help her get Flapjack out of the pasture. If he could have turned even paler just then, he would have. She took him by the hand; they walked to the gate and entered the pasture looking for Flapjack. He was grazing on some willowy grass in the marshy area towards the far end of the pasture before it turned into woodland. Raymond kept looking all around them as they walked, glad that horses couldn't climb trees and get him if he tried to hide up in one if a steed should attack. Amber slipped Flapjack's halter over his head, fastened it and started to lead him away. She reached back and grabbed Raymond's hand once more. His palms were sweaty. She chatted excitedly as they walked, getting herself all prepped for the big day ahead. He nervously laughed and nodded, still looking all around as they approached the gate…and…ahhhh…safety! Amber had decided that she *would* go to Mary Anne's party, no matter how tired she might be. She would need the relaxation and at least one mint julep after today. She had not mentioned the party to Raymond. She had thought she would wait to see how things went at the show. It promised to be a very interesting day, for sure.

Amber was able to get Raymond's help in bathing Flapjack, although he kept a fairly safe distance. She walked her beautiful and now-clean horse around to hurry the drying process and then she groomed him from muzzle to tail. Lo and behold! Raymond slowly reached out and ever so gently petted the horse on the nose. He quickly pulled back his hand, as though he had just received an electric shock. Amber shook her head and laughed. Zara had offered to loan her one of her many saddles and accompanying tack. Mary had also offered some of her gear, too, for which Amber was grateful. English saddles and tack were costly and she had already spent a small fortune to look beautiful today. Zara was there at the stable before Amber had arrived, which surprised many of the other boarders. They knew that Zara was a very late sleeper and they thought that daylight must be a real shocker for her. Zara had picked out an appropriate English saddle for Flapjack, polished it up and it now had the clean scent of Neatsfoot Oil combined with the smell of leather. Wonderful, refreshing horse scents.

The tack was loaded into the compartments in the trailer. Flapjack was an easy loader and walked right up as Amber led him to the ramp. Raymond stood back and watched. Zara came running up to Amber, giving her a big hug and wishing her good luck at the show. "I'll try to get over there in time to see you ride," she told Amber "and perhaps…just perhaps I can persuade grumpy old Remy to join me." The rear gate to the trailer was closed and secured with chains. Flapjack was happy to be munching on a flake of hay that Amber had placed in the basket inside the trailer. And off they headed to Double D, Raymond following in his own pickup.

"I been knowin' Doe-reen since grammar school," Amber's dad had reminded her as she left home this morning. "Give 'er a big hello and a hug from me, will ya?" He had said this exact same thing every year.

Mary Anne started the preparations for her Derby Parties days in advance. This was definitely an adult-oriented party…no Cater-Tots for *this* one! The menu hardly varied from year to year, with her guests looking forward to a once-a-year treat or two. Her specialty was the traditional burgoo, a hearty stew with a variety of meats and vegetables. She kept her particular recipe a well-guarded secret despite many requests from guests. She made several derby pies; pecan and chocolate chip sensations that were so rich that people could almost pass out from the shock. The fact that practically everything she served on this day was liberally laced with bourbon didn't help matters. Even the whipped cream that topped the pies was made with a splash or two of bourbon. Then, of course, were the mint juleps. She grew her own mint in her vast garden and this was the perfect time of year (and purpose) for harvesting beautiful, long stems. This year, she had purchased more expensive, aged bourbon for the event. Needless to say, she had been sampling it, in little sips, as she went about setting up the tables and decorations. She normally hired a bartender to keep the juleps flowing but not this year.

The party decorations were all Derby-themed…banners, napkins, drinking glasses…and no expense was spared in making sure everything looked just perfect. Her guests would be arriving late in the afternoon, many of the ladies wearing the most flamboyant hats they could find…or make. A Kentuckian by birth, the Blue Grass in Mary Anne's roots came to the surface in all its glory on this day. Money flowed like bourbon at this party, with bets being placed by everyone, including the racing novices. Information on the horses, their jockeys, the owners and trainers was bantered about as if it was the hottest gossip in town. Of course, there was always good dirty gossip being discussed throughout the day as well. Inhibitions went out as the bourbon went in.

There were festive tables set out in her beautiful back yard, surrounded by dozens of huge rose bushes, now in full bloom. A small vase was the centerpiece on each table, with the color of the roses in each vase matching the tablecloth and napkins. Mary Anne loved coordination. She also loved the compliments that would echo throughout the event. And she was very eager for her stable friends to meet her special guest…her new bartender.

Trailers were pulling into the parking area at the Double D by the dozens, stirring up the dust from the dry terrain. The sounds of eager riders, laughing and talking, mingled with the sounds of nervous horses whinnying and snorting. All the places under the shade trees had been taken since very early in the morning, practically at the crack of dawn. Amber found a spot she liked, backed her trailer into it, parked and hopped out into the bright sunlight. Raymond, who obviously never attended a horse show in his life (nor had ever intended to do so), was awestruck by all activity. He pulled his truck alongside Amber's trailer and parked. He sat there for a moment, chewing his lower lip again.

He opened the door to his truck, thought about it for a second, then cautiously stepped down. He ambled up to Amber. "Dang! Ain't seen *this* kind of stuff before," he muttered, almost to himself.

Gotta work on his grammar sometime in the future Amber thought to herself. If, of course, there *would* be a future with Raymond. He was cute. He was fun. But, as she was quickly discovering, he was…well, dumb as dirt. She unloaded Flapjack and hitched him to the side of the trailer. With eyes wide, he surveyed the surroundings, snorting and sniffing the air. He was a seasoned horse when it came to shows but he always reacted the same way as soon as they arrived. Amber figured that all horses do the same thing. She hung a hay bag on the side of the trailer and Flapjack started munching on it right away, forgetting about the other horses around him, all hitched to their respective trailers…all munching their respective hay.

Amber checked the show sheet again, although she had scanned it when it had been posted online on Double D's website. Noting the classes in which she would compete, she meandered away to the registration window to pay the required fees. There were two large show rings at Double D; one was for the western classes, the other for the English events. The classes run concurrently and Amber was pleased to have seen that she would not have a conflict with the timing of her chosen classes. Each ring had its own judge, ringmaster…sometimes called a steward…and its own announcer. It would soon get dusty and noisy. She was very familiar with the western pleasure classes and was glad that those would be first, before her big challenge of the day. She would have to make a mad dash and a quick change from her cowgirl appearance to her English lady appearance. She had really liked how she looked in her bedroom mirror as she tried on this new attire several times at home, and was now eager to show off this new look in public. She would also have to change Flapjack's tack quickly. Her heart began to race. She changed into her fresh, clean western attire for the first event, then saddled and bridled Flapjack. They were ready to go. She led her mount to the lineup waiting for their first event, Raymond walking beside Amber, on the far side from the horse. He kept looking around, nervously, and chewed on his lower lip again…still.

"Amber!" called Doreen Ambridge. "I just knew I'd be seeing you here today. How the heck ya been doin'?"

"Oh, just great, Miss Doreen, thanks. Daddy says hey, by the way. Looks like you're going to have a super turnout today. Oh, this is Raymond," Amber blurted, indicating her friend. "He's a new friend of mine and would you believe it, Miss Doreen, he's never, ever been to a horse show before." and she laughed a nervous little laugh.

"Well, hello, Raymond. Hopefully you'll see some terrific riders and horses here today. Your little friend here is one of them. Oh, and Flapjack, too, of course."

"Hey," mumbled Raymond as he nodded his head.

"Gotta go," Doreen called as she hurried away. "Good luck, Amber!"

The gate was open for her class. Amber climbed up into the saddle, clucked, kicked her heels and Flapjack moved into the ring. Big class, Amber thought to herself. There were fifteen horses in the class and the dust was kicked up as they first walked slowly around the ring. Judging starts as each horse enters the ring. The ringmaster and the judge were standing side by side. The judge would let the ringmaster know which gait he wanted to see, then the ringmaster would signal that call to the announcer who would then let the riders know via the PA system, loud and clear. The horses will be judged on the rail at the walk. Then the judge will call for a jog and soon a lope. These gaits will be judged in both directions, clockwise then reverse, around the ring. When the call to reverse the horses is given, the riders must keep their mounts moving at all times, never stopping to turn around. Flapjack stumbled just a little as the "reverse your horses" was announced and Amber hoped that the judge was looking elsewhere at the time. She recognized this judge from years past and she liked him. He was always very fair. The command was given to line up in front of the judge. The horses must stand still at this time, to give the judge the opportunity to look at each horse and rider individually, sometimes walking around to see all sides. The judge may also request, directly to the rider, to back up his or her mount. Ringmaster and judge conferred for a moment, the judge rereading his notes and the scribbled grades in the score sheet. The ringmaster took the scorecard and ran across the ring to the announcer's stand.

The awards were announced, with Amber and Flapjack placing second. Amber was pleased. Evidently the slight stumble had gone unnoticed. Raymond hooted and hollered from the sidelines at the announcement, which sort of embarrassed Amber. She collected her ribbon and moved out of the ring, waiting for her next class.

Two more western events, with Amber and Flapjack taking two more ribbons: a first place and a third place. She slid down off of Flapjack as soon as she exited the ring. It was her final western class, now she had to get back to the trailer, change tack and change her clothes. Raymond had been holding onto the ribbons she had won and he handed them back to her on the way back to the trailer. Although he was still a bit apprehensive, he no longer appeared so nervous being around so many horses. He came to the realization that, at least for today, these horses had other things on their minds and they weren't going to seek him out and attack.

Amber's eyes lit up when she saw Mary and Zara walking around the area, obviously looking for someone.

"Mary! Zara! Over here!" she squealed. "Over here!"

"Hello there, young lady. What's that I see in your hand? What are all those ribbons?" Mary said with a huge smile. Zara gave Amber a really tight squeeze and a kiss on the cheek.

Amber proudly held up the ribbons for her friends to see and shrugged her shoulders.

"Yeah. We were lucky, I guess. Flap tripped a bit in the ring during the first class but I guess the judge was looking the other way or something. Anyway, I'm excited. And I am *so* excited to see the both of you here!" she exclaimed, almost jumping up and down with excitement. Mary nodded towards Raymond.

"Oh, gosh," Amber gulped, "I almost forgot my manners…I am so sorry. Mary, Zara, this is Raymond. Raymond, please meet my really, really good friends Mary and Zara."

"Hey, ma'am," Raymond said and nodded to each lady in turn, shaking their hands. He was taken aback by the strength in Mary's handshake and by her beauty. Mary was wearing light tan jodhpurs, high black leather boots and a pale blue sleeveless blouse that was unbuttoned just enough to reveal a provocative neckline.

"Wait," asked Amber, looking at Mary's attire. "Are you riding in the show today too?"

"Nope. Not today. I just wanted to look like I fit in," she laughed. "Oh, no. Today is *your* day, Amber. I came here to check out all those things I taught you back at the stable…to see how good you are under pressure, you know? Besides, Zara and I thought you could use a cheering squad but I guess you have one here already," indicating Raymond. Raymond smiled a toothy smile, not taking his eyes off of Mary. Although no one would ever know it, he dreamed about her later that night.

"Amber, you better go get yourself ready," Mary said, suddenly realizing the time. "I'll change Flap's tack for you. You gotta hustle before they start that class without you."

"Aw, that's so sweet, Mary. Thanks so much. Gosh, I didn't realize time was getting' away from me." Amber grabbed her new English attire and hustled off to change. Raymond stayed close to the two ladies, looking around to make sure no horses were close enough to bite or kick.

Mary and Zara glanced at the show sheet. Mary shook her head. "Uh, oh," she said.

"What?" asked Zara.

"The English judge," Mary responded. "I've encountered her before at other shows. Veronika Snapp." She almost expected that the mere mention of the name would frighten small children and spook the cattle. "She's a good judge, but…," she trailed off.

"But what?" asked Zara, frowning.

"Well, aside from being about a hundred and ten years old…she's good, as I said, but she has a few quirks and isn't always fair. But that's just my opinion, from what I've observed. I know there have been complaints about her in the past. I didn't know she was still judging. Perhaps Amber should have gone just for English Pleasure and not jumping just yet. But… too late for that now, isn't it?"

Mary quickly changed Flapjack's tack from western to English and was cinching up the girth when Amber made her first public appearance in her new attire.

"Wow!" gasped Raymond when he saw her. "You look amazing. Wow!"

And she did. Both Mary and Zara agreed and each gave her a big hug. Mary pulled out her smartphone and snapped a couple photos of Amber.

Then she took a couple selfies, including Zara. Raymond photo-bombed one and they all laughed.

"You'll have to adjust your stirrups when you mount," Mary said to Amber. "I estimated but you'll know what feels best. Hurry into the ring and take some practice jumps before the class starts. There are already several others in there now too."

Amber pulled the stirrup leathers out so the stirrup was in her armpit to gauge the length, climbed up into the saddle and made the final adjustments. Mary smiled. Her student learned very well…and very quickly.

"Good luck, sweetie," Zara said.

"Remember, Amber," Mary instructed. "You are being judged the second you enter the ring. Keep your head up, your heels down, get Flap into a good, steady gait, focus, focus, focus…and have fun! This is your very first time riding English in a show. We can hope for the best, but this will be great learning experience for you even if you don't place."

Amber smiled a great big smile, blew them all a kiss and headed into the ring to practice.

Amber had already memorized the jump pattern the riders were to follow in the class. There were several other riders in the ring practicing as well and Amber wanted to avoid getting in their way…or having them get in *her* way. Ten jumps, none too high, but a couple a bit intimidating. The jumps back at CedarView were old, rickety and not as colorful as these but Amber felt confident that Flapjack would do just fine. She got him into a nice, steady trot, then a canter as she approached the first jump. Up and over he went with ease. A few more jumps, all cleared perfectly, and Amber was having a great time. She directed Flap towards that strange jump, the one with triple bars and he leaped, knocking down one of the bars. Damn, she thought. She tried a few more jumps, all of them clean, and her confidence was renewed.

The announcement was made to clear the ring. This class would begin in five minutes. The horses and riders filed out of the ring as the ringmaster and judge entered and took their places. Veronika Snapp, who was closer to sixty rather than a hundred and ten, was dressed entirely in brown. Standing all of 4'9", she was trim, with a hooked nose, leathery skin, wearing tight dark brown trousers, a lighter shade of brown silk blouse and a cloche hat with three long, brown and white feathers sticking out from its brim. She looked like a falcon seeking its prey. The ringmaster signaled to the announcer to introduce the first rider. Amber would be riding fifth.

The first horse had a good round, clearing the jumps with ease, rider confident and she received a restrained round of applause as she finished. The second rider, a man who appeared to be in his mid-forties, although this class was for riders 18-35, didn't do so well. His horse clipped several bars, knocking down a few as he rode. No applause for him as he left the ring. Amber's heart rate began to speed up. Two more riders, then it was Amber's turn. She took a deep breath, leaned over and gave Flapjack a hug on his neck and whispered "I love you…let's do this!" into his ear as she was announced to begin her run. Mary took out her smartphone again and videoed Amber's ride.

The first guests began to arrive and Mary Anne plopped a great big billowy hat on her head. Her wardrobe's color scheme for the day was black and white, with a huge Kelly green bow on the side of her floppy white bonnet. Kisses and hugs were exchanged and the aroma of burgoo wafted throughout the house and out into the yard.

"Damn, Mary Anne," laughed one of her guests, "I could smell your party half a block away! Love it…you are the best!"

Mary Anne was flattered and smiled broadly, giving the speaker another big hug and a squeeze. Inwardly, she laughed out loud. He says the exact same thing every year, at every party.

"Well, thanks! Don't make me blush, now, ya hear? Go hit the appetizer table, guys. Oh, and you remember where the bar is, don't you?"

Mary Pat and her husband, Derrick, parked their car in the expanse of front lawn that Mary Anne had reserved for her guests. Living on three acres of property, with a huge front lawn was a benefit at least once a year. Mary Pat wore a full-length bright blue dress with matching hat, ribbons flowing from its brim and down her back. Another guest, who Mary Pat hadn't seen since last year's party, pulled in and parked next to them.

"And a gracious good afternoon to you, my deah," Mary Pat declared in the deepest, fakest southern drawl she could muster. "Imagine meeting y'all heah!"

The ladies air-kissed each other and giggled like schoolgirls. Their respective husbands just shook their heads and smiled. The two ladies linked arms and headed towards the house chattering like magpies, husbands walking behind. They stopped to chat with another guest, an older woman with an outrageously flamboyant hat.

"I don't know why I come here every year," she joked, "just to be harassed and embarrassed by a houseful of drunks...me, included, of course." And they all laughed.

"Well, I declare!" Mary Pat continued with her southern belle act. "Talkin' 'bout drunks, let's go on in and get a julep. I'm parched." She fanned her face with her hand.

The cars were beginning to add up and, obviously, so were the guests. The house was filled with conversation and raucous laughter. And drinking.

"Where's Mary? Is Mary here yet? And I haven't seen Zara yet, either." Mary Pat asked Mary Anne.

"Not yet. They both went to watch Amber at that show today. They'll be here later, I hope. Hey, come on over to the bar. I want to introduce you to someone".

Mary Anne took Mary Pat by the elbow and led her to the bar. A tall, heavy-set man was busily making the prettiest and best mint juleps that had ever graced this party. He was chatting with a few of the guests as he poured the bourbon, and wild laughter would follow almost every one of his statements.

"Mary Pat," Mary Anne announced proudly. "Please say hello to Don Edwards." And she did the tah-dah motion. "Recognize this handsome guy?"

Mary Pat had a quizzical look.

"Oh, you silly. Perhaps you don't recognize him because he's not wearing his EMT uniform."

"Oh, my god!" exclaimed Mary Pat. "You were that shadow standing over Mary Anne in the riding ring after she pulled that asinine stunt."

"Yes, ma'am, indeed. That would be me. I thought she was the prettiest knocked-out-cold lady I had ever seen," smiled Don, with a toothy grin. "And besides, I'm a sucker for redheads."

He held out two mint juleps to the ladies. "To be honest," he said, "Margaritas are my *real* specialty but this is the poison du jour, so here you go!"

Mary Pat switched her head back and forth, looking at him, then Mary Anne and back to him again. She took the drink and sipped it loudly through the straw, finishing it in a gulp.

"Well, I'll be damned, Mary Anne. You little vixen, you," laughed Mary Pat, switching to her drawl once again. "Wouldn't y'all know it, though?" She leaned in, almost whispering in Mary Anne's ear. "The best way for y'all to find a guy is flat on your back with your legs spread! Oh, did I just say that out loud?" Then she laughed. Mary Anne gave her "the look", and made a fake frown.

"He's so sweet," Mary Anne purred, rubbing Don's burly arm. "He called me every day after I got back home to see how I was doing. Son of a gun…one thing led to another and, well, here we are!"

"And where, exactly, *are* y'all, Mary Anne?" drawled Mary Pat.

More guests were lining up at the bar, so Don went back to making his drinks. The two ladies walked across the room, arm in arm, chatting.

"He's great," cooed Mary Anne. "He's a real gentleman. He's taken me out to dinner a few times. And a couple movies, too. He's been married before and has a young daughter. She and her mom are out in…oh, shoot…somewhere out west. Can't remember which state. He sees her a couple times a year, though. He loves my cooking. Oh, and he's so smart… and articulate. I haven't had a problem with *any* pronunciations!"

"Well, that settles it," Mary Pat blurted. "Marry Mister Diction the minute he asks you!"

Amber took a deep breath, held her head erect, tapped Flapjack's side with her heels and headed into the ring. The falcon in the cloche hat started taking notes. Flap's steady walk became a trot, then eased seamlessly into a canter as they headed for the first jump. Up and over with ease. The adrenaline was pumping and Amber felt great. Could Flap actually know he's being judged? She had never felt such energy and electricity in his strides. The next jump. Perfection. Eight more jumps to go, including that tricky oxer that Flap shied at earlier and the triple bars, which he had nicked in practice. No problem! Amber rode flawlessly. Mary watched with pride as her young student, and mount, performed like seasoned pros. Zara could barely watch and closed her eyes every time Flap approached a jump, cracking them open just in time to see the horse hit ground again. Raymond was impressed and completely forgot he was surrounded by horses, even though none were too interested in taking a bite out of him…or kicking him in the ass.

The round was over and Amber trotted Flap out of the ring to wait for the other seven riders to complete their runs. Mary couldn't help but smile. She felt that, even this early in the class, that Amber would certainly place. Amber slid out of her saddle and stood by her horse, kissing him on the nose and patting his neck. Raymond came up to her and actually petted Flap on his side, albeit cautiously. Mary and Zara came running up to them and they both gave Amber a tight squeeze.

"Well done, Amber…*very* well done," Mary exclaimed breathlessly. "Can't wait to hear the results. Snapp is only going to place three horses, and you will surely be one of them. I hope!" Then they all laughed.

"Amber, I know the show gets over late this afternoon. Are you planning…,"

Amber was standing slightly behind Raymond. She started gesturing wildly and silently, rapidly shaking her head no. She knew what Mary was about to ask. She had not told Raymond about Mary Anne's party. Amber mouthed the word NO, pointing to Raymond. Mary understood.

"Ah…are you planning on being at the stable…ahh…early tomorrow morning?" Mary continued.

"Probably. Yeah, I guess so. Why?"

"Well, I thought perhaps we could have another lesson." And, nodding her head, she winked at Amber.

"Yeah! Cool. I'd love it." Then she thought about the rest of the riders in her class. "I'm getting nervous. I guess I should watch but I just can't bear it. I heard a couple rails being knocked down while we were talking. I guess we must be pretty far along with the riders, aren't we?"

The announcement was made that the final rider had completed the course. Zara and Mary crossed their fingers as the ringmaster carried the score sheet from the judge to the announcer. The winners were announced, from third place to first. Amber was wearing number 22, her lucky number. But neither her name, number, nor Flapjack's name were called. Amber was crestfallen. Zara gasped and Mary was stunned by the decision. Mary ran to Amber to comfort her the best she could.

"I'm so sorry, honey," trying to put a positive spin on it. "But you looked awesome and Flap did a great job. "Look, this is your first time in English. Chalk it up for experience. You should be proud of what you did. There's always the next show…and the next. If you'd like, why not ask the judge for some pointers. Ask her why you didn't place. After all, you had a faultless, clean round. Find out what she was looking for that you didn't do. It couldn't hurt. Follow protocol, though. Ask the ringmaster to request to speak to the judge. That's polite. There's a break between the classes and there he is. Ask the ringmaster. Go ask," she prodded. "Don't be shy. Zara and I will take Flap back to your trailer for you and get him cooled down. Raymond will come with us, won't you, Raymond? Or do you go by Ray?" Amber didn't want to tell her what his friends call him.

"Sure!" said Raymond, still awestruck by Mary.

Amber approached the ringmaster with her request. He agreed readily, knowing that the judge often did this with young riders. She approached the judge cautiously.

"Excuse me, ma'am. Ms. Snapp," she said with a catch in her voice.

Veronika Snapp stopped in her tracks and turned to look at her. She was carrying the clipboard with the information from all the classes she was judging and the results.

"Yes?" was her simple reply, looking up at Amber.

"I was wondering if you might be able to give me a few pointers… or…ah…suggestions about what I might be doing wrong. I thought I did everything perfect and we had a clean run. I didn't place in the class and I was wondering why. Could you please tell me what I did wrong?"

The little bird of prey looked at Amber, checked the number on Amber's back, then glanced at her notes. Amber tried to see the score sheet but the judge was too quick.

"Nothing, missy. You didn't do anything wrong. I just don't happen to like palominos."

And that was it. Veronika Snapp turned on her heels, with no further word, and walked away. Amber's shoulders slumped and her heart sank. Discrimination. At a horse show…because of the horse's color. Amber watched in disbelief as the judge walked away. If she had still been holding her riding crop she would have liked to hit the old bird with it.

Mary, who had hitched Flap to the trailer, was approaching Amber just as the conversation, such as it was, ended. She watched the judge walk away and, seeing Amber's body language, knew instantly that a bit of consoling was in order.

"Okay, honey. What did she say?"

Amber, holding back the tears, told Mary the short, terse pronouncement that the judge had made.

Mary scrunched up her face, put her hands on her hips and shook her head.

"Ah, well, just damn. That's politics, Amber. Love it or hate it, it's everywhere," Mary sighed, remembering similar situations in the show rings of her past.

"But, that's just so unfair!" Amber said with a sob.

"Unfortunately, Amber, life isn't fair. I'm surprised that you haven't discovered that by now. It's a rude awakening, I know, but hey, it's blunt, it's painful and that's life. Sometimes life's a shit. Period. Yes, you did everything perfectly. Perhaps the blue ribbon went to someone who *didn't* do everything perfectly. But we'll never know. We don't know what that judge saw or didn't see. There are assholes all around the world reaping accolades and rewards daily. Fair? Hell, no! Fairness and perfection won't elect presidents. You know…and I know…and Flapjack knows that you did the *absolute* best you could. I'm proud of you, Miss Givings and I'll award you with my personal blue ribbon."

Mary bowed to Amber with a sweeping gesture, and then gave her a big hug.

Raymond had come up behind them and felt left out. Amber, actually, had forgotten that he was here.

The three of them walked back to the trailer where Zara was gently grooming Flap and making sure he had plenty of hay.

"Aw, Raymond," Amber said, suddenly remember that she had packed a picnic lunch for them both. "I totally forgot about our lunch, with all the excitement and everything."

"No problem," he responded. "I knew you were too excited. And I was too nervous. But, you know what? Being around all these horses today and none of them comin' chargin' after me…and seein' how sweet Flapjack is…well, maybe I'm getting over my fear. A little bit any way. I may have been too quick to judge all horses by that one old mare. I owe it all to you, pretty lady."

Amber sighed "Oh, how sweet, Raymond. I'm so glad. Really!" She thought about it for a moment, felt a little ashamed, then said, to the surprise of both Mary and Zara "I wasn't sure I would be going or not after the show today, Raymond. So I didn't even mention it to you beforehand. But one of our friends is having a Derby Day party this afternoon. Would you be interested in going with me? There will be a ton of people there. Horse folks and otherwise. It's always a lot of fun."

"Dang, Amber. I'd love to. Thanks. Shoot, yeah!"

Mary and Zara glanced at one another and smiled. Ah, youth. The excitement, and then the disappointment of the show drained her spirits. Now Amber really wanted to go to Mary Anne's party and gulp down as many mint juleps as she could.

She looked at her other two friends. "I hope you're going to the party too so we can get drunk together and you can give me some more life lessons, Mary," she laughed.

"Go get Flap back to the stable. Don't bother changing, you look great…and so horsey," Mary giggled. "I won't change either. Give the guys something to ogle…especially if I carry my riding crop and smell like leather," she winked broadly. "I'll meet you there…and be ready to drink up, young lady. I can really handle my liquor!" and she let out a big guffaw.

Zara said that she would go on too. Go home, change and try to convince Remy to join them at the party.

Mary's car pulled up along side Zara's as they both hunted for a place to park on Mary Anne's now-crowded front lawn. They found spots furthest from the house, parked and got out.

"Where's that southern gentleman of yours?" Mary asked Zara.

"Ha! The old grump is sitting home. Alone, as always. No matter how much I try to tell him that he'll really enjoy himself here, he won't budge. He probably feels that if he laughs…hell, if he *smiles*…his head will explode. Besides, I can have more fun without him…watching all of you drunks." And the ladies laughed. The strongest drink that Zara took was diet cola.

It was nearly post time by the time they had arrived at the party. The raucous laughter and conversation greeted them as they approached the house. It was a segregated party. Boarders from CedarView Stable clustered around each other and it was a large crowd. The other clusters were comprised of neighbors, friends and some clients of Cater-Tots, but without the tots in tow. They weren't the horse crowd, but they enjoyed the derby and a good party.

"Mary! Zara! You finally made it!" shouted a bourbon-filled Mary Pat from across the lawn. "Come on an' I'll buy y'all a drinkie-poo."

The three ladies linked arms and ambled towards the bar. Mary's attire, still in jodhpurs, plunging neckline and high black leather boots, drew stares from most of the male guests, many of whom worked their way towards her throughout the evening, hoping to engage her in conversation.

"Mary Anne has taken a lovah," Mary Pat whispered with a thick drawl. Mary stopped short and looked directly at Mary Pat.

"Say what?" was the incredulous response.

"Yay-us," Mary Pat drawled her best drawl. "That big lug who helped her to her feet after the tumble at the stable has now swept her *off* her feet!" now dropping the drawl. "Actually, he seems really sweet in a big old bear way."

Mary Pat led Mary and Zara to the bar, which had now become a regular mint julep filling station. Sprigs of mint, powdered sugar and empty bourbon bottles were everywhere. Don was still making them and swilling them down as well.

"Don. Don, boy," Mary Pat tapped Don on his shoulder. "Don, I'd like y'all to meet two of my nearest and dearest friends. Don, Mary. Mary, Don. Zara, Don, Don, Zara." And the boozy introductions were made. Don shook hands with both of them, each with a firm grip. Mary was impressed. Guys, so often, limp-handed women, afraid of breaking their tender little hands. Mary liked guys who were strong, took command and weren't afraid to be themselves.

"Very nice meeting you, Don. Are your juleps as strong as your handshake?" asked Mary.

"Well, hell. They're practically straight bourbon," Don replied with a bit of a slur to his words. "I'll make yours a double if you'd like."

"I'd like," grinned Mary. "It's been a long day. Hey!" she suddenly realized that it was almost race time. "Where do I place my bets? Where's the bookie?"

Zara asked Don for a diet Coke.

Mary Anne came up behind them and gave each a big hug. Lots of hugs going around today, for sure.

"Come with me. Grab your drinks and come upstairs. There are TVs in just about every room, but the big screen one is in my living room. So's the bookie. Riders up! Bets are about to be closed, so hurry."

The ladies grabbed their drinks and ran, giggling, up the stairs. Zara planted herself on the floor, right in front of the television, eager to hear her favorite sound: Assembly of Buglers.

Bets were placed, spirits were up and drinks were downed. Amber and Raymond made it just in time and she looked beautiful. She *had* changed her clothes when she had gotten back to the stable. The English-riding showgirl from a short time before was now in a pastel-colored, flowered-print dress. Her hair was tucked into a big flamboyant hot pink hat with ribbons and bows piled high.

"Whoa, Miss Givings!" shouted Zara when she saw her. "Don't you look like a vision." Raymond smiled. He thought so too. Maybe, he thought, I should try one of those mint things that everybody is raving about. Just one, though.

The horses were being loaded into the gate. The bell sounded and the race was on!

Almost as soon as it began, the race was over. There were hoots and hollers from Mary Anne's guests as the horses dashed around the track. There were always winners and always losers, but everyone was having a good time. Even Raymond got in on the betting. The most casually dressed there, in jeans, a snap-front western shirt and a big Stetson, he fit in perfectly. Several of the CedarView boarders recognized him from the feed store. Mary passed around her smartphone so everyone could watch Amber's ride at the show. They complimented her...and consoled her. The beautiful, pleasant spring day had mellowed into a perfect spring evening. Spring blooms filled the air with intoxicating fragrances. Mary Anne's garden always got raves. Amber took Raymond's hand and led him to a wrought iron bench in the middle of the rose garden. Perhaps she had been too hasty in her assessment of this guy after all. He *was* sweet and very attentive. He was also very drunk. For someone who never had a mint julep, he sure took a liking to them in a hurry. Actually, Amber was feeling a bit wobbly herself and got the "giggles" easily. The bourbon had helped ease the pain of her brief encounter with Veronika Snapp. As they sat there, two other ladies came wandering through the garden.

"Mary Anne told me she had chocolate mint out here somewhere" one guest was saying to the other. "Chocolate mint, did you ever? I never knew that existed, except as a candy," and she, too, had the giggles. There were more than a couple drunks in the garden.

"Yes, I saw it last year," responded the other guest. "It really and truly smells like mint...well, chocolate mint. Really. Oh, here it is. Look, there's a whole bunch of it growing here. Smell it. You won't believe it"

The first lady bent way over, then knelt down, to smell the plant, almost losing her balance.

"Oops!" she squealed and laughed. "That damn ground just won't stay still. Oh, my. You're right. That aroma is amazing. I'd like to take a big bite out of it."

The ladies giggled some more, nodded a greeting to Amber and Raymond and meandered back into the house, chatting non-stop. Raymond was intrigued.

"Chocolate mint? Really? A plant that smells like chocolate mint." He got up to check out the situation and located the plant in question. Amber was feeling very, *very* mellowed out. As Raymond stood up, she slowly, gently rolled over onto the seat and drifted into a woozy sleep. Raymond bent over to smell the plant. He just kept right on bending until he was prone. Oh, it felt so good to be lying down. So he simply passed out.

The guests switched from drinking to eating now, surrounding all the tables, filling their plates and finding places to sit. Even though it was a warm spring evening, Mary Anne lit a fire pit out in her back yard, attracting several guests as they pulled lawn chairs around it. The party was mellowing, the conversations were getting quieter. A stereo, with outdoor speakers, was playing quiet jazz that wafted gently throughout the yard. The bar area down stairs was empty, Don having joined in with the eating and talking. Zara excused herself to go to the ladies room but went downstairs instead. When she got to the bar, she refilled her glass part way with diet Coke. She looked around, poured a little bourbon into her glass. Stopped, looked around again, then poured some more.

Marty Howce walked around all the tables of food that Mary Anne had prepared, surveying her handiwork and grabbing samples as he walked. Not only were all the tables beautifully decorated, but also the food was pretty as a picture.

"Mary Anne," he mused. "I know I say this every year, but will you *ever* consider being a food stylist? I've worked with some great ones from coast to coast on my food shoots and, frankly, this table right here." as he spread his arms, "could be on the cover of any food magazine I know."

"Aw, thanks, Marty. I appreciate all the kind words. Who knows? Maybe someday…in my next life. But I really don't know all the tricks of making food photogenic like the pros. I've read about them. I've even seen some videos about them. And I've certainly seen *your* work. *Your* results.

No, I'm just having so much fun now with my kid parties. Maybe I could freelance…or sit in on one of your food shoots sometime."

"Sure, that would be terrific. I'll let you know." He glanced out into the garden, squinting his eyes to make sure he was seeing what he *thought* he saw. "I might be mistaken," he laughed "but I think poor Raymond might have passed out in your rose garden."

Mary Anne roared with laughter. "Oh, good lord! I hope he didn't fall into my rose bushes. One of my friends, Jeannine, did that last year. I'd hate to have to pull thorns out of *his* ass like I did with poor Jeannine!" and she howled with laughter again.

"He's safe there," Marty said, shaking his head and laughing. "Just let the poor guy lie there to sober up. Should be interesting to see his reaction when he wakes up."

The food was disappearing and dirty plates were appearing everywhere just as quickly. The sun was long gone, the moon was rising in a cloudless sky. A perfect ending to an exciting day. Amber had told her story of the day's events countless times, eliciting sympathy and encouragement. The groups of horse people and non-horse people mingled, chatted, laughed and agreed that this was Mary Anne's best derby party ever. But then, they said that last year too.

It was getting late. The fire in the pit was reduced to just a small pile of warm, smoking embers. The party was winding down and the guests were sobering up. Good-byes were said. Hugs and kisses given. Handshakes shared. Winnings had been distributed to satisfied bettors, amongst the grumblings from the losers. Cars were driving off into the night, their headlights bouncing off the trees as the cars navigated the bumpy terrain of Mary Anne's front lawn. Mary Pat and her husband thanked Mary Anne for the great time and looked around trying to see if Amber or Mary…or Zara were still here.

"Oh, well," said Mary Pat. "I guess I missed them if they've already left. Anyway, good evening, dahling" she drawled. "It was a blast. Have fun with Don!" and she winked.

"Get out, you two," Mary Anne laughed. "Get out and stay out!" They all laughed.

Mary *had* left a bit earlier. She had walked Zara to her car.

"Are you sure you're alright?" Mary had asked Zara. "You seem a bit… well, shaken."

"Oh, yes. I'm fine. I think I might be on a sugar high or something. Too many sweets there for me. Especially that derby pie. Yes, it does it to me every year. I just don't learn. Don't worry, I'll be fine. That black coffee will kick in before I'm even out of the neighborhood. Really."

Mary watched as Zara drove down the bumpy driveway, almost hitting a fence post. "Must be a rut in the road," Mary thought. "I'll have to be careful driving out."

About an hour later, Raymond, still flat on his back, fluttered his eyes open. He stared straight up into a dark, star-filled sky with a beautiful crescent moon overhead. A shooting star streaked by and faded quickly. He smiled a goofy smile as he surveyed the heavens. The sweet fragrance of roses and gardenias filled the air.

"Hey!" he said suddenly, sitting up. "Where the hell am I?"

JUNE

The Lost River

"After a certain point, all natural bodily changes are for the worst."

Mokokoma Mokhonoana

Bryan Dennison awoke each morning with aches in his legs and ideas in his head. Belonging to an inventors club, he possessed a few patents on products that went absolutely nowhere but made him proud of his endeavors nonetheless. Basically retired, he was constantly in search of things to keep his mind occupied. He needed a purpose. Repairs or improvements would be made on things when none were really necessary. It seemed that he was always walking around his place with a hammer in one hand, a cup of coffee in the other and his eyes peeled just trying to find a loose nail somewhere to hit. He had trained his horses lovingly, primarily having them do "circus tricks", as his wife called them. One of them would actually sit down on a bale of hay on command. He had been thrown from, stepped on or fallen from more horses than he could recall. He had even felt a bite or two on rare occasions. Whether it was arthritis, bursitis, advancing age or simply a matter of hypochondria, he had a complaint about some pain, in some part of his body, on a daily basis. Brandy, his wife of thirty years, had been genuinely concerned when these aches and pains started appearing several years ago but had become immune to his perpetual whining. She'd listen politely to his daily morning report on his condition but she had, more than likely, tuned him out after the first sentence. The fact that he was at least twenty pounds overweight didn't help maters any.

Brandy was slender, with shoulder-length brown hair, which she wore in a stylized pageboy. An intelligent, well-read woman, she worked as a print broker for a large industrial press. She was very well compensated for her talent but she was also very frugal. She and Jessie Howce often laughed about and compared notes about their respective frugality traits. Bryan, on the other hand, loved to spend money. He would invest in one crank invention after the other. He had been a building contractor before "retiring" due to his many ailments. Through wise past investments, they were comfortable and led a good life.

Brandy and Bryan each had two horses, which they had boarded at CedarView Stables long before Remy and Zara became the owners. They faithfully cared for their "babies" twice a day. As a rule, Bryan would feed and groom them every morning and Brandy would have stable duty in the afternoons. Often, though, they would accompany each other. Whenever their two young grandsons would stay with them for a weekend visit, or during the summers when their visits were longer, they would join them. School had just gotten out for the summer and the boys were staying with their grandparents for two weeks. Jason was 11, dark-haired and brash. Terry was 9, blond and a bit shy. They both idolized their grandparents and looked forward to the times when they could visit.

"Hurry up, boys," Bryan urged his grandsons. "Finish your breakfasts and let's head to the stable. Looks like it's a great day out there and perhaps we can go for a little trail ride. You up to that?"

"Sure am, Gramps!" answered Terry.

"Me, too!" responded Jason enthusiastically.

"Well, then…let's get!" said Bryan as he pushed back his chair and stood up. "Oops, sorry." He said quietly.

Brandy shot him a glance. She had heard the telltale sound.

"Did you just fart?" she asked, glaring at him. The two boys stifled a laugh.

"Well, yeah…guess so. Take short sniffs and there'll be enough to go around!"

The boys almost choked from laughing.

"Oh, boys, please don't encourage the old goat," said Brandy, shaking her head and trying to hold back a smile. "That was disgusting, Bryan… especially at the breakfast table."

"Oh, please," smiled Bryan. "A deaf man would have been happy to hear it."

"The sound is one thing, Bryan, but…" she trailed off. She finally smiled, leaned in to him and gave him a peck on the cheek. "But I love ya anyway."

Bryan looked at the boys, shook his head, rolled his eyes and smiled too.

"Qui a coupé le fromage?" he asked, looking around.

"Bryan!" Brandy scolded. "Honestly, Bryan. Sometimes you annoy the hell outta me".

"Yeah?" he responded. "Well, sometimes *I* annoy the hell outta myself too. Get over it." He continued, with a laugh. "You think that living with *you* is any pink tea, girly-girl?"

"Living with me, you old fart, is a privilege. You should bow down and kiss my feet every day."

"Yeah? Well, you should kiss my ass in front of the post office at high noon!" laughed Bryan, again. And the boys just howled.

"What does that mean, Grandpa…that thing that you just said?" asked Terry. "What was that, French?"

"I'll tell you when we're out riding. I'll teach you how to pronounce it properly so you can surprise your parents when you get back home."

"Oh, lordy," said Brandy, as she shook her head…again.

The air was clean and fresh. The sun was shining brightly in the clear blue sky. The bird feeder in their back yard was alive with chirping activity. The pathway leading to their detached garage was lined with young, alert variegated hostas, just awakened from their winter slumber. Brandy's perennial garden had already started blooming despite the prolonged drought.

"Get your gear together, kids," Bryan called to the boys. "I'll be out there in a minute…once I can get myself going. My back is killing me already." This was his usual morning complaint, this time isolating his back.

"You joining us today, dear?" he asked Brandy.

"You and the boys go on. Maybe I'll join you in a little while. I'm going to stop by and visit my parents. I chatted with Dad a bit on the phone before you got up and Mom seems to be slipping a bit more. I want to chat with them both. Or, rather, talk to Dad about the situation. He's going to put up resistance, I know, and put up a fight. But somebody has to think about this and address the issue…and soon."

"Oh?" said Bryan, genuinely concerned. "Don't you want me to come with you?"

"No, that's okay. I can handle this, really. It's been coming for some time and I've just been putting it off for too long. But *please* keep your eyes on those two," indicating the rambunctious boys getting ready for their day. "You know how excited they get…and how careless they can be."

"Yeah, yeah, I know. They are *truly* boys, though, aren't they?"

"As opposed to what, monkeys?" laughed Brandy.

"Come on, boys!" Bryan called loudly. "Damn, you're slower than mole-asses!" and he heard the boys giggle again.

"I call shotgun!" Jason shouted as he hopped into the passenger side front seat. Terry, always too late on the call, slid into the back seat, folded his arms and silently called his brother a bad word.

"Everybody in and buckled up?" asked Bryan as he started the engine. Both boys answered to the affirmative. Remembering what he had done with the boys when they were much younger, Bryan started to back the car out of the driveway and halted abruptly halfway.

"Are we there yet?" he called out.

The boys, remembering this also, answered loudly in unison, "No!" and laughed. Bryan drove halfway down the block, glanced into his rearview mirror to make certain there were no cars behind him and came to another very abrupt halt. "Are we there yet?" he called out again.

"NO!" answered the boys again, louder this time and they all laughed. This was a game the three of them had played as the boys were growing up. As any parent or grandparent knows, the question of impatience: "are we there yet?" has been asked throughout generations. Bryan started singing a little ditty. The boys, knowing it only too well, chimed in. All three sang and laughed.

"Had a little monkey; took 'im to the country; fed 'im on gingerbread. Masso, fasso, kick 'im in the asso, now my monkey's dead!"

"Eew, a squished possum," Terry announced as they passed the remains on the road.

"Ah, that's so sad, boys," Bryan began another tale. "Ya know, Georgia used to be overrun with those damn little critters. Possums comin' outta the woodwork. But, over the years, they have vanished entirely from the state. Don't know why. Don't know where they went. Now, those wildlife folks," he paused, shaking his head, "they don't want to panic us Georgians with the thought of no more possums. So, they pick various neighborhoods throughout the state and late every night a truck comes around and throws out a dead, squished possum…just so folks think they are still rooting around. Those stupid critters are slow and they love to sit in the road just waiting to be squished, you know?"

"Gramps," said Jason, looking back at Terry and rolling his eyes. "Exactly how gullible do you think we are?"

"Shoot!" answered Bryan. "Two years ago you would have believed me. And you wouldn't have known the word gullible."

And from that point on, whenever any of them spotted a poor dead critter in the road, one of them would say: "A truck came by."

Brandy finished doing the breakfast dishes, picked up a packet of information from her desk and grabbed her car keys off of the hook by the back door. Her parents, both in their eighties, lived a twenty-minute drive away. She had postponed this conversation with her dad as long as she could. Both of her parents had been vital, interesting people all of their lives. Her mother, especially, had been socially active in various organizations…garden clubs, reading circles, welcoming committee for their neighborhood. But she had slowly, yet steadily slipped into another world. Little clues, at first, had given Brandy pause. A forgotten word, not that unusual for someone of that age…then forgotten names…and times of disorientation. She would have good weeks, months even, when she would be perfectly lucid. Then, without warning, she'd slip. A bit further each time. She must be slipping more, considering her dad's phone call. Brandy feared this illness. She constantly bought and completed monthly puzzle magazines. She played mind-challenging computer games daily. Keeping her mind active, she figured, could…*should* stave off any mental deterioration.

Her parents, Cliff and Sara Ambridge, had been best friends and marriage partners for sixty-two years. They had raised and educated two loving and loved children. They now had six grandchildren and two great grandchildren. They had maintained a beautiful home for decades, a chore now taken on almost entirely by Cliff. Their house, a stately colonial with ivy covering the front brick wall along the road, was situated in a neighborhood shaded by decades-old oaks and elms. Brandy pulled her car into their long driveway, shut off the engine, collected her thoughts, released a deep sigh and headed for the house.

The lawn had been freshly mowed and all the hedges lining the front of the house were neatly trimmed. There were pine islands surrounding several large trees in the lawn, edged by caladiums poking through the straw. Here and there, lacy ferns showed off their fresh green fronds.

Brandy closed her eyes and slowly inhaled the aroma of the fresh cut grass. She had always loved that crisp, clean scent. Out of politeness and respect, she tapped on the front door before opening it to enter. She slowly walked through the foyer. Sara was seated on the sofa in the living room, watching television, as Brandy stepped into the room.

"Hi, Mother," she almost whispered, not wanting to frighten her.

"Oh, hello, dear," was the calm response, as she turned around. "I didn't hear you come in. Is Bud with you?"

"Bryan, Mom. My husband is Bryan."

"Ha!" laughed her mother. "I knew that. What's wrong with me?" and she laughed again, shaking her head.

Bud was Brandy's younger brother. He had died suddenly from a massive heart attack four years earlier.

"No, Mom. Bryan is taking Jason and Terry over to the stable for a ride this morning".

"Jason and Terry?" Her mother looked confused. "Do I know them?"

Cliff was entering the room and heard this. He turned to look at Brandy.

"Yes, Mother. Jason and Terry. They're on summer break now. They're our grandsons."

"You have grandsons already? Oh, dear. How did I miss *that* piece of news?" and she laughed again. "Are you taking them to the lake?"

"No, Mother," Brandy was getting frustrated now and switched back and forth from calling her Mother, then Mom. "We haven't lived near the lake in nearly thirty years." And that lake in question had been in New Hampshire. "How are you feeling, Mother?"

"Well, just fine, dear. Why do you ask...don't I look okay?"

"You look beautiful as ever, Mother. I was just asking. You look just fine."

"Oh, I'll be right back, dear," Sara said as she got up and headed out of the room, suddenly seeming to remember something. "I found something and I want to show it to you. I had a feeling that you would be here today."

Brandy and Cliff exchanged glances as Cliff shrugged and shook his head. Cliff was a dapper gentleman. His thinning, not entirely gray hair, smooth complexion and stylish moustache belied his age. As always, he was dressed as though he was still going off to business. Fashionable dress slacks, white shirt and a perfectly tied bow tie, not a clip-on. He was a charmer with the ladies and almost always had a twinkle in his eye. But there wasn't much of a twinkle today.

After giving him a warm hug, Brandy launched right into her speech. "Dad, I have something to show you, too. Please do *not* get mad at me but something has to be done. We've delayed this way too long."

Cliff almost knew what was coming; yet he wanted to avoid it. It was a fruitless endeavor. Brandy opened the packet she had brought with her. A beautiful color photograph was on the cover of the brochure. River's Edge Assisted Living was within fifteen minutes of where they now were standing. Brandy had visited and revisited the facility on several occasions checking every detail.

"Dad, I know that you're strong and in good health today. At least, I assume you are. But what if something happens to you? Suppose you fall. Suppose you become ill. Who will take care of *you* on a daily basis?

Certainly not Mother. I still have a job so I can't be here 24-7, now, can I? We need to act before this turns into an emergency situation."

"I know," started Cliff, so quietly that Brandy could hardly hear him. "I know that Sally has been going downhill". He had called his wife Sally since the day they first met. "I've been doing great with her. She still listens to me and we manage fine. Sure, she has her moments…there might be times when she goes into a rage for no apparent reason. But, dammit, I can handle her well enough."

"The question is, Dad, how long will you be able to handle her? When is enough too much? Sure, you can handle her today…but what about a tomorrow that might not be that far off. How many tomorrows will become more and more difficult for you? That's going to happen *someday*."

Her father teared up and let out a plaintive sigh. "I'm at that age where I don't have that many somedays left. Then I worry, at times, that I have too *many* somedays left," he said, staring off into space. "How many more springtimes will I enjoy? How many more winters will I endure? I don't think we were intended to live as long as we do." He paused for a beat. Brandy looked puzzled by that last remark. "I mean, us humans. Centuries ago if you lived to be forty or fifty, you were considered damn old. Great advancements over the years. Were they really all that great? Pills…machines…and more pills keep us old folks going and going until our bodies say enough is enough. Knee replacements…hip replacements… everything but brain replacements. That will come sometime, I'm sure. Sometimes enough is too much. You know, if we could just check out when we're ready, that would be great. You're too young to remember your mother's old aunt, Maud. Actually, she may have passed before you were even born. Anyway, she was *way* up in years, in the hospital for one ailment after the other. She was lying there in her hospital bed, watching all of us yack our heads off. She just turned to us and said 'Well, I've had enough', closed her eyes and quietly died. Perfect! What a wonderful way to go. I think about this every day. Every damn day. I lie awake at night thinking *one day closer*. Either I'll be gone or she will. One night, in the not-too distant future, one of us will climb into bed alone. An empty bed. I pray to God, for poor Sally's sake, that it will be me. If I go first, Sally will be lost and you will be burdened. I'm sorry for sounding so morose,

Brandy. But, you know? No matter how good a life one has had, sometimes old age just plain sucks."

Sara entered the room with an old black handbag slung over her arm.

"Look what I found in the back of my closet the other day. Lord knows how long it's been there," she said, holding out her newfound prize. She had long since forgotten the purpose nor had the need for a purse for the past couple of years. "Come. Sit next to me, dear," she beckoned to Brandy and patted the seat. They both sat on the sofa as Cliff settled, sadly, into his big recliner, watching them both.

Sara opened the purse. She pulled out a faded but still beautiful lace handkerchief, an old pack of Black Jack chewing gum that had hardened with age, a lipstick, a dime, a penny and an emery board.

"Did you say you were taking the boys to the lake this afternoon?" she continued before Brandy could correct her. "You and Bud used to have so much fun there. Remember that wonderful old amusement park they had...on that little island? You used to *love* that boat ride through the tunnel. What was that called?"

Brandy was taken aback by the question and had to stop to think for a moment. She hadn't thought about that amusement park in years. Her favorite ride had been on a rickety old wooden barge-like boat that floated slowly through a long, dark, dank, twisting wooden tunnel, emerged into the outside again and then went up a steep incline like a short roller coaster. The boat would pause at the very top, for an eternity thought the young Brandy, then released and went zipping down, kids screaming with glee, making a big splash in the water at the bottom. She and Bud would ride that the first thing as soon as they got to the park and it would be the last ride, again, before they headed home.

"Oh, my," answered Brandy. "I haven't thought of that place in years. Let me think." She paused for a few moments. "It was the Lost River. That's it. That's the name of that ride. The Lost River. Wow...it was so much fun. We loved that ride." And for a brief instant she was riding it once again.

"Oh, what's this?" her mother asked, with a puzzled look on her face, as she pulled a crumpled piece of paper that was stuck in the corner at the bottom of her purse. "Now why would I keep this?" She opened it up.

On the paper was a long-forgotten grocery list. Her mother looked at it for a second, and then slowly turned the paper over, as if to examine it.

"Ah, that's why! Look, dear."

She handed the paper to Brandy. She read it and was struck speechless by the sad irony. A warm tear rolled down her cheek. Her mother must have seen a quotation years ago and thought enough of it to make a note of it. On the paper, in her mother's handwriting was *"Time takes all but memories."*

Bryan's car rumbled down the bumpy driveway at CedarView. Several other cars were parked there and Bryan could see a few riders trotting around the ring.

"Good golly," he blurted. "Looks like everybody and his brother are out for a ride today, too!" He opened the car door, stepped out and farted. He looked around as if trying to find something on the ground.

"Did ya hear that, boys? Must be a bullfrog around here someplace."

"Gramp," retorted Jason. "I swear, you must be a bullfrog magnet. They seem to follow you wherever you go." And both boys laughed.

"Smart-ass!" Bryan snickered. "Who do you want to ride this morning, boys? I'll be on Sassy."

Sassafras was a black and white Paint and she was Bryan's favorite horse. She was spirited and very smart. Buck was a large buckskin quarter horse. Patches was a brown and white Paint and Dolly was an older, gentler, very sweet flea-bit gray Arabian. All of the horses were well trained and well behaved. Bryan had used them all as schooling horses.

"I want…ahh…Bucky!" decided Terry. Jason selected Dolly for today's ride. The boys had been riding since they were very young and had even competed in children's events at a couple of small, local shows. They knew how to properly groom their horses first, and then saddle and bridle them.

The boys ran toward the stable, frightening Mother Clucker, the hen, who must have hatched some of her eggs. A flurry of little chicks swiftly followed her as she scurried away for safety. The boys chased after her, making clucking sounds and laughing.

"Watch out for that old rooster," called Bryan. "He'll peck your backside if you're not careful!"

Their horses had seen them come down the driveway, so they were waiting for them at the pasture gate. The boys helped Bryan retrieve the horses, put on their respective halters and tied them to the fence railing while the saddles and bridles were gotten from the tack room. Bryan chatted for a few minutes with Mary Anne, Mary Pat and "just plain" Mary, who were riding this morning also. They were going to be staying in the riding ring, with Mary giving her friends a few lessons in dressage.

"Your grandsons are getting *so* big...and handsome," said Mary Anne. "It's always so nice to see them out here. And I know that you enjoy their visits too."

"Y'all look so darlin' in y'all's Stetsons," Mary Pat chimed in, laying on her southern drawl, flashing a huge smile and fluttering her eyelashes.

"Aw, shucks. Thank you, ma'am," answered Bryan, tipping the brim of his hat, giving her a wink and using his best John Wayne impression.

"Grandsons?" Mary added. "You're *way* too young to have grandsons this old."

"Oh, I'm gonna like *you!*" Bryan responded without missing a beat.

The boys had the horses saddled and ready to go when Bryan came out of the tack room.

"Remember to give Dolly the knee before you finally tighten her girth, Jason. You know she likes to fill up with air and the girth will be too loose for ya."

"Yep, I remember, Gramp." Jason responded, pulling the girth, and then giving Dolly a swift knee to Dolly's side. The horse let out a low grunt as Jason pulled the girth as tight as he could get. Bryan double-checked their girths and bridles, just to make sure the boys had done everything correctly. They had.

"Want to head down to the river this morning, fellas?" asked Bryan. "Not sure how much river is still there considering the drought. It might be gone...or just a trickle. But it's a fun trail. Give us a chance for a nice trot and perhaps a short canter. Just have to be careful, remember, about that short stretch that we have to walk along the main road 'til we get to the trail. Sometimes ya have to put up with crazy-ass drivers, honking their horns and all. Keep a tight grip on your reins but I know you kids will be fine. Ready to get lost in our jungle out there?"

Both boys were eager to ride. In the past, all three of them pretended that they were brave, intrepid explorers, forging new trails through virgin territory. When his grandsons visited, Bryan was a teenager again and he loved every minute of it. And, for at least the duration of the ride, he would forget about his aches and pains.

The boys were up in their saddles in a flash. Bryan put his foot in the stirrup, gave a slight bounce and farted as he hoisted his weight up. Sassy let out a grunt and a low nicker.

"Oh, hush, you," he said to her. "I'm not *that* heavy! Let's head 'em out, boys," he called, as he led the way up the driveway, towards the street and the awaiting jungle.

"Goddammit, Brandy," said her dad quietly. Sara had left the room in search of some other forgotten, lost treasure. "Sally and I are going to stick it out as long as we can. I can't possibly conceive of a world without her in it. Even if she does get…well…lost at times. I'm still a damn good cook…we eat great. The house…well, perhaps it's not as neat as *you'd* like it, but it isn't a pigsty either, is it? I'm not ready for this. She's not ready for this. I'll know when it's time for the next move. She'll tell me, in her own way, when it's time."

Sara came back into the room and saw the two of them sitting side-by-side talking softly. She stopped and watched them both for a moment.

"Don't think I don't know what's going on here," Sara said, eyeing them suspiciously.

"What do you mean, Mother? Dad and I are just talking about silly little things. You know. The weather…and the horses. Stuff like that."

"Really? You two are conspiring," responded Sara, still looking at them and slowly shaking her head. After a pause, she continued. "First, Bud calls yesterday and asks to speak to your father, then you show up today."

"Bud…what?" Brandy turned and looked at her father. He shook his head and whispered, under his breath.

"Jack. It was Jack, from across the street. His dog had gotten loose and, often, when she does, she ends up in our back yard. He was asking if I had seen her. Sally never answers the phone any more but she did yesterday. Poor Jack was confused as hell until I got on the line."

"Oh, yes. You three are up to something," Sara continued again. "You're planning a surprise party for my birthday, aren't you?" and she smiled.

Sara's next birthday was ten months away.

"Mother, your birthday is in April."

"Ha! Don't you think I know that? Who forgets their own birthday anyway? *Niemand ist zu hause,*" she said in perfect German. A language she studied decades ago. *"Niemand ist zu hause,"* she repeated, laughing and tapping the side of her head. *Nobody is home.* "Well, don't worry. I'll pretend to be surprised. I won't spoil it for the others. Just remember…I love chocolate cake" she winked at them both. "And pistachio ice cream."

Brandy felt a lump in her throat. Chocolate cake and pistachio ice cream had been Bud's favorites. Her mother always preferred angel food cakes with strawberry ice cream. Brandy noticed that her mother had put on some costume jewelry before returning to the living room. She must have been rummaging around in the closet again.

"Look at this beautiful bracelet," Sara said, as she held out her wrist for inspection. Her watery pale blue eyes sparkled but she seemed distant. "It's a pretty little trinket, don't you agree? You and Bud gave this to me one Christmas years ago, remember?" and she gazed lovingly at the cheap bauble. Jason and Terry had bought it with their own money for Sara's last birthday.

"Want some coffee?" asked Cliff, trying his best to be a bit more cheerful, but failing at it. "Just brewed a pot before you got here."

Brandy just shook her head slowly, as she watched her mother admiring the bracelet. She wondered what goes on in people's minds when they begin to slip away like this. What do they think about? What do they see? Is it youthful innocence returning? Are they *aware* of what's happening… or, worse yet, are they aware of what lies ahead?

"No. No, thanks, Dad. I'll pass on the coffee. Smells really good, though. Please consider what I've said today. And please, *please* look over the stuff that I brought. I don't want this to take a toll on you and lose you too."

"And I don't want to lose Sally. Not yet, anyway. I simply cannot bear it," her Dad responded, looking back and forth between his daughter and his wife.

Sara wandered back towards her bedroom again, Brandy assumed. Cliff stood and embraced Brandy, hugging her tightly. He smelled of Old Spice and she smiled, kissing him lightly on his cheek. When did my parents get to be this old, she thought. When did *I* get to be this old? A few minutes later, Sara slowly wandered back into the room.

"Oh, hello, dear," she said to Brandy. "I didn't hear you come in. Did you just get here?"

Bryan and the boys broke into a lazy lope through the woods, heading towards the river. It was a perfect morning. They rode through stretches of tall, thin bamboo…moving in and out of patches of sunlight streaming through the big, old trees. A large great blue heron flew up from the rustling reeds that were waving to and fro in a soft breeze and a circling hawk squawked loudly overhead. A doe and her young fawn scampered off into the woods in the distance. A little red fox spotted them as they approached and it ducked down behind a rotting log and cautiously watched as they rode by. They reached what had been a wide stream. Last year they had facetiously called it a river, when they were mighty jungle explorers, and pretended that no man had ever set eyes upon its waters. It was slowly flowing but the stream, now just a creek, was only half as wide as in the past.

"Damn," said Bryan. "We need some rain bad. This'll be nothing but a dry riverbed in another couple of weeks."

They crossed the creek, with Dolly stopping midway to "play". She pounded her front right hoof into the water, splashing her rider. Dolly was a real water horse, loving to splash and roll in it whenever she got the chance. Whenever it *did* rain, she rolled in the mud until she was covered in the red Georgia clay. Bryan cursed the fact that her white mane and tail would look pink until she was bathed again.

"Urge her on, Jason. Kick her in the ribs or we'll be here all day watching her play!" called Bryan.

They trotted, with an occasional canter, for a couple of miles before Bryan headed them back towards the stable. He glanced at his watch and was amazed how quickly the last two hours had vanished. He pointed out various birds along the way and told a few more tall tales. The boys chatted and laughed loudly, too, filling their grandfather in on school and sports back home. Bryan also gave them a brief lesson in French.

"How are you guys doin' in school? Gettin' good grades, I hope. Don't want any dummies for grandkids, you know."

Jason and Terry almost answered together. "Straight A's, Gramp. We're both on the Honor Roll."

"Damn, you're fart smellers...er...smart fellers!" a spoonerism too good to waste.

They made it back to the main road and walked their horses leisurely on the narrow shoulder, facing oncoming traffic. A small piece of white paper on the ground ahead of them caught Buck's eye and his nostrils widened with a snort. The other two horses paid no attention to it. Horses can spook at the simplest of objects. Horses' eyes are set on the sides of their heads, so they have exceptional peripheral vision, even being able to see the riders on their backs. But there is a blind spot directly in front of them. They might catch sight of an object with their right eye. If they should turn their head, ever so slightly, and then that object comes into view with their left eye, to the horse, that object has suddenly jumped. A slight breeze caught that piece of paper just as Buck and Terry approached. It fluttered just a bit...and, to Buck, it moved quickly from one side of his path to the other. Buck halted abruptly, snorted, reared up and then took a rapid leap to the right, several feet out into the road directly in front of a fast approaching little red sports car. Terry maintained his balance and control of his horse. The young lady driving the car slammed on the brakes, causing the car to spin completely around three times, with white smoke billowing from the burning rubber and squealing tires. The car came to a halt less than five feet in front of the horse and young rider. This all happened so quickly that Bryan didn't have a chance to react until the incident was over.

Bryan jumped off Sassy, holding onto her reins and rushed to Terry's side. He could feel his heart pumping wildly in his chest. The young lady sat, visibly shaken, in her car. Jason rode up along side Terry as well.

"Holy, shit!" exclaimed the young boy, still holding onto Buck's reins with a firm grip. "I think I peed myself!" Then he gave a nervous laugh.

"Hell, I know *I* did!" answered Bryan, although he really hadn't. But he *had* farted as he jumped from the saddle.

The young driver pulled her car off the road and onto the shoulder, to compose herself. The top was down on her convertible and the sun bounced off her silver jewelry, casting sparkling reflections on the black leather upholstery.

"You okay, miss?" asked Bryan. "That was quick thinking on your part and, man, you handled that car like a pro." He actually thought she was an idiot for driving down this road at that speed and, probably, on her cell phone, not paying attention to what or who was ahead.

"Yeah, I'm cool…I think," she answered breathlessly, looking up at the three horsemen and their mounts. "I'm so, so, *so* sorry! I know I was going faster than I shoulda. I see horses riding along here all the time and I should be more careful. I'm so sorry," she repeated.

"Hey, that's fine," Bryan tried to reassure her, though still thinking her an idiot. "Nobody got hurt. It could have been awful, though. Really awful. But it wasn't. Maybe we all learned a bit today. You always have to be careful around horses…whether you're on them or on the ground. Or in a car, for that matter. No harm done. You sure you're okay?"

"Yes, I'm fine. My heart is still beating like crazy, but I think I'll live." She gave Bryan a wan smile. "Again, I'm so sorry."

"We were the ones out by the road," Bryan answered. "It was our fault that we were in the wrong place at the right time for that to happen. Just collect yourself and drive carefully, little lady. Everybody's fine. See? Even the horse has calmed down."

Buck had found some grass to nibble on while everyone was chatting. His ordeal was over and forgotten.

"Cool," Said the girl, as she restarted her engine, put the car in gear and slowly pulled away, back out onto the road. She waved to them as she went. Bryan watched as she *very* slowly drove away. He then turned to Terry.

"Okay, so how are *you*? You handled yourself and Buck beautifully. Now, after it's all over and we're sorta calmed down, I can say that I'm proud of you, Terry. And, Buck…well, I need to have a talk with him about getting spooked at silly shit. Which reminds me. Better not let your Grandma hear that language of yours, young man! She'll blame me, sure as shootin'! You okay?"

"Yep, Gramps. I'm fine. It all happened so fast. I didn't think about it until the car stopped. By the way, I was just kidding about peeing myself." And Terry laughed a nervous laugh.

"You know, boys," Bryan said as he bounced himself back up into the saddle. "Perhaps this might be a story that we *don't* tell Grandma. We don't want her to have an attack and get her panties in a wad, do we?"

They were back at the stable in a few minutes and Brandy was there waiting for them. She had been chatting with the three Marys and Jessica Howce. Bryan and the boys slowly walked their horses down the driveway and ambled up to the chatting ladies.

"Well, here come the explorers back from the lost jungle. Have a good time?" Brandy asked.

"Sure did," said Bryan quickly, as he glanced at his two grandsons. He hopped down from Sassy and farted.

"Damn, Sassy. Did you just step on that poor bullfrog?"

"I heard some squealing brakes up on the road a couple minutes ago. Did you see anything?" Brandy asked, ignoring his previous statement.

The three guys looked at each other and shrugged, shaking their heads nervously…and guiltily.

"Must be some crazy-ass drivers, you know?" Bryan blurted. "How'd it go with *you* today?" he asked hastily.

"Well, about as I expected. I just need to keep a closer eye on Dad. If Mother gets too bad, I'll intervene. Who know's? Tomorrow she might be just like her old self. Dad says that happens. She takes good care of herself; hygiene-wise, that is. That could go on for days, weeks even. Then she slips back into her own personal haze. I guess I'll know when the time is right. Dad says she starts talking German every once in a while now. She studied it in high school and never used it since. She's Scots-Irish, for Pete's sake! Why would she be doing that? But I lost the battle…for today, anyway. How's your back, by the way?"

"What?...oh...killing me," he responded, almost as though he suddenly remembered about his morning complaint, as he reached around to straighten and brace his back. "And my ass hurts like hell too, while we're at it!"

JULY

Rance Rants –
The Savage Within

"In reality, the source of all these differences is, that the savage lives within himself, while the social man lives constantly outside himself, and only knows how to live in the opinion of others, so that he seems to receive the consciousness of his own existence merely from the judgment of others concerning him."

—Jean Jacques Rousseau

The fire in the grill was dying down, the aroma of hamburgers, bratwurst and hot dogs still drifted in the air. The trash can along side the deck was filled to overflowing with paper plates, napkins, and empty bottles and cans from beer, soft drinks...and even a couple empty wine bottles. The horses grazing in the pasture no longer reacted to the sounds of exploding fireworks in the distance. A bright, half-moon barely kissed the tops of the tall pines at the western edge of the pasture and would soon disappear below them, while a cloudless sky full of stars twinkled overhead. Fireflies flickered through the woods, creating an almost magical sight. Warm, mellow jazz streamed through someone's iPad on the deck. Dave Koz, on sax. A summer symphony of crickets and various other nighttime insects serenaded the area as well. Summer holidays were always good excuses for the boarders to get together for fun and conversations that would linger into the night. There were a few sparklers left in the last box and kids and grandkids begged to have them lit.

Spouses, lovers, friends, children and a few dogs had gathered earlier in the afternoon with covered dishes of all kinds. Folding tables had been spread out with the requisite red, white and blue plates, cups, napkins and candles. The weather had cooperated with a blisteringly hot day that offered very little relief as the sun set. It hadn't mattered. The day had been filled with ball games, badminton, volleyball, horseshoes, bocce and, despite the heat, a lot of riding. Smartphones had been used in abundance…photos, selfies and videos of horses and boarders. The horses had been cooled down, fed and put back out into the pasture. Remy was always concerned at these gatherings that the amount of drinking combined with horseplay could lead to someone getting seriously injured. So far, everyone had been lucky. And so had the horses. Zara was never concerned. The three Marys were chatting in the center of the riding ring as they picked up some discarded drinking cups left by the kids. The air was punctuated occasionally by their laughter. Amber Givings and the love-struck Raymond sat side by side on a blanket that Amber had spread out on what was left of the lawn surrounding the deck. He had brought a guitar with him to the festivities and had totally surprised everyone by his soft, beautiful singing voice as he strummed and serenaded them all as they ate and drank. And drank. And drank. Many of the long-time boarders had been friends for years, socializing away from the stable as well. Everyone enjoyed each other's company. With one exception.

Rance Hurakon was not a popular man. He was the husband of Julia Constance, a boarder, who went by her maiden name. Rance rarely made appearances at the stable, to the satisfaction of the other boarders. He was 5'7" tall, yet he acted as though he was 6'4". Belligerent, abrasive, sarcastic, cocky, he had an attitude that immediately put people off and put them on the defensive. He would argue with anyone for the sake of argument; debate any topic, whether he knew anything about it or not; swore worse than any sailor, no matter who was around to hear and always smelled of cheap tequila. The truly surprising thing was that he owned a very successful liquor store, The Velvet Hammer Bottle Shop, and, obviously, could afford the best tequila available. He preferred the cheap stuff. On rare occasion, he would manage to get some very good marijuana and, secretly, let a few good customers know about it. And, secretly, they might make a purchase or two...booze and otherwise. They didn't mind that he was an asshole. Rance had rationalized that since one state after the other was legalizing recreational cannabis, Georgia would surely follow. Someday. Soon. Perhaps. But he would be ready when it happened. Although a few of the boarders frequented his bottle shop, none were aware of the goings on in the back room. Julia was aware that Rance got and smoked pot on occasion, but she was unaware that he was selling it...on occasion. Nobody could see what Julia, a beautiful woman, could have seen in this vile little man. Julia was always beautifully groomed; Rance wore no color other than black. Today it was a black t-shirt, with the graphic image of a large skull created from musical instruments, and black jeans cut off just above his knobby knees, revealing his scrawny, pale legs. He was constantly trying to grow a beard because his face had a perpetual grizzled look to it. His thinning hair was always disheveled, giving the appearance that he must have just stuck a fork into an electrical outlet. His hair had been black at one time but gone to an early whitish gray. He was very thin and ashen and looked much older than his 35 years. Behind his back, and certainly out of Julia's earshot, all of the boarders called him "Rancid". He and Julia were the parents of a 10-year-old son and an 8-year-old daughter. Their son, David, was exceptionally smart, very observant and exceptionally shy. An extreme introvert if ever there was one. He had his nose buried constantly in his smartphone and, as much as he could, he would remain in his room, behind closed doors. He truly loved his mother but, when it came to his dad...well, David didn't trust Rance and had been embarrassed by him on countless occasions. Becky, their daughter, resembled a smaller version of Julia and loved riding. She would accompany her mother to the stable often. David, on the other hand, wanted nothing to do with the stable, horses, other people, or the outdoors in general. And he longed for the day when he could move out and be on his own. He sat, sullen-faced, in the darkest corner of the deck he could find, trying desperately to disappear into the darkness. Against his protestations, his parents had made him attend the picnic, although he knew from past experiences how his father would try his best to be his worst.

Two of the younger boarders, Gary and Linda Smart, were packing up their gear, saying their goodnights. Linda was a few months pregnant with their first child. She and Gary were extremely excited about the event. Linda was the equestrian; Gary never rode. Gary would come out to the stable only when Linda couldn't make it or for party functions such as this one. Both of them were very good-looking and very friendly. Gary was a salesman, working for the same packaging company as Marty Howce and, despite their slight age difference, were very good friends. Gary *did* have a tendency towards egoism, however, and was teased about it often. He didn't care. He loved the attention. His car sported vanity plates that boldly and proudly spelled GARY. All of his custom-made dress shirts had his monogram, GS, either on his pockets, sleeve cuff or both. He would have preferred the stylish look of a three-initial monogram but, with the middle name of Allen, he decided otherwise. He had an engraved nameplate on his laptop case and on his now old, no-longer-used attaché case. Despite his ego…or because of it…Gary was very good at what he did. He also had a passion for watches. He had dozens of them, ranging in cost from a few hundred dollars, that simply told the time, and to a few costing thousands of dollars that, aside from the time, measured his heart rate, counted his daily steps, sent and received emails, kept track of his stock portfolio and the current, up-to-the-minute population of China. Well, okay…perhaps that last one was a slight exaggeration. His favorite, however, was a genuine, original classic with the image of a world-famous mouse on the face.

"Have you decided on any names yet?" Mary asked, as she helped them pack up their car

"Well," answered Gary, "If it's a girl, we're going to call her Gari. G-A-R-I."

Rance saw his opportunity and pounced. "And if it's a boy you're going to call him Linda, right?"

Gary shot Rance a look. Then, realizing with whom he was dealing, decided it was best left ignored.

"Man, I gotta piss like a Russian race horse!" Rance suddenly announced to no one in particular. He stumbled off to the tack room bathroom. Within a few minutes he was back, but it had given the Smarts ample time to drive off into the night.

"Hey, Remy," called Bryan Dennison. "How's old lady Critchley doin'? Any of your horses get out and end up in her yard lately?" He chuckled.

"Nope. Everybody's been behaving lately," Remy answered matter-of-factly.

"I hear she practices witchcraft or voodoo or something like that," Continued Bryan.

"Voodoo?" asked Marty with curiosity.

"Yeah. Somebody told me once that if she doesn't like you, she writes your name on a piece of paper and puts it in an ice tray in her freezer. Something bad is supposed to happen to you if she does that," Bryan answered.

"Ha! If that's the case," said Zara, "I must have at least a couple of places in her freezer."

"Is that sorta like deja-voodoo?" Joked Marty.

"Funny, Marty," quipped Zara. "But that doesn't even make much sense."

"Why, Zara? What have *you* done to the poor old lady?" asked Bryan with a confused look on his face. "You're the nicest person around."

"I wave to her every time I drive by and she's out in her yard," Answered Zara with a grin.

"So?" asked Marty.

"I wave with my middle finger!" Zara responded, demonstrating. "She comes from that little Podunk town up in the mountains but she has that holier-than-thou attitude like she's royalty or something."

"Ha!" shot Marty. "The duchess from Suches!"

Everybody chuckled and Bryan proposed a toast.

"A patriotic salute, then, to commemorate this day to the duchess!" and he shot his arm straight up, middle finger extended. They all looked around to make certain that none of the children were watching.

Suddenly, everybody's arms were in the air, their middle fingers pointing to the stars.

"Here's to the duchess!" they shouted and then collapsed into convulsions of laughter.

After regaining their composure, Marty and Jessie started chatting with Zara about computers and the amount of time Marty spent online. Jessie was always complaining to Marty about it and Zara agreed, saying that Remy, too, seemed to be addicted to the computer whenever he was home. They were a small group who remained seated on the deck now. They could still hear fireworks exploding in the distance and see colorful glows in the sky.

"It's obviously a guy thing," said Marty defensively.

"It's such a waste of time," Jessie responded, with Zara nodding in agreement again. "I know you do all of your work on the computer. That time, obviously, is justifiable. But all the nonsense time. All the social media crap. I hate Facebook. You claim you're reading. Reading what? Garbage stuff, no doubt."

Marty had always been a voracious reader. His dad had razzed him about that constantly. "Damn, Marty," his dad would say, "You can get more information off a cereal box than anybody I know."

A couple of the other husbands came to Marty's defense regarding the computer.

"Hell!" chimed Rance, who looked as though he had dozed off but was apparently listening…waiting for his chance to rant. "You women will just complain about anything us guys do. Don'tcha think that guys just seem better informed? The fucking computer is a treasure trove of information. You women yackety yack about beauty and hair and shit like that. And what the fuck your kids are doing and how smart they all are. And who's fucking who in Hollywood."

"Whom," said Mary Anne.

"What?" asked Rance.

"Whom. It's who's fucking *whom* in Hollywood. At least use proper grammar." She laughed.

"Oh, bite me! You knew what I meant. English is English. If I said I ain't got no money, you'd know exactly what I meant, wouldn't you?" retorted Rance.

"Yes," said Mary Anne smugly, "And I'd know exactly *why* you don't have any money!"

Laughter all around, punctuated by more fireworks exploding in the distance.

"See? That's what I mean," continued Rance. "Silly stuff. Men talk about ideas. Do you ever talk about what's going on in this fucked up world? I doubt it. You're probably asking your husband," indicating Jessie, "Do these pants make my ass look big? Do you like my hair? Am I getting old looking? Am I ugly? Am I fat? Aw, bullshit, that's all."

"Rance," Marty decided to chime in, "you're about as pleasant as dysentery."

"Who gives a shit?," answered Rance.

"Well, there ya go," quipped Zara, slapping a hand down onto her knee.

Rance had a talent for putting a chill on any party, and it certainly didn't take much for him to ruin a perfectly good day. Although people had the tendency to ignore him, sometimes that was difficult. The fact that everyone had been loosened up with beer or wine…or stronger spirits took the edge off of Rance's venom. Alcohol had dulled *their* senses and sharpened *his* tongue. They had heard it so many times before, at previous stable parties. He prattled on and those who knew him let him vent. Those who might not be so familiar with him often left the parties with their mouths agape. Julia was often surprised by the fact that some guy, tired of his tirades, hadn't beaten him to a pulp. She often wondered why *she* hadn't beaten him to a pulp.

"That's an idiotic thing to say," said Mary Pat, as she approached the deck, trying to remain calm. "We women care about big issues, too. For that matter, if women took over, the world would be in a hell of a better shape than it is now, don't you agree, ladies? We should have had a female president by now, too!"

All the ladies agreed.

"And, besides," Jessie added, "I tell Marty all the time that men are totally incapable of multi-tasking."

"Not true," replied Rance. "I can sneeze, fart and pee all at the same time."

The guys snickered, even though they didn't want to give Rance the pleasure of laughing at his inane remarks. Besides, that line was older than dirt.

"Have you ever *tried* to carry on an intelligent conversation with a woman?" asked Mary Anne. "What about with Julia? You know,…your wife! We all know *she's* intelligent. We've had lots of conversations that never, ever touch on the nonsense you're spouting."

"Oh, trust me," Julia chimed in. "We've had *lots* of conversations. None of which need sharing here tonight!" and she laughed heartily.

Julia, having been married to Rance for years, knew that his rants, quite often, were fake, just to stir up controversy and arguments. She was patient with him but, at the same time, he embarrassed her. He had not always been so cantankerous. This unpleasant persona had appeared within the past couple of years. She thought, at first, that he might be having an affair and, hence, the mean streak to cover up his guilt. But that had not been the case. Then, perhaps, she thought that he might have discovered that *she* was having an affair. Which she was. So many secrets around this place!

"Oh, for Pete's sake, Mary Anne," Julia said, shaking her head. "He's an asshole when he *hasn't* been drinking…and he's polluted tonight. Bear with him. I have for way too long…but I love the jerk anyway," Julia had lied about that last part.

"Mary Anne," Rance pounced. "I'd like to hear some intelligence come out of *your* mouth for a change. You're always yacking about your little tea parties for the kiddies every time I hear you. Damn, what a rip-off." Then he laughed and Mary Anne seethed. She wanted to, but refrained from kicking him in the groin.

"Julia," Mary Anne purred with sarcasm. "I'm sorry that I must have provoked your poor husband in some way. He must really hate us women for some reason. I have either insulted his intelligence or his manhood, both of which are in serious question. You are as sweet as can be but… and I am not usually so bold… frankly, I don't see what you ever saw in that man."

"Hey!" snapped Rance immediately. "I'm right here. I can hear that. Hell, I'm her knight in shining armor."

"Oh, yeah," snorted Marty, who had been enjoying this repartee. "You're a regular Sir Rants-A-Lot. Or, how about Rance the Recalcitrant?"

Everybody but Rance laughed.

"You know," spoke up Zara, trying to bring some friendly chatter back into the evening, "speaking about computers. I know…that conversation seemed ages ago. But, anyway…somebody posted on Facebook the other day a story that Mars was going to be closer to Earth than it had been in decades. It's going to happen sometime around the end of August, I think. And this is the best part. They said that Mars would appear as large as the full moon in the sky. Won't that be spectacular?"

"Oh, bullshit…bullshit…BULL. SHIT!" blurted Rance. "See? More nonsense. That's a hoax, folks. Okay, maybe Mars *might* be having a close encounter with us, but it simply cannot…I repeat…cannot appear as large as the full moon. Im-fucking-possible. Do you realize the gravitational pull on Earth if that were the case? Who the hell ever starts these fucking things on Facebook anyway? Why? What's the purpose? Probably some small-brained bitch somewhere trying to have fun. Anybody who believes that shit is an idiot. That moronic story seems to resurface every couple of years to get a whole new tribe of idiots all jazzed up and excited. There is so much fake news on that damn Facebook that's sickening."

"Is it possible, Julia," Marty asked, gesturing towards Rance, "That he could have Tourette's syndrome and not know it?"

"You know what else gets me pissed?" Rance continued.

"Oh, Christ!" Bryan Dennison muttered to himself.

"Good god, man. Have you left no rotten rant unspoken?" Marty asked.

"All this fucking politically correct bullshit," Rance continued, without missing a beat, ignoring the comments and completely ignorant of the fact that he was putting quite a damper on what was a fun day. "I'm sick of it. You just can't call a spade a spade anymore, if you know what I mean. No pun intended. Look at what goes on downtown every year. A goddamn Black Arts Festival. Well, what the hell would happen if someone wanted to put on a White Arts festival? Huh? Think about it. What about those BET Awards on television…why aren't there any WET Awards? Miss freakin' Black America? Hey, with what's going on at our southern borders pretty soon there'll be a Miss Hot Tamale America. Before you know it, the air will be filled with the smell of cilantro and chilies. And our kids will be going around saying "hola", for chrissake! And don't even get me started on those frickin' towelheads who are invading our country now. I'd love to stuff their mouths with slabs of bacon. See how they like *that*."

"Honest to God, Rance," Marty said bluntly. "I swear, you could start an argument in an empty room. Someday somebody is going to shoot you. And we'll all testify that it was justifiable homicide."

"Oh, fuck y'all!" Rance said loudly.

"Rance! Shhh," admonished Julia. "There are young kids around. *Please* watch your language."

"Oh. Well then…fuck y'all," he whispered.

"I'm going for my gun," said Marty, laughing. "I'll put us all out of our misery."

"What?" asked Rance haughtily? "Are you going to shoot everyone up here on the deck?"

"Nope. Just one bullet will take care of it, man."

"Oh, please," teased Rance. "You're a buncha bitchy little girls. There's a little bit of me in every one of you." And he pointed a bony finger at each one, jabbing it for effect. "I have the balls to say the things you only think about, but are too afraid to say out loud. Everybody probably has these same thoughts every once in a while but keep them hidden… secret. Ashamed or otherwise. Everybody has secrets. And, I'll just bet that everybody has done at least one thing you're ashamed of."

"Secret thoughts and secrets, perhaps," Mary said. "But I don't have anything to be ashamed of. As a matter of fact, I'm kinda proud of a couple of my vices." Then she laughed.

"Oh? And what would those vices be?" asked Rance."

"Ha!" Mary responded without missing a beat. "Those, little man, you will never…ever…know."

Marty chimed in. "And we're certainly nowhere nearly as prejudiced about everybody and everything as you are, that's for damn sure."

"Oh, bullshit. I'm not prejudiced. I just hate idiots and fat people," Rance snapped back. "I mean, just the other morning I saw this tub of lard waddling out of McDonald's. If anybody told her to haul ass she'd have to make two trips."

"Y'all can kiss mah sweet l'il Gawja ayass, Rance," piped in Mary Pat, using the best faux southern accent she could muster.

"Horse shit, Mary Pat, Miss Magnolia Mouth of the South. Aren't you from some place up north? Where was it? Dumpster, New Jersey or some cesspool like that?"

Mary Pat pretended she didn't hear him.

"Hey, Rance," Marty interjected, "isn't your shop open today? Shouldn't you be in there managing it so your employees can enjoy the holiday, too?"

"Nah, they're a good bunch…and, besides, they get time and a half. I'm a decent boss. Fuck 'em if they don't like it, anyway."

"Well, that's too bad, I guess. You'd rather be here, prattling on and trying to cause a kerfuffle amongst all these fine folks," Marty answered.

Say what? All heads immediately turned to Marty and three smartphones whipped out, going straight to Google.

"Kerfuffle?" asked Rance. "Kefuffle…what the fuck? Is that even English? Sounds like some kinda German pastry, to me."

"Rancid…er…Rance, you know, you give credence to that biological conundrum," Marty said, with a wide grin.

"Oh, yeah? And what would *that* be?"

"How can there be more horses' asses on this planet than there are horses?"

Laughter all around. Except Rance.

"Ha, ha…very funny," sulked Rance. "And there you go, using your hundred-dollar words. Conundrum. Kerfuffle. Wow! What a couple of biggies. Think you're so hoity-toity with your big words and your expensive Rolodex watches and all. Very funny." His malaprop, with a direct slam at Gary Smart, was intentional.

"Say, Rance," spoke up Remy, finally becoming part of the conversation. "Being that you're so anti-PC, that must apply to handicapped folks as well, right?"

"What do you mean by that?" asked Rance, with a quizzical look on his face.

"I was filling up my car at that convenience station up around the corner a couple days ago," Remy said, with a sly, uncharacteristic grin. "Wasn't that your car I saw come zipping in and park in the handicapped spot? And wasn't that you I saw jump out of your car and dash into the store?"

"I always considered having a small dick a handicap. Next question?" snapped Rance, with a wry smile.

"Why am I not surprised?" Mary thought to herself.

"Oh, that reminds me, Marty," picked up Rance, on a roll again. "How's *your* Peter?"

"What? Excuse me?" gasped Marty.

"Peter. Didn't you say a month or so ago that you hired a new young guy? A Peter something or other?"

Marty recovered. But he knew that Rance had baited him just to be an asshole.

"Yeah, I did. Didn't know you were around to hear my conversation but, yeah, I did hire Peter. As a freelancer. Peter Scott, the guy with two first names as I teased him. Heck of a nice guy and great designer. So funny, though…," he was talking to the others on the deck at this point and avoiding Rance. "His partner stopped by to have lunch with Peter last week. Get this. His partner's name is Scott Peters." And Marty chuckled.

"Gay, huh?" said Rance, smirking. "Was he always gay or just since it's become popular? They are everywhere these days. Were they always there and we never noticed them? Now they're coming out, pardon the pun, of the woodwork and announcing it to the world. Christ all mighty, they even parade themselves up and down Peachtree Street every year, don't they? Now they can even decide whether or not they're a boy or a girl…or both at the same time. What the hell? Hey, if you look inside your shorts and you have a wee-wee, you're a boy. If you don't, you're a girl. The only good thing about them marrying each other is that they sure as hell can't procreate. Although I'm sure they try hard enough. No pun intended. I just wonder how long it'll be before there's a goddamn rainbow flag flying over the White House."

Rance was silent for, perhaps, thirty seconds then he blurted out "Oh, and one more thing!"

"What now?" Brandy Dennison chuckled, "You think you're Columbo all of a sudden?"

"Ha, ha…ha!" answered Rance. "No. What's with all these idiots walking around with pink, purple, turquoise and whatever other color hair these days? They look like freakin' parrots escaped from their jungle."

"Well, I'll be damned," exclaimed a surprised Mary. "As much as I hate to say this, I actually agree with you on that one, Rance."

Rance sat back, folded his arms and looked like he had just scored the winning goal at the World Cup.

"Take it easy, take it easy. Don't let it go to your head, buster," shot Mary.

Marty just shook his head and wished he had not even mentioned Peter. He wished that he wasn't even here, this late, arguing with this moron. Marty wished that the old widow across the street, Mrs. Critchley, had a dozen slips of paper with Rance's name on it tucked away in her freezer. Not that he wished bad things happening to anyone…but…well, with Rance that needed rethinking. Why were they all just taking this verbal abuse from this wretched person, he thought. What's the point of even arguing with him? It just seems to egg him on…and on. He was surprised, really, that none of the other guys there just didn't simply deck the loudmouth. Why didn't *he* just deck the asshole? Why bother. Rance wasn't worth it. But then, he thought, if everybody simply ignores bigots such as him…if no one complains…if everyone remains complacent then these guys will continue, persist and succeed. The thought that if you ignore these assholes, maybe they'll just eventually slink silently away doesn't work. The bigots just prattle on, maybe just to hear their own venomous thoughts. You shouldn't really start to argue with them either. It's like poking that proverbial sleeping bear. Marty was sure that everyone else sitting here on the deck at this very moment was in agreement with him. Except for Rance, needless to say. He was all revved up and ready for more. But, then again, Marty thought, maybe Rance just wants to be noticed. In the worst way.

Don, Mary Anne's "lovah", had dozed off before all the hoopla with Rance heated up. Hot sun and cold beers had lulled him to sleep early in the evening. Every once in a while he'd jolt awake, eyes wide, then slowly drift back into a summer stupor. Derrick, Mary Pat's husband, had sat quietly listening to Rance's ravings and the heated responses from everyone else. He stretched out in his folding chair on the deck, leaning back and cradling the back of his head in his hands. His legs were outstretched with his ankles crossed. He didn't want to get involved in this part of the discussion. Although he wasn't *totally* ashamed of it, in actuality, he agreed with a lot of what Rance said. But he would not have been so…well, so fucking vulgar about it.

Trying to change the subject and ease Rance out of the conversation, Marty asked if anyone else had seen the recent news story about a husband and wife who had missed their flight to Europe. They had been stuck in heavy traffic due to an accident on the way to the airport and their flight had departed by the time they got there. The plane they were scheduled to be on crashed into the Atlantic, killing everyone on board.

"It just wasn't their time to go," said Zara. "It was fate."

"Well," said Marty, pausing for dramatic purpose. "Fate, indeed, stepped in. The wife was killed in an automobile accident two weeks after they got home. She was driving a little red sports car and a drunk driver smashed into her head-on. Evidently, she was intended to die on that plane but, obviously, her husband was not."

"God works in mysterious ways," Zara said softly…always a devout Catholic… "It was kismet. Jesus said…"

"Oh, crap!" Rance interrupted. "Kismet. Kiss my ass. Who the hell knows what Jesus said or when he said it…or if he even did? Who the hell was his secretary? Who was taking notes?"

The others simply stared at him.

"What do you mean by *that*?" asked Zara.

"I mean, who was there writing down every word…every blessed word?"

"Well, it says in the Bible…"

"Yeah, well. The Bible was written years, decades after these things *supposedly* took place. Every event seems to be there in black and white. But what is true, if anything? And what was made up by some joker smoking wacky tobbacky and or eating magic mushrooms, eh? And all those wonderful quotations attributed to Jesus? I repeat, who wrote them down on the site…at that time? Weren't most of those folks illiterate anyway? If you say that folks remembered what he said years after the fact…well, then…I say bullshit. Do you remember what you said to Remy last Saturday night at 9:35? Think about it, folks. Think about it. I simply cannot believe that so many millions of people have bought into this cruci-fiction crap."

There was an embarrassed silence. Absolutely nobody wanted to get into a religious debate with him at this point. They didn't want to get into *any* kind of debate with him. For that matter, they didn't want to talk to him at all. It had been too festive a day. And they were all feeling the effects of the heat and the drinks.

"Rance, you're incorrigible," Marty finally said.

"Why, thank you," he answered smugly. "I try my best."

"Have some more tequila, Rance," interjected Bryan. "Drink up. Keep drinking. We'll all be better off here if you're unconscious."

Everyone laughed and applauded the suggestion. Rance shot them the bird.

"Marty," Zara said, really trying to liven their spirits after Rance's rants. "You're a creative guy. You've certainly got a way with words. You should write a book about this place. Oh, the stories you could tell!"

Marty smiled and slowly shook his head. "Just because I'm creative design-wise doesn't mean I can be creative when it comes to writing, you know. There are a couple different disciplines working there. Besides, no one would believe it anyway." He had an immediate flashback to a little boy and a man on a bridge...and the seashell sound and fury. He shuddered.

The night with Rance had taken its toll. Everyone was tired and emotionally drained from his ramblings.

"Julia," Mary Pat began. "Zara, Mary, Jessie and I are going on a trail ride tomorrow. We haven't been to Yahoo Hill in ages and we thought tomorrow would be the day. It will be cooler in the morning, so if we go early we can beat the heat. Want to join us?"

"Sure, that sounds great! Thanks for asking me. But what about you, Mary Anne", Julia asked.

"I would really like to join you, but I have a Zumba class in the morning and I love it. I don't want to miss it." Mary Anne responded. "Also, I have a party to do tomorrow. I have to prepare for that. I'll probably bring the kids out to the stable to see the horses. They're city kids, I think."

"Hey," interjected Rance. "What's Yahoo Hill?"

"Hasn't Julia told you about that yet?" asked Mary Pat.

"I did," said Julia, "but, as always, he probably wasn't paying attention. Or perhaps he was stoned." She laughed.

"That's not so," he said. "Can I go too or is this just a girly thing?"

"*You?*" exclaimed Julia. "When was the last time *you* were on horseback, you jerk?"

"It's just like riding a bike, right? Can I go?"

Zara, Julia, Jessie, Mary and Mary Pat all thought a collective "Hell, no!" But Zara thought about it for a moment more, smiled a sly smile and said, "Well, okay. It will be an experience, for sure." And she winked at the other ladies.

"Come on, boys," Marty called to their two sons who had been running around in the riding ring kicking a soccer ball with Bryan's and Brandy's grandsons and Mary Pat's three sons. They were all dripping with sweat. "Get in the car. Let's go."

Everyone collected the remaining food, cleaned up as much of the area as they could see in the dark, with only the floodlights from the stable shining out over them. Julia's and Rance's son David had fallen asleep on the far end of the deck and, fortunately, had missed the entire evening of rants from Rance.

Mary Pat's husband packed up their car and said his goodnights to everyone. The three Marys, Jessie, Julia and Brandy hugged Zara, said their polite good night to Remy and pretended that Rance had fallen into a bottomless pit.

"See you in the morning, ladies!" he called out, waving to them as they walked to their cars.

He had no idea what kind of day lay ahead of him.

The sun rose in another cloudless sky. It was, after all, summer in the south. Considering the late night the early morning riders had kept the evening before, they all arrived at the stable perky, sobered up, filled with energy and anticipation of a thrilling adventure. Today their ride would take them through densely wooded terrain that ended up at the base of an extremely steep uphill trail. They called it "Yahoo Hill" because each rider would take turns, one at a time, at the bottom of the hill. They would collect their horse, kick it hard to start the action and yell "Yahoooo!" as they galloped as fast as they could up the incline. Those who rode with a western saddle, and could grip the horn, had it easier than those who rode English.

Julia was actually concerned about Rance's safety, considering the length of time since he had last been on horseback. She tried to convince him to change his mind, but he resisted. He wanted to go. They owned only one horse, so Rance would borrow one of Zara's. The morning was pleasant when they all arrived at the stable, but they knew that the temperature would rise quickly. The ladies got their respective horses from their stalls and started to groom them.

Mary Anne got to the gym and did some warm-up stretches to prepare herself for the hour of intensive cardio. She loved this Zumba class and never missed it, taking it three times a week.

Julia helped Rance groom Cinnebar, Zara's big, black Tennessee Walker. Zara picked this horse for Rance on purpose. He was a well-trained horse, one that Zara had ridden up Yahoo Hill several times. Cinnebar seemed to love the thrill of Yahoo Hill and he was the fastest to reach the top. Every time.

The other members of the Zumba class were arriving, stretching, sipping water and waiting for the instructor to get the music going. The room was filling up and everyone was ready.

The horses were being saddled. They pranced around in eager anticipation of a nice workout. The trail rides would make them a bit nervous at first. They would snort and sniff the air as they started out of the paddock area, heading towards the woods.

The music started. A slow warm-up salsa. There were thirty members getting into the rhythm. Within minutes, they would all be sweating.

The horses walked at first, nose-to-tail through the woods. There was a clear sky overhead and rays of sunlight pierced through the leaves, casting beautiful patterns on the ground and over the horses.

The music became a faster beat. A cha-cha. The instructor urged her followers on, faster…and faster…with hoots and hollers. Mary Anne felt the sweat dripping down her face. "Single, single, double…single, single, double…"

The horses were now trotting. Rance had been placed in the middle of the line so they could keep an eye on him in case something happened. He tried to look comfortable, although he now wished that he had been talked out of this ride. Too late, obviously, to turn back. And he was definitely not going to show any fear or apprehension in front of all these ladies. Why didn't any of the other guys want to come on this ride, he thought?

"Get some water, guys," the instructor said during a quick break between songs. "We're going to kick it up a notch. This next one's a new one." She called her group "guys" even though it was about 60% female.

The horses were at the base of Yahoo Hill. Rance looked up...*way* up the incline.

"Holy shit!" he said in disbelief. "That looks like a fucking steep grade! The horses do that?"

"Hell, yes," yelled Mary Pat who was first in line. She hit her horses's rump with her riding crop, let out a loud "Yahooooo!" and up the hill she went, leaning as far forward in the saddle as she could to ease the strain on her horse. She disappeared into the woods at the top. Julia was next, then came Mary, hooting and hollering all the way up the exhilarating ride.

"Damn. Shit. Fuck," thought Rance, almost out loud.

"Okay, guys," called out the instructor, "this is it. Here we go! The music was getting faster, louder...the dancers were whipped into a frenzy and dripping with sweat. The pulsing Latin beat was irresistible! "Up, down, squat. Lift! Lift! Up, down, squat. Lift! Lift!" The group called out the moves in unison, getting louder with each repetition.

It was Rance's turn in line. Cinnebar was ready. Rance was not. "I... ah...let's...maybe I'd...," he muttered.

The music became a frantic merengue. The room was bouncing!

Zara, who was behind Rance, reached out and swatted Cinnebar on the rump with her riding crop as hard as she could, yelling "GO!" The horse bucked, farted and bolted straight up the hill at a full gallop, with Rance hanging on for dear life. A very loud "Oh, fuuuuuuuck!" was the only thing Zara heard as the horse raced to the top.

"No," called Zara. "You're supposed to yell Yahoooo!"

"It's cool down time now, guys," said the instructor. The music was a calm tempo and heartbeats began to return to normal.

After Zara and her horse raced to the top, the ladies found Cinnebar further down the trail with no one in the saddle. Rance said he hadn't fallen off but he wasn't sure, exactly, how he had gotten on the ground, flat on his back. His legs seemed a little wobbly as he tried to stand up. He lay back down and took a deep breath. The ladies laughed. It was a mean trick, for sure, that Zara had played and could have ended in a serious accident. At least everyone was wearing their riding helmets. Even Julia enjoyed seeing her husband uneasy and, frankly, visibly shaken.

"Awww, poor Rance," Zara exclaimed, shaking her head, as she looked down at him on the ground. "Bless your heart."

As anyone from the south knows, the expression "Bless your heart" has several different interpretations depending upon the situation. It could be an expression of genuine affection, sympathy, concern, fear, or, in this particular case, it could mean "You sorry sack of shit. You have the intelligence of an acorn and you reap what you sow."

It was a less strenuous trail back towards the stable. They all walked at a leisurely pace, chatting and laughing loudly amongst themselves, riding side-by-side. Rance brought up the rear this time and he did not utter one word all the way back.

Mary Anne showered at the gym and felt really refreshed. She was eager to hear how the ride went and called Mary Pat on her cell. She was taking a big gulp of water when Mary Pat got to the part in the story about Rance and Yahoo Hill. She nearly choked laughing.

"Oh, and I found two dimes in the middle of the locker room floor at the gym," said Mary Anne. "I'm feeling lucky! Ha!...sounds like a line from an old Clint Eastwood movie, doesn't it?"

Mary Pat kidded, "Twenty cents worth of lucky, eh? Oh, there's a country-western song in there somewhere, I just know it."

"Ya think? Well, maybe I'd better buy a lottery ticket today. Ya never know." And they both laughed.

"Gotta go, Mary Pat. I have to pick up my party kids with the van. Maybe I'll see you later at the barn."

"See ya!"

Julia had decided to spend more time at the stable after the ride than Rance had anticipated. They had both driven there in the same car, so he was stuck. He thought perhaps that he could just relax on the deck…the same deck where he had gotten everyone worked up just the night before. His backside was sore, though, and sitting was uncomfortable. He offered to groom their horse, Taffy, while Julia just chatted with the other ladies. Taffy was in her stall, having been cooled down sufficiently and was slowly eating a flake of hay as Rance gently groomed her. Mary Anne's Cater-Tots van slowly drove down the driveway and parked. Rance turned to watch as eight black children tumbled from the vehicle.

"Oh, Christ. Niglets," he muttered, rolling his eyes. He returned to grooming Taffy.

Mary Anne cautioned the children to be very careful around the horses. Not to make any sudden moves or sounds, otherwise they might get frightened. They all had just come from a local park where the children had played games, had their cake, ice cream and sodas and were now on sugar highs. Lots of giggles and jumping around. Again, Mary Anne cautioned them. Each child had been given a helium-filled balloon and the kids skipped passed the empty stalls with them firmly grasped in their hands. They were eager to see the horses, through the fences, in the pasture.

Rance ignored them as two little girls approached his stall.

"Oh, look at this pretty one," one girl exclaimed, calling in to Rance. "What's his name?"

"*Her* name is Taffy," responded Rance tersely, hoping that the answer would satisfy the little twits and they would move on. He had not noticed that the two balloons, bobbing in the breeze, which the girls were holding were making Taffy a bit nervous. Her nostrils flared and her eyes widened.

The girls moved closer to the stall door to see the horse better. A small, sharp piece of wire protruding from the side of the stall door came into contact with a balloon, resulting in a very loud pop.

Taffy spooked and turned sharply in her stall, hitting Rance with her rump, pushing him hard against the stall wall. The girls screamed, frightening the horse even more. Taffy swirled around again, knocking Rance to the ground.

"Holy fucking shit!" shouted Rance.

The commotion brought Julia and Mary Anne running up to the stall as Rance burst through the door.

"You fucking goddamn cunt!" he screamed louder, directing his tirade towards Mary Anne, and leaning uncomfortably close to her face. "You bitch, bringing that tribe here. What the fuck's in your head, horse shit?"

The two little girls just stood with their mouths agape, staring up at this raving lunatic. Mary Anne was seething. She retained her composure and gathered up all the children. It was an abbreviated visit to the stable that day. She turned to glare at Rance as the children were put safely into the van and buckled in. The van hastily drove up the driveway, leaving a cloud of dust and disappeared into the heat of the day. Julia couldn't believe that Rance had acted that way. Yes, he *was* quick to lose his temper but doing so in front of 8-year-old girls was inexcusable. She was mortified.

Later that evening, reeking of cheap tequila and Tiger Balm, Rance padded across the living room in his stocking feet to answer his doorbell. He was surprised to see two police officers standing on his front porch.

"Are you Rance Hurakon?" questioned one of the men.

"Yes. Why? What's wrong?" responded Rance, worried that something had happened to Julia or one of his kids.

"A summons has been issued for your arrest. A complaint has been registered against you. I'm afraid you're going to have to come with us."

"What the hell for?" Rance asked incredulously.

"Public lewdness, profanity and endangering minor children," answered the policeman.

"You've got to be fuckin' kidding me!" spouted Rance.

The mid-July heat was intensifying. Even after her afternoon nap, Zara felt drained as she headed to the stable for her late-day chores. As she drove down the dusty street towards the stable, she noticed Mrs. Critchley standing rigid out on her front lawn, keeping an eye on the road and her hands on her hips. The widow, somewhere in her mid to late seventies, was slender, tanned from working out in her yard constantly and dressed in her usual attire: khaki slacks, a men's-style denim shirt, untucked, with rolled-up sleeves, and a bright red bandana tied around her neck. Her face was lined but not wrinkled and the skin was drawn tight over a firm jawline. Her frizzy salt-and-pepper hair looked as though she had combed it with an eggbeater.

"Oh, shit," thought Zara. "Did some horses get out again? Good lord, she's waiting to pounce on me."

Mrs. Critchley recognized the truck and motioned for Zara to pull into her driveway.

"Crap!" Zara said out loud. "What does the duchess want now?"

She pulled in and rolled down her window.

"Hello, Angela," she said coolly, wondering what to expect. "Beautiful day, isn't it? Despite the heat, I mean." She tried to force as natural a smile as she could.

"Zara," she said succinctly and nodded her head. Her voice was brittle. "I know we haven't seen eye to eye over the years and that probably won't change much. But I think I should bring something to your attention."

"Oh?" was Zara's cautious response, wondering where this was going.

"I know that you had some stuff stolen from your place a while back." "Yes. Yes, we did. And…?" Zara said, then thought, well yes, but that was months ago.

"Well, I don't sleep good these nights and I'm up and about several times. There's hardly any traffic down this street at night. For that matter, there is usually *no* traffic late at night at all. Now, this might not mean anything at all, I'm just saying."

Zara was suddenly *very* intrigued by where this was going. She got out of her truck and leaned against it, folding her arms.

"And…?" she prodded the old widow.

"Well, off and on there *has* been a car come down the road late at night…very slowly. It will stop right at the top of the drive going down to your place. Sometimes, if anybody is there late at the stable, the driver goes on and, I guess, drives around for a while. Then that car comes back. Slowly again. When whoever is driving that car sees that your place is now dark, with nobody still there, then that car goes down the driveway. It's only there for a couple minutes, then it high-tails it outta there."

"Hmmm," said Zara, as she furrowed her brow. "What kind of car was it? Could you tell what color?"

"Oh, heavens," answered Mrs. Critchley. "I don't know one car from the next. Unless it's a white one, all cars look black to me at nighttime anyway. I don't know any makes of cars anymore at all. But…," dragging out the word and hesitating for dramatic purposes.

Zara stood up straight. "But…?"

"Did you know I'm a birdwatcher?" Asked Mrs. Critchley.

Now where the hell is this going, Zara thought to herself. Is she going batty? Has senility finally settled in?

"No, Angela, I had no idea you were a birdwatcher. We sure do have a lot of pretty ones around here, though, don't we?" Placate her, Zara thought.

"The point I was going to make," Mrs. Critchley continued with just a hint of irritation, "is that I always have a pair of binoculars handy. It was dark, of course, when I saw the car, but the streetlight down the road a bit is just bright enough to see things…things like the license plate. And, well, the license plate has a light on it too. Maybe they're casing the joint. Maybe I just watch too many of those damn cop shows on TV. Who knows?"

"Really?" asked Zara, with enthusiasm. "Could you make out anything? Any numbers?"

"It's one of those weird ones," answered the old lady. "You know. Don't they call them vanity plates or something like that? The ones that sometimes make words or names?"

"Yes, yes!" exclaimed Zara, realizing that at least part of the mystery might be resolved or understood. "What could you make out? Anything?"

"Oh, yes. I use *very* good binoculars, Zara. A Nikon Monarch 5. I'm serious about my birding. The plate read CRZY1. Would you have any idea who that might be? Of course, we *could* call the cops to report it and *they* could trace it."

Zara was taken aback. She thought about it for a moment, and shook her head as she started to tear up. Just as quickly, she collected her thoughts and regained her composure.

"I'll take care of it, Angela. Thanks. You've been a tremendous help and I really, *seriously* appreciate it." She stopped to take a breath and think about her next words. "Look, I'm so sorry that I've been such a bitch in the past. And…," she was almost ashamed to say the rest. "And I'm so, so sorry that I waved at you the way I do."

"Well," huffed Mrs. Critchley in return, standing as rigid as she could get and folding her arms. "I guess you've never noticed that I've waved back at you, too. In a similar manner."

They both looked each other squarely in the eye…and then burst out laughing. Then they hugged.

"Again, I'm so sorry, Angela," said Zara apologetically.

"Oh, shoot," answered Mrs. Critchley, pulling back with a broad grin on her face. "I guess we're just a couple of sour old bitches. We won't change. Don't intend to. Now git! And keep your scrawny nags off my lawn…or I *will* call the cops!"

Zara got back into her truck, pulled across the street and down the long driveway to the stable. She turned off the engine and sat, in silence, for five minutes, thinking about her next moves. She picked up her cell phone and punched a number on speed dial.

"Chris," she said quickly as her daughter's husband answered. "Please don't hang up. Please, please, *please* put Taylor on and, *please*, I implore you, make her promise that she won't hang up on me."

There was silence for a moment.

"Hang on." was the simple reply.

Zara waited for close to five minutes, with her heart beginning to race. She could hear muffled talking in the background, some of it sounding angry.

"What?" Taylor said suddenly and loudly into the phone, startling Zara with its abruptness.

"Taylor," Zara said nervously. "I need to see you. We need to talk and I'm serious. Something is happening."

"Like what?" was the succinct reply.

"Can you come by the house tomorrow morning? Your dad is going to be out of town."

A long, very long pause was followed by the sound of an exasperated sigh.

"What time?"

"Oh, hell. How about nine or so?"

"I have to bring the kids."

"That's fine," said Zara. "No problem. I haven't seen them in ages. Remy will be sad to have missed seeing the boys, but that's not my concern right now."

"Care to give me a clue about what's up?" Taylor asked.

"Tomorrow. At nine. I have another call to make now. Don't eat before you come. I'll fix a nice breakfast, okay?"

"Sure. See ya," And Taylor clicked off.

Zara fought back the tears as she hit another speed dial number.

She got Kristine's voice mail. She left a message pleading with her youngest daughter to *please* return her call tonight…no matter how late it was.

The house was filled with the aroma of coffee and the special French Toast Casserole that Zara had prepared the night before. She had kept her emotions within her for too long, she thought. We need to resolve these issues once and for all. How fortuitous that Remy should be out of town this week, visiting his brother in Pennsylvania, with things finally coming to a head.

Kristine, the first to arrive, was a school teacher and had the summer to loaf around. Although the fall session of school begins in early August in Georgia, she still had a couple weeks of pleasure. She had planned a return visit to Europe at the end of this week and, always the planner and well organized, she was packed and ready to go. She had hesitated, at first, to accept her mother's invitation when they had spoken around midnight. But Zara had sounded more forceful than usual, so Kristine agreed to be there. They hadn't spoken or seen each other in months.

Taylor and her boys, following her usual pattern, were fifteen minutes late. That had given Zara and Kristine some time for idle chatter.

"Coffee?" she offered them both, holding an empty cup aloft, after Taylor finally arrived.

"Sure," answered Taylor.

"Yes, please," added Kristine.

The two sisters exchanged a few pleasantries, but they had never been especially close. At least, not recently.

Zara poured three cups of coffee, offered them cream and sugar, and then got the casserole out of the oven.

"It's very hot," she explained. "Better wait a couple minutes before I serve it. Will the boys eat this?" The last was asked of Taylor.

"Oh, yeah. Those goof balls will eat anything. I think they'd eat shit if I put ketchup on it. If only we can get them away from the television."

"That's okay. Let them stay in there for a while," said Zara, collecting her thoughts. She took a sip of her coffee, and then took a deep breath.

"You both remember Brandy Dennison from over at the stable, don't you?" she asked the girls.

They both nodded and answered in the affirmative.

"Why?" asked Kristine. "Did something happen to her?"

"Oh, no, no," Zara quickly responded. "Nothing like that at all. You probably *don't* know that she almost constantly has her nose buried in puzzle books or magazines. She thinks it will prevent her mind from going as she gets older. I found that kind of silly but…damn, if I didn't get hooked on them too."

The two girls looked at her with a questioning expression. And this is the reason for Mom's breakfast? Is *Mom's* mind going?

Zara scooped out servings of the casserole onto some plates and poured some maple syrup over each piece.

"Here. Take these into the boys," she said to Taylor, handing her two plates. "They can eat in front of the TV, no problem."

The plates were delivered while Zara and Kristine sat in silence, waiting for Taylor to return and sit down again.

"As I was saying," she began again. "I've gotten hooked on those damn puzzle books and, consequently, I look at *everything* like I'm trying to solve a puzzle of some sort. It might be a logic problem…or word scrambles…"

"Mother, where are you going with this?" asked Taylor impatiently. "Surely you didn't get us here this morning to discuss your *latest* addiction? You said on the phone yesterday that something was happening. What the hell is it? Cut to the chase."

Taylor had always been abrupt which, at times, annoyed Zara and Remy both. Taylor could also be hateful in her sarcastic comments, without a care for other's feelings. Kristine shifted uneasily in her chair. She hadn't touched a bite of her breakfast.

Zara got up and retrieved a large manila envelope from the counter.

"I thought that someone was trying to embarrass me," she said, as she opened the envelope. "Instead, I think someone is asking for help in a very uncomfortable and unusual way."

She spread four pieces of bright yellow paper on the table in front of the girls. It was apparent that one of the pieces had been crumpled into a ball, then opened up and flattened out again.

"I have finally put the pieces of the puzzle together," Zara said, staring at them both.

Kristine gasped and stood straight up, almost knocking her chair over. She turned and stared at Taylor. Taylor stared at Zara.

Rance stared at Julia. She was packing for one of her many business trips to California. In pharmaceutical sales, Julia's job took her across the country but Rance noticed that she had been going to California more often recently. He had also begun to pick up other signals and was beginning to put pieces of the puzzle together. He was still seething from the incident at the stable with Mary Anne and her partygoers. Although he had made a court appearance, paid a hefty fine and issued an apology, it festered in his brain like a cancer.

"Y'all going out to the coast for a good fuck?" he finally blurted out to Julia.

Julia turned abruptly and gave him the iciest stare he had ever seen.

"You're crazy," she said coolly. "You haven't got the foggiest notion. This is the largest account I service...and you're being an asshole."

"I guess the operative word there was *service*," snapped Rance.

"You really are such a shithead, you know?" Julia snapped right back at him. She zipped her luggage, grabbed her cell phone and headed towards the door. "*Please* don't forget to pick up the kids from Mom and Dad's on Sunday...please try to offend as *few* people as possible while I'm gone... and try not to poke your eye out with your sharp tongue!"

"No kiss goodbye?" Rance asked sarcastically.

"Kiss my ass!" was Julia's response as she hurried out the door.

Julia got into her car and Rance watched, sadly, regretfully, as she drove off to the airport. He had nothing to say. To anyone. He sat down.

"Sit down," Zara said softly to Kristine, as all three of them stared at the papers. Kristine sat.

"At first, your father and I thought that these were some strange notes left for the boarders…for God knows what reason. And then these puzzle books got me to thinking. I don't know, maybe doing those damn things has sharpened my senses somehow…beyond horse sense, that is. I'm actually surprised that nobody else over at CedarView has picked up on it. At least, in part. I assume no one over there is aware of my…well,… my history."

The two girls were getting worried, but for different reasons.

"In actuality, the first two lines of each of these notes should have been a clue right off. But it *does* take a little bit of brainpower, I guess. The last is first…the first is last. Now, let's think, shall we? What could that mean, huh?"

She glanced back and forth between her two daughters. Taylor looked puzzled. Kristine avoided eye contact.

"Okay. Think about the alphabet. Any clues yet?" and Zara was ready to lay the truth out in the open. "The last is first. The last letter, Z. The first is last. The letter A. And, guess what? Is this a fill-in-the-blank thing? Now, that part is easy, isn't it?"

Maybe Taylor wasn't as swift as Zara thought. She still looked confused.

"Mother…," Kristine started, then thought better of it.

"Once I figured that out," continued Zara, "I thought those notes were *about* me. Then I realized those notes were *to* me. They were telling me something. These are, really, very angry notes and…and very hurtful and sad. Pathetic, frankly. They indicate that I haven't been there for someone. I know that I haven't been so much recently…and I know that, at one time, I wasn't there at all. But why hasn't that someone come to me. Directly to me. Things have changed. I have changed…sort of. We need a dialogue. These were calls for help, weren't they? To make a public announcement, so to speak, in bold type…on yellow paper…making my boarders leery about heaven knows what."

"What the…?" commented Taylor, still shaking her head in confusion.

At that moment, Kristine jumped up, ran from the house and got into her car. Zara heard the tires squeal as they hit the pavement and speed away, the bright morning sunlight glistening on Kristine's CRZY1 license plate.

Zara buried her face in her hands and wept. Taylor suddenly making sense out of the situation was struck silent. Her heart pounded in her chest.

•

Years earlier, before leaving Pennsylvania, moving to Georgia and eventually buying CedarView, Zara had a problem. A drinking problem. And she became a very nasty and abusive drunk. Remy Major had actually been the friendly one…the happy-go-lucky guy who everybody enjoyed being around. Kristine had noticed, recently, little telltale signs that perhaps Zara was drinking again.

A CLOUDY FUTURE,
AND A STORMY PAST.

Aside from a few very close friends still back in Pennsylvania, nobody in Georgia was aware of the Major family situation. As the situation intensified, for some reason, Zara would become extremely abusive to her daughters, with Kristine in particular. She thought that Kristine was Remy's favored child and became jealous of Kristine's beauty and bubbly personality. It got so bad, at times, that Kristine would hide under her bed so Zara couldn't reach her…or run away and would be gone for days. She was a teenager…a confused and sensitive teenager who longed for her mother's acceptance and love.

A THOUSAND TEARS
CAN'T QUENCH A THIRST

Aside from the physical wounds that took time to heal, Kristine's emotional wounds presented a different matter…and a different problem. Zara continued to seek alcohol. Remy continued to seek help. Kristine continued to seek love. Kristine got pregnant. Remy was furious. In her drunken rages, Zara would beat Kristine. Even went into her room at night while the girl was sleeping and pounded her. Remy and Taylor tried to keep Zara and Kristine apart daily. Tried to get Zara to seek help. Both Remy and Taylor would end up trying to cover their bruises. During the third month of her pregnancy, she hemorrhaged; complications and infection developed. The baby, along with her uterus, had to be removed.

A TINY LIE
GROWS LARGE TOO FAST

The teenage father of Kristine's baby never knew of the pregnancy. For that matter, neither Remy nor Zara knew who he was for certain. They had surmised, correctly though, that he was the son of one of their very good friends. Friends of the Majors grew distant, became less friendly, turned away from them. Friends became strangers. They seemed oblivious to the fact that Zara had a serious problem. Remy was finally able to get Zara committed to a rehab center, but against her wishes. She fought it. Called him every name in the book. Lashed out at him and her two daughters. When asked, Remy lied to their remaining friends, telling them that Zara was taking an extended vacation to visit family who she hadn't seen in years. When they eventually moved to Georgia, long after rehab, Zara had seemed to have her problem under control. To keep herself occupied and happy, Zara bought horse after horse and Remy bought CedarView. But Remy had become a different person. He distrusted people, because of what their friends had done. He became sullen and, for the most part, withdrawn. And, Kristine thought, he got a bum rap.

HOPES ARE LOST,
DREAMS ARE BURST.

Kristine had always loved children and had dreams of the day when she, too, could be a mom...and she had jokingly planned on having six. Her therapy slowly erased the horrors of long ago, but it created a different person. In reality, with her family she had become withdrawn and sullen. However, when she was in public...at school...at social gatherings...a "new" Kristine emerged. Her friendly outgoing effervescent persona was a façade. And she was extremely frightened of young men.

She hated the fact that her mother was, now, the popular one at the stable, and her father was not. She overheard boarders chatting about Remy and his sourpuss ways and his unfriendly manner. She remembered the way he once was. The fun-loving, cheerful guy…almost always with a smile on his face. Her mother was to blame. And she hated her for it.

With Remy's pathological penchant for privacy, he had made certain that Zara's past would remain…well,…in the past.

Years earlier, Taylor had thought that Zara's behavior, liquor-fueled or otherwise, was reprehensible. They had had words and parted ways. Taylor and Remy would often talk on the phone…or meet at the stable when Zara wasn't there. She, too, had thought that perhaps her mother had started drinking again. Zara had.

As it turned out, the situation with the stolen saddles and bridles was a random and unrelated crime, never to be solved.

As much as Zara enjoyed hearing everyone's tales of woe at the stable, *nobody* there had a clue about her truth…her past.

•

Zara composed herself as her two grandsons came running back into the kitchen.

"This was yummy, Grandma!" shouted Blare, the youngest, holding out his empty plate.

"Good for you, young man," responded Zara. "Come here, give Grandma a great big hug. You're getting *so* big!"

"Mom," Taylor began. "I don't know what to say. What the hell, really, is going on here?"

Zara sat back, rubbed her face with her hands and pushed back a stray strand of hair from her forehead.

"I don't know why Kristine approached the situation this way, Taylor, really I don't. Why did she have to make such a strange puzzle out of it? I had my suspicions and should have acted on them. But…well,…I didn't. As you know, your dad and I have been at odds for years. Yes, it's my fault. Yes, I had a problem. I guess I still do. I was a horrible mother. Kristine is obviously going through something all over again. Maybe this has something to do with her continuing therapy. Maybe she's just trying to embarrass me. Show me for what I really was…am…whatever. I really don't know. A strange way to ask for help is all I can say. A phone call… or a conversation would have been so much less dramatic…or weird. My guess is that she wants it to be more public now. She's tired of living a lie and wants…needs to share her…our story with others. And, frankly, that's fine with me too. I never wanted to be keeping this horrible secret inside either. Damn, *you* know what it did. To us. To your dad and me. You and Kristine blame me for the way Remy has become. The person he has become. Well, you were right. And I am so, so sorry. Life's a shit, isn't it?"

Rance was drowning his sorrows in tequila while Julia was out of town. With no one to admonish him, he would forego a glass and drink straight from the bottle. The telephone rang and he stumbled across the room to answer it, without checking caller ID. Yes, they were the rare few to still have a landline.

"Good afternoon. Is this Mister Rance Hurakon?" asked an unfamiliar friendly-sounding male voice.

"Yes?" answered Rance, wondering who the hell this might be.

"Hello, sir. I hope you're enjoying this beautiful day. This is Officer Pendleton from the Policeman's Benevolent Associa…"

"FUCK OFF!" Rance yelled, as he slammed down the receiver.

AUGUST

Between Lovers

"...There is the heat of Love, the pulsing rush of Longing, the lover's whisper, irresistible—magic to make the sanest man go mad."

Homer, The Iliad

It was the fifth straight week with daytime temperatures in the 90s. The drought that had gripped the south for nearly two years showed no signs of relinquishing the territory. The horses found as much relief from the blazing sun as possible by staying in the wooded areas and especially around the stretch of creek that still flowed. Some simply stood in the water, others lazily grazed on the remaining weeds that were unaffected by the lack of rain. Yellow and black butterflies fluttered through the trees, in and out of the rays of sunlight streaming through the foliage, landing occasionally on fresh droppings to extract the moisture. Cicadas buzzed loudly, unseen.

The herd found no pleasure, on days such as these, to play their "come chase me" game. In cooler weather, one or two horses might start prancing around each other, playfully nickering and reaching out to nip one another. This would start a chase that eventually included the entire herd. Horses, with thundering hooves, would gallop from one end of the thirty-acre pasture to the other. Through woods, leaping over fallen trees, splashing through the creeks, coming to a screeching halt at the gates leading to the stable. There would be snorting and stomping…and tossing of heads. Then, just as abruptly, turn around en masse and dash off again. The game had not been played for weeks.

Most of the boarders had elected not to ride, especially during the heat of the day. This was a precaution for themselves as much as it was a concern for their horses. Unless Zara or Remy were going to be taking care of their horses, the boarders came to the stable to feed and groom early mornings or late evenings, when the heat was not as oppressive. Dust from the red Georgia clay settled on everything. The days were lazy at the stable, with most of the activity coming from large carpenter bees that buzzed around, always trying to bore their way into the rafters above the stalls. Much to the chagrin of other boarders, Gary Smart would swing at the bees with a narrow strip of timber, knocking them senseless or killing them. He called it his "Bee-Bop Board".

"Hey, Gary," yelled Mary Pat when she saw what he was doing. "Those bees are harmless. They won't hurt anything. Leave 'em alone!"

Gary would laugh, toss the board aside and wait until the coast was clear before he would start swinging again.

At 3 o'clock this afternoon, Mary's pick-up truck came rumbling down the driveway, stirring up a trailing cloud of dust. She hoped that she might be the only one at the stable and was surprised to see that Mary Pat and Jessie were there too.

"Hey, girls," she called out as she strode from her truck towards the tack room. "Whatcha doin' out here in this freakin' heat?"

"Oh, I just came out early to feed the babies," Jessie responded. "Marty and I are going to the Braves game tonight."

"Yeah," said Mary Pat. "I was surprised to see Jessie here too. I'm feeding early, then staying in the pool until midnight. I don't care if I look like a prune when I get out. This heat is really, *really* getting to me!"

They all laughed.

"And what brings *you* out here at this time, Mary?" asked Jessie. "We haven't seen you for weeks. Where the heck have you been?"

"Ah. Well. I've been a bit…busy the past few weeks. Haven't had much time to spend here at all. I've been coming out at odd hours. Sorry that I haven't even called to chat for a while. Time really got away from me. Thunder seemed to be favoring a leg last night when I brought him in and he has a cracked hoof. I'm meeting the farrier out here to take care of it. I know that it's a bit too hot for that kind of work, but he had to fit it into his schedule."

"Oh," said Mary Pat, "I wish I had known that Crazy Billy was coming out here today. I'd have him take a look at Jake's hooves too. I'm sure they must need a trimming. Haven't had that done in a few months. Do you think he might have time for that?"

Crazy Billy was William Farmer, the farrier who had taken care of their horses for years. Practically every horse owner in the surrounding counties knew him. The girls joked that he must be at least a hundred and ten years old. He knew everything anyone could possibly know about horses and their hooves. But he had been showing his age, whatever his real age might be. He had gotten careless over the past couple of years and the upper part of his right ear was missing because of it. He had trimmed a hoof a bit too short on one feisty mare and she let Crazy Billy know it by turning around and taking a big bite. He, in turn, gave her a swift kick in her side as the blood streamed down his neck. Although he was loved, it was probably about time for his retirement.

"Uh, no. It's not Crazy Billy who's coming out," said Mary. "I ran into a guy at The Tack Shack who was raised doing this stuff, so I thought I'd give him a try."

"Oh, cool," said Jessie. "If he's any good, perhaps we can all switch over to him. And let Crazy Billy drift off into that retirement village with his poor wife."

"We'll see," Said Mary, with the hint of a smile on her face.

Mary Pat and Jessie went out into the pasture to retrieve their horses. As they were leading the horses to their stalls, an unfamiliar pick-up truck slowly came down the driveway and parked. Mary Pat and Jessie came to an abrupt halt as the young man jumped out of his vehicle. He went around to the back of his truck to get all of his paraphernalia and the ladies did not take their eyes off of him. He was tall, obviously well muscled and wore the tightest jeans either of them had ever seen. His snug, light gray t-shirt contrasted with his tan and his thick, dark brown hair.

The ladies quickly put their horses in their respective stalls and dumped the feed. They each came rushing back to greet the stranger.

"Jessie, Mary Pat, this is Stet Brandson," introduced Mary. "Stet, this is Mary Pat and Jessie."

Stet reached out and firmly shook their hands.

"Hey, ladies," he said with a very deep, sexy voice. "It's a pleasure meeting you both."

If Mary Pat and Jessie could have melted, they would have. They both stared into his sparkling blue eyes.

"Hey, Stet," smiled Mary Pat and she felt her knees give a little.

"Nice meeting you, too, Stet," Jessie practically drooled.

"Okay, Mary. Let's have a look at Thunder and see what we can do," said Stet, eager to get to work and get out of the heat.

Mary haltered him and brought Thunder out of his stall, firmly grasping the bright red lead line as Stet examined the horse's hooves.

"Yeah, this heat takes its toll on these poor guys sometimes. Their hooves get dry and, unless you keep putting that gunk on it, they have a tendency to crack. Looks like he picked up a stone bruise, too. No big deal. The crack isn't too bad and I can file it down, give him a little trim and you're good to go."

Stet had been around horses all of his life and loved everything about them.

"Man," he had said to a friend at one time, "I love to bury my face in a horse and get a good whiff. I love the smell of a horse. Horse scents are a big turn-on for me. Hell, I even love the smell of horse farts. Sounds weird, I know, but I love the smell of manure too. Sick, eh?" and then he had laughed.

By the time he was finished trimming Thunder's hooves, his t-shirt was soaked with sweat.

"Stet?" asked Mary Pat sheepishly. "Any chance you might have the time to just take a look at my hooves, too...well, I mean my *horse's* hooves?"

Stet laughed, glanced at his watch and said "Sure. Bring him out here and let's have a look."

Stet started to examine Mary Pat's horse, but the heat and perspiration were getting to him. Sweat was dripping down his face. He raised his right shoulder, buried his face in the t-shirt sleeve, wiping it to remove the wet.

"Sorry, ladies, but this heat is a killer. I just have to do this," he said, as he pulled off his t-shirt.

Mary Pat and Jessie let out a collective, but silent gasp. His smooth, well-defined chest glistened with moisture. Topped by broad, muscular shoulders, his torso tapered down to a tight, narrow waist. He looked like a Michelangelo sculpture in the flesh. His pecs rippled as he moved his arms. They couldn't help but observe that his right nipple was noticeably larger than his left.

"They just need to be filed down a bit. Otherwise they look good. I can do it quickly for you, but then I gotta scoot," said Stet.

"Great…cool," said Mary Pat. Anything to keep you and that body of yours here as long as possible, she thought. Take off those jeans, too, if it gets too hot for ya.

He finished up and said to Mary, "I'll catch up with you later. I gotta run."

"Wait!" exclaimed Mary Pat. "I have to pay you and I don't even know what your rate is."

"No problem," smiled Stet. "This one was a freebie. If you like what I do, we can work something out."

"Really? Wow, that was awfully sweet of you, Stet. I hope we'll see you again."

"Oh, you will, I'm sure," Stet answered as he turned to give Mary a wink. "Hey, I really need to get the hell outta Dodge. I'll call you later, Mary." He patted her on the shoulder and called over his shoulder "See ya, ladies!"

Mary Pat and Jessie stood beside Mary and watched as Stet got to his truck, wiped his sweaty face and chest with his t-shirt, hopped in and drove up the driveway, leaving a trail of dust in the air. Jessie failed to see the glint in Mary's eyes. But Mary Pat *didn't*.

"Oh. My. God," exclaimed Mary Pat. "Don't tell me that you're doin' 'im!"

"Okay," answered Mary.

"Okay what?"

"Okay, I won't tell you that I'm doin' 'im." Said Mary with an innocent grin.

"Jesus, Mary and Joseph. How the hell old is he anyway?"

"He's twenty-nine. Almost thirty. Now don't you *dare* go judging me, Mary Pat!"

"Ha!" Mary Pat responded loudly. "I'm not judging you. I'm jealous as hell!"

•

She had not intended to be flirtatious. But she was. It really wasn't her style. But it was. Mary had gone to The Tack Shack for some fly repellant and to price a new bridle. She liked the place and had become fairly good friends with Brenda, the owner. She loved the way the shop smelled of leather and she would usually kill time there just browsing through their clothes racks. She was a very good customer. On this particular day, she had noticed a young man chatting with one of the sales girls. The man was obviously very humorous, as the girl would giggle and laugh, clapping her hands. He was showing something to her in a little book, which he snapped shut when the girl started laughing. Mary had needed to ask that girl a question about one of the bridles, so she waited until she caught the clerk's attention.

"I'm sorry to interrupt, but can I butt in for just a second? I have a question," Mary asked.

"Oh, sure," said the girl. "I'm sorry that I wasn't paying attention. What do you need?"

The young man turned and smiled at Mary. Click!

He was wearing the tightest jeans Mary had ever seen on a guy, western boots, a hunter green t-shirt and a cowboy hat that was pushed back off his brow. He stood at least 3" taller than Mary. When he smiled, dimples formed on his tanned face…and he smelled fantastic.

Mary asked the young girl about a couple types of bridles and questioned the cost versus quality differences. The girl was actually very knowledgeable about the products that were offered. As the girl spoke, Mary couldn't help but let her eyes drift past her to look at the young man again. A few times she saw that he was looking at her as well. She made her decision about the bridles, thanked the clerk, got the container of fly repellent she was after and started to take her choices to the check-out register.

"Thanks for letting me butt in," Mary said to the man, and flashed a big smile.

"Hey, no problem," he replied, returning her smile.

He reached out his hand. "Hi, I'm Stet Brandson."

Their hands touched. Click! Was the temperature really rising in here?

"And I'm Mary Gordon. Nice meeting you, Stet."

"I'm in this store a lot," continued Stet. "How come I haven't seen you in here before?"

Sounds like a pretty standard pick-up line from a not-so-standard guy, Mary thought.

"Timing, I guess," she answered. "I'm not really in here a lot."

They chatted for a while longer about tack, fly repellent, the heat and horses. He was interesting and had a lot of good thoughts about the care of horses. Mary noticed, however, that he didn't try to make her giggle and laugh as he had with the young sales clerk.

"Hey, I gotta go," she finally said. "I enjoyed our chat. Perhaps we'll bump into each other again in here."

"Sure thing," said Stet, reaching out his hand again. This time the handshake was held a bit longer. They both smiled, looking each other in the eyes, and nodded.

Whoa, what the hell was *that*? Mary asked herself as she walked back out to her truck. A feeling stirred in her that she hadn't felt in years.

Calm down, lady, she thought. He doesn't look any older than my son.

Two days later, Mary was shopping and stopped in at her favorite luncheonette for a sandwich before heading home. She had intended to take it with her, but decided to sit there and continue reading a mystery she had started the night before. It was too hot to ride anyway, she reasoned. She sat at a table in the corner of the shop, started her sandwich, took a sip of iced tea and buried her nose in the book.

"Wow, talk about timing!" said a deep voice.

She glanced up to stare into Stet's smiling face.

"Ha! Are you following me?" Mary laughed.

"Ah, it's fate, Mary. Serendipity," he responded. He was carrying what looked like a sketchbook. "Are you too engrossed in your book or can I join you for a while?"

"The book can wait. Have a seat, Stet."

Stet ordered a sandwich and a Coke. "Thanks, Alexis," he said as the waitress delivered them to the table a few minutes later.

"You come here that often that you know the servers by name?" remarked Mary.

Stet laughed. "Name tag. It's small, but it's there," he said, pointing to an imaginary badge on his shirt, then pointing towards the server.

"So, Stet is an unusual name," said Mary. "Is it an abbreviation? For Stetson, perhaps? A nickname?"

"Nope. Stet is Stet," he replied. He grinned. "My Mom wasn't married when she got pregnant with me. I was a mistake. A *big* accident. She really didn't want kids at all. She was going to get an abortion. Had it all set, too. Then she changed her mind. She was a young copywriter at a big ad agency out in California. Stet is a proofreader's mark. It means something like leave as is…retain. If somebody decides to take something out, then changes their mind. Actually, I think it's pretty cool!"

"In that case, I'm glad your mother decided to keep you, then, Stet," said Mary.

"Well, she *had* me but didn't keep me. She really, *really* didn't want to have kids. But my dad did. He was the one who raised me. It was his last name that I took. He was the full-time farrier at a big horse breeder's place in California. Still is, for that matter. That's where I learned all that I know. He taught me a *ton* of stuff. We had a great time and travelled all over the country."

"Oh, that's so sad, though, that your own mother didn't want you."

"I've adjusted. She was honest. Said that she was just too selfish to raise kids. My dad had plenty of help with me as I was growing up. Plenty of ladies around." He laughed. "And, as it turns out, I see my mom from time to time. We keep in touch. She and her husband have lived in Atlanta for years. He's a really cool guy and she's a hell of an interesting person. We've actually become good friends. Weird, eh?"

"Well, it isn't the norm. But, hell, these days, what's the norm?"

"Exactly! Hey, I have no complaints," he said, as he bit into his sandwich. "And what's *your* back story, Miss Mary?"

Mary filled him in on her husband and Stet seemed genuinely moved. She mentioned her son in Chicago.

"Oh, wow, that's so cool," Stet remarked. "I actually thought about architecture at one time but I'm lousy at math. Rather, I *hate* math! So, that pretty much nipped it in the bud for me."

"So, what is it that you *do* do?" asked Mary. "…aside from following older ladies around town, that is."

They both laughed and met each other's eyes.

"Oh, a bunch of different stuff really. But, if I had to put a profession on a blank line in some sort of application it would have to be farrier."

"Great," said Mary. "I may have to give you a call sometime. The farrier everyone at the stable has been using for the past century is getting on. We're all afraid that we might call him one day only to discover that he's dead!"

Stet let out a loud laugh. "You can only be referring to Billy Farmer," he said. "Good lord, everybody knows him. He's a cool guy and sometimes I go out with him if he has a lot of horses to do. But I know what you mean. All of his long-time customers are as afraid to *not* call him as they are *to* call him. You're right, though. It's time for him to say goodnight, Gracie."

Stet pulled out his wallet, got out his business card and handed it to Mary. "My cell is the number you'll have better luck reaching me at."

Mary glanced at it. "This is certainly a role-reversal, isn't it? A guy giving his number to a lady?"

Stet blushed. After a short pause he asked. "So, Mary. Any guys in your life right now, aside from your son, that is?"

"Just between you, me and the proverbial fencepost, nope. None at the moment. Sort of in a between situation, as the old cliché goes. How about you?"

"Between you, me and the hitching post, I'm a betweener too, I guess." And he sighed. "I hope you'll use that number sometime soon, Miss Mary." Stet smiled and winked. "But now I gotta run."

Mary was enjoying his company and was sorry that he had to leave. He picked up his sketchbook, grabbed the check for lunch and headed toward the cashier.

"Hey," called Mary. "I think *my* lunch is on that tab too."

"Next time, you pay," said Stet with a very broad smile and another wink. "Call me."

Stet paid and was out the door, waving to Mary as he left. Okay, Mary thought, what the hell is happening here? Really, what *is* going on? She suddenly realized that she hadn't finished her sandwich. She had sat, intently listening to and staring at Stet. What do I do now, she pondered? She picked up her book, opened it to the last page she had been reading and simply could not remember anything about it. Damn, Stet fried my brain!

Several times throughout the next day or two she toyed with the idea of calling Stet. She thought: Is this a good thing or a bad thing? Am I a good witch or a bad witch? Am I about to make a wrong turn at the junction of Smart and Stupid? Cautious or foolhardy? Curiosity, at times, overrides logic.

"This is Stet," he said, as he answered his cell phone.

"Hey, Stet. This is Mary." She was a bit nervous, and a bit concerned that she may come across as a little too aggressive. Or too eager. Or too needy.

"Oh, hi!" he answered with enthusiasm. "I was hoping I didn't scare you away."

"Hell, it takes much more than a guy your age to do that, sonny!" she quipped, wondering if that was too flip. Ease up, Mary.

"What's up?" he asked.

"I was wondering if you might be interested in heading to that little sandwich shop again. It's almost lunchtime and I could stand some company. That book that I was reading turned out to be a real dud."

"As it so happens, I was in the process of fixing some lunch here when you called. Don't take this the wrong way...I hope I'm not being too forward. Why don't you come on over to my place? It's not too far from that sandwich shop."

"Hmmm...well,...where, exactly, is your place?"

"I have a small house out here in Between. Probably no more that seven or eight miles from where you are right now. Right up Route 78 a bit. You can meet my horses, too. Hey, I'm safe. I'm not a pervert and I won't bite... unless provoked or requested to."

They both laughed. Mary didn't want to let Stet know how much that excited her.

"Well…I suppose," she said. "Give me your address. I have a GPS in the truck."

Thirty minutes later she turned her truck down the driveway that her GPS had indicated. It was located on a twisting road, with no other houses or driveways in sight. The long, gravel driveway wound through beautiful oaks and poplars. It was very shaded and noticeably cooler here. She didn't know what to expect at the end of the driveway, but was totally shocked by what she saw. She had been anticipating, perhaps, an old, rustic cabin of some sorts. In a clearing stood a very contemporary one-story structure. The house had a variety of angles and a lot of glass. She could actually look straight through the house, into the woods behind it. The steep-pitched roof had seven skylights that she could count. Who knew how many were on the far side of the roof. There was no lawn. Instead, the gravel driveway ended by forming a large, circular turn-around directly in front of the entry. A low, one-step-up porch was crowded with several enormous pots, containing overflowing greenery and exotic-looking blooms. Despite the continuing drought, these were well tended.

"Whoa!" she exclaimed out loud.

Off to the side of the house was a small paddock area with a just-as-small shaded riding ring and a pole barn. She could see two horses in their stalls, their heads leaning out and over the bottom half of their doors.

As she braked to a slow stop, a large red Doberman came running towards the truck, barking loudly. Mary was hesitant to get out.

"Luger! In the house," called Stet as he came out of the front door. The dog immediately turned and ran back through the open door.

"Don't worry about him," said Stet as Mary slowly got out of her truck. "He's a big pussy cat. Albeit a loud one. Folks have a bad impression of Dobes. Nazi dogs and all that. They are actually a very docile and loving breed. Great guard dog, though! Scares the shit outta the UPS guy every time."

"Strange selection for a name, then, if you're trying to dispel that image," said Mary, not quite sure.

"Come on in. I'll introduce you to the horses after lunch."

He ushered Mary into his house and she was momentarily at a loss for words. This was *not* what she had expected at all. Dark hardwood floors throughout…and stark bright white walls…very contemporary furniture everywhere. It was most definitely masculine in a very artsy way. Even had a huge, wall-mounted flat screen TV. She turned all the way around, drinking it in.

"Love the Barcelona Chair. My son has one, too, in his Chicago apartment." She exclaimed, pointing to the living room.

"Good eye, lady. I'm impressed. Yeah. They're great, aren't they? Terrific design that holds up decades after the fact. Hey, have a seat. I'll get you a drink first before lunch. You like iced tea, right?"

Mary laughed. "It's obvious neither one of us is originally from the south. Otherwise you would have asked if I wanted sweet tea."

Stet just shook his head and laughed too.

Mary looked around the room. Original oil paintings hung on every wall, sometimes in large groupings that took up the entire wall, ceiling to floor. Some of the paintings were abstract; some were images of trees, plants or animals. Each one was exquisite, and each one was framed beautifully as well. Mary noticed a stack of sketchbooks on one of the tables. She opened one and flipped through the pages. Stet had had one of these books with him at the luncheonette. Were these *his* sketches? Damn, she thought, these are gorgeous.

Stet brought two tall glasses of iced tea into the open expanse that he called the living room, and handed one to her.

"This is quite a surprise," she said, sweeping her arm around the room.

"Just 'cause I live amongst the hicks in the sticks doesn't mean I are one," he joked.

"I love all of these paintings," she continued. "Obviously you're a collector."

"Obviously you didn't look close enough," Stet laughed. "Obviously I'm a painter."

"Holy crap! These are *your* paintings?" Mary was incredulous; as she leaned down to see, in painted block letters at the lower right corner of each painting the name STET.

"'Fraid so" he grinned bashfully.

"Well, just damn and double damn! When you said you dabbled in lots of things I didn't expect this. I sure as *hell* didn't expect this! Are those sketchbooks your dabbling too?"

He nodded. "Yep. Come on back. Lunch is on. Let's head out to the kitchen. We can chat further while we eat."

Mary hadn't noticed it when she had first entered the house, but soft, mellow jazz was playing on a stereo.

"Nice music," she commented. "I enjoy jazz as well."

"My taste," responded Stet, "goes way back to the classics in jazz as well as some of the current stuff. The old standards. Not too fond of the funky stuff, though."

There was a large concrete countertop island in the center of the kitchen with bar stools surrounding it. Two plates, with sandwiches on them, were placed at one end.

"And what do we have here?" asked Mary, eyeing the thick sandwiches.

"One of my favorites," answered Stet. "Cold roast beef, sliced really thin but piled high, muenster cheese and tomato on rye. Hope you like mayonnaise. I first had this at a little side-street deli in New York City when I lived there for a while." He tore open a bag of potato chips and poured some into a bowl.

"Wow, sounds delish!" said Mary, quite impressed. "God, I *love* this house. I had no idea these things existed out here in the boonies."

"Well, I had this property for a while and only built the house last year."

"Oh, so you had the house built recently. I guess that explains it," said Mary.

"No," returned Stet. "I built the house."

"Wait. What? You built it? I thought you said…"

"Well," interrupted Stet. "I sorta lied about the math bit a few days ago. I happen to love architecture too, but really couldn't get into all the studying that goes into it to make it a full time thing. My dad actually taught me a lot about building things as I was growing up. I told you, he was a great teacher. I designed this house and a couple buddies helped me build it. It pays to have talented friends, doesn't it?"

"What other surprises do you have up your sleeve?" Mary asked laughingly.

"Time will tell," Stet replied, giving her a big wink. "Time will tell."

They chatted and laughed for several hours following lunch. Mary was growing very fond of this young man. Apparently he was growing very fond of her as well.

"I'd better get going," said Mary, glancing at her watch. "It's almost feeding time at the zoo."

"Oh, come on out, before you go, and let me introduce you to *my* two big babies," said Stet, scrambling to his feet.

They walked to the stalls, with Luger following behind, sniffing Mary's jeans.

"This is George," he said, pointing to a large black Tennessee Walker. "He's the old man of the place. He's a little over thirty. He's been a part of my life since I was a kid." He then pointed to a dappled gray mare. "And this sweet young lady is Gracie. She's only ten."

Mary laughed. "Funny names for horses."

"I told you I like the good old standards." And he smiled.

George ambled over towards Mary, sticking his head out of the stall door and widening his nostrils, taking in her scent. She stroked his neck and gently rubbed one of his ears. He seemed to enjoy it. Gracie paid no attention to Mary at all.

"You said that George is thirty?" asked Mary, surprised to see such an alert horse for that age.

"Yeah…well, he's probably a couple years older than that. Anyway, he's the oldest horse that my vet sees in this county. He's definitely beginning to slow down, I'm sad to say. I don't put him through anything strenuous. Just some easy trail rides, now and then. I've been concerned about his well being and watching out for his quality of life. I don't want to have him linger or suffer if he should go downhill in a hurry. Doc Morrison… that's my vet…said that George will tell me when it's time. He would let me know in his own way."

Mary had a quick thought about Thunder. She had never had to put a horse down and didn't even want to think about it. Bonds between horse and master are extremely strong, especially if one has had the horse for a long time. She couldn't even imagine the emotions that poor Stet would be going through when George closes his eyes forever.

"I really need to go now," said Mary, still stroking George's neck and rubbing his muzzle.

Stet slowly walked Mary to her truck, continuing to chat as they walked.

"Wish you didn't have to rush off so soon. I hope you'll come back." They both reached for the door handle at the same time and their hands touched. They looked into each other's face.

"Come back soon," he whispered.

He turned and walked back into the house as Mary drove away. He didn't look back. Neither did she.

•

A couple days after the luncheon, Mary's cell phone rang. It was Stet.

"Hey, you gave me *your* number...I don't remember giving you *my* number." Mary said.

"Nope, you didn't. But you called me a couple days ago. What's the matter with you, lady? Forgotten about caller ID? I have a full day tomorrow, but how about you coming back over here for dinner tomorrow night?" answered Stet.

Mary hesitated. *Where is this going? Where could it go? Where do I want it to go?*

"Well...okay...sure. Why not? What are you having? Can I bring some wine, or something?"

"Nah. You don't have to bring anything but a hardy appetite. May I assume that you like steak?"

"Absolutely!" she responded.

"Good. Now, don'tcha go 'spectin' no Moon Pies for dee-ssert, neither, ya heah?" he said in his best redneck accent. "See ya at 6."

Mary was absolutely giddy. *What the hell, girl*, she thought. *What the hell.*

The next evening at 6:05 Luger jumped off the front porch and came running out, barking loudly, announcing Mary's arrival. Stet opened his front door, stepped out onto the porch and called the dog back into the house. He was wearing dark khaki shorts that stopped above his knees, a navy blue sport shirt opened by a few buttons and he was barefoot. She liked that look. A lot. Actually, it excited her. A lot. Hot damn, Mary thought, you look hunkalicious. She, too, was wearing khaki shorts, a magenta halter-top and sandals. She had chosen colors to accentuate her tan. She brought him a bottle of Chardonnay and a bottle of Montoya Cabernet…just in case.

"Hey, thanks, Mary. I told you not to bring anything. Are you trying to ply this poor young guy with liquor?" he laughed.

Jazz piano music was playing quietly on the stereo in the background. The late, great Marian McPartland. Mary wasn't sure where this night might lead, but the sight of his bare legs got her mind, and libido, racing. His beautiful…masculine…muscled bare legs.

"You want some of your wine now?" he asked. "I'm already drinking something else."

"Yeah…yes, please. A glass of wine would be great. The Cabernet. They're both chilled, by the way."

Stet headed into the kitchen for a corkscrew and a glass. Mary settled into the big leather sofa in the living room. On the coffee table in front of her were more sketchbooks. She opened the one on top of the short pile and thumbed through a few pages. It piqued her curiosity.

"What are these?" she asked as he padded back into the living room with a filled glass of wine in one hand and a crystal decanter in the other. "These look like caricatures."

"Well, then. I guess that's what they are," he chuckled. He picked up a small glass that had been on the coffee table and poured some liquid from the decanter.

"Wait a minute. I think I know these people," she said, almost laughing. "Isn't that Brenda from The Tack Shack? And those are a couple of the girls who work there, right? Wow, these are fun. Oh my god, these are so freakin' funny. Don't tell me that you do these too?" she was laughing and clapping her hands like a schoolgirl.

"Oh, just one of my many, many talents, little lady." Stet replied. "But I have to be really careful about these funny, crazy things. Really careful."

"Why?"

"Well, not everybody can handle caricatures. Some folks don't realize they are *not* portraits. They're exaggerations that the artist brings out in comic form. Not wanting to brag or anything, but it really isn't so easy doing good caricatures. I know, guys do it at amusement parks and places like that but…well, really good caricatures take a really good artist. My absolute favorite caricaturist was famous for doing theater and movie stars. Al Hirschfeld. I have a book of his work somewhere around here. His work was my inspiration. Guys, as a rule, love 'em. They'll laugh their asses off at their own caricature. Women…well, that's another matter. Women are far more sensitive and, quite often, can't take them. If they have any kind of self-esteem issues, they might go ballistic. Sometimes they downright hate them. Sometimes they go bat-shit crazy. Trust me, I've seen it."

Mary flipped another couple of pages. "Holy shit!" she exclaimed. "That's me, isn't it?"

Stet smiled and sipped his drink.

"Oh my god, that is *so* funny. I love it! I'm not bothered by that all. What's wrong with some women, anyway?"

The simple black ink lines captured the essence of every person portrayed in the book. Mary recognized a few more faces, including a great caricature of Crazy Billy, missing ear and all, trimming a horse's hooves while bending over a walker.

"These are so fantastic. Do you do anything with them?"

"Another one of my dabblings," Stet answered, with a bit of a cocky air. "I have connections and get hired out for corporate meetings and trade shows office parties. Stuff like that. Corporate functions can pay big bucks, even these days. As a matter of fact, I already have a gig lined up for New Year's Eve. A private party. Wanna come with me?"

Mary stared at him for a second, then smiled. "You mean, like a date?"

"Well, like, yeah." he responded.

"That's, what, four months away? You think we'll still be friends by then?" she joked with him.

"I was hoping we would be more than friends by then, Mary," he said, turning a bit more serious. He looked her square in the eye.

"What have *you* been drinking?" Mary asked, trying to bring a little levity back into the conversation, although she knew what was happening.

He laughed. "This is Cabo Uno," he said, holding his glass aloft. "Some of the best tequila you can buy, in my humble opinion. You'll have to try some later. Now, as we were saying. Do you already have a date for New Year's Eve?"

"Ah…that would be a no. I usually don't plan that far into the future." Mary replied. "But if you were…*are* serious, sure. Why not?"

"Great!" said Stet. "I promise, Mary, I am *not* a predator. I don't usually pursue a girl like, frankly, I'm doing with you." After a beat, and staring at her, he jumped up and exclaimed, leaning into her and whispering, "I think my coals are hot!"

"Excuse me?" Mary said with a startled look on her face.

"The grill. The charcoal is ready for the steaks."

They lingered for a long time over dinner. The steaks were cooked to perfection. Stet had put together a hearts of palm salad with raspberry vinaigrette and baked potatoes with crispy, crunchy skins. Stet started to clear away the dinner plates and Mary could feel her heartbeat quicken. And who will be dessert, she asked herself.

Stet came up behind her chair, leaned over and gently kissed her bare shoulder. She closed her eyes and she knew that she was getting aroused.

"Wait…wait, wait, wait. Do you think…," and she hesitated.

"Yes, I think. On occasion." Stet answered, with a soft, deep voice. "And sometimes I act."

Mary continued. "Don't you think we might be moving a little too quickly here?"

"Then stop me." His voice was even deeper than it had been a moment before.

Sometimes libido overrides logic.

She got up and turned to face him. He was holding her shoulders and slowly drew her nearer to him. Their lips were close. He stroked her cheek with one hand as he pulled her even closer with his other arm.

"Damn, you smell good," he said with a warm smile.

"Funny," she responded, "I was about to say the same thing to you."

Their lips finally met. They were extremely close and Mary was certain that he, too, was aroused. She started to unbutton his shirt and put a hand on his warm, smooth chest. He untied her halter-top and let it fall to the floor. She pulled his shirt back and off his body and it, too, fell to the floor. He smiled, took hold of her hand and led her to his bedroom. They stood there silently and kissed as Mary unbuckled Stet's belt, unzipped his shorts and let them drop to the floor. He kicked them aside. He was wearing boxer briefs and Mary could tell, even in this low light, that he had a massive erection. Her shorts and panties were off in a heartbeat and, as she lay back onto the bed, he slid off his briefs and tossed them across the room. He lay on top of her, suspending his weight with his arms, and smiled. She was wet. He was hard. She felt his cock on her belly as it probed for her opening. He slowly, ever so gently slid into her. Jesus Christ, she thought. I have never felt like this before. He didn't thrust. His motion was slow and steady. He went deeper. She caressed his chest, letting her finger tips just brush his right nipple. Earlier in the evening he had told her about his tick incident and they had laughed about it. His cock grew even more rigid and straighter than when it had first entered her. Damn, he was right, she thought again. He didn't want his first experience with Mary to end too quickly. He withdrew and slowly kissed his way down her body. He buried his face between her legs and she let out a little moan of pleasure. Intense pleasure. He loved her taste…her aroma. His tongue was talented and she arched her back, hoping he would explore further, deeper. But she, too, didn't want to come too quickly.

"Come up here," she whispered. "Lie back."

He stretched out, flat on his back, his head resting on a pillow. Mary sat up and took in his entire body with her eyes. God, she thought, this man is perfection. She then started gently caressing his body, from chest to feet, with her hands. Over his chest, down passed his waist…down each strong, beautiful leg. She took his erection in her hands and leaned forward…and down. The tip of her tongue touched the head of his cock. She tasted the sweet, salty flavor of his pre-ejaculate. It was his turn to moan. She opened her mouth and let his cock slide in, running her tongue around it as it entered. He was incredibly large. She could feel his cock throb as she slowly moved forward and backward, working the shaft.

"Jesus Christ," he moaned louder. "Mary…Mary…Mary…you are fucking awesome!"

Her face was deep in his pubic hair. She could feel his balls against her chin. He pushed her away gently, spun her around, laying her back on the bed and thrust his cock into her again. She leaned forwards and upwards, licking his right nipple. She then squeezed his nipple between two fingers. Stet let out a scream of ecstasy. Mary had not been prepared for the explosion of pleasure that followed. Stet's cock felt like a hot steel rod. His ejaculation was nothing like Mary had ever experienced. His multiple spasms of pleasure brought her the most intense orgasm simultaneously. She thought that he would never stop coming. She almost cried because she felt so great. His orgasm finally ended and he fell back onto the bed, exhausted and sweating. Mary, too, lay back and finally took a breath. She could feel his warm semen flowing from her body and onto the sheets. His cock was wet, still throbbing, with a few remaining drops of semen oozing onto his belly.

They turned to look into each other's face. They both smiled.

"Well. Well, well, well. I have just been properly seduced," whispered Mary, wrapping the sheets up around her.

"Well. Mary…Mary…Mary," Stet said gently, as he lay there, naked, with his hands clasped together behind his head, cradling it on the pillow. "Mary, Mary, Mary…"

•

"Mary. Mary?...uh, MARY!" said Mary Pat loudly. "You seemed to be off in La-La-Land somewhere. You Okay?"

The dust from Stet's truck zipping up the driveway had barely drifted away.

Jessie came back from letting her horse out into the pasture again. "Did anyone else seem to notice that it got a bit hotter when Stet was here? Damn, he looks like he just stepped out of an L.L. Bean catalog…an X-rated one, though. He's a real cutie-patootie." Then she giggled. "Marty has a six-pack too, but his has Budweiser printed all over it."

"Okay, so what's been going on?" Mary Pat looked Mary squarely in the eye. "Is this why you've been sort of scarce lately? That big hunk occupying your time?"

"I *have* been seeing a fair amount of him lately, yes," was the coy response.

"Yeah?" Jessie added her say in the matter. "Judging by that stupid-ass look on your face, I'd guess that you've seen just about every inch of him."

Mary scrunched up her face and shook her head. "You ladies are too much."

Mary told her friends how she and Stet met, about his beautiful home, his artwork and about his horses. "I had no idea," she said, "how many riding trails wind their way through the woods in Between. Actually, I really never gave that town a second thought before, except about its funny name. I guess the name means, what? The town is right between Atlanta and Athens? Is that it? I don't know." She shrugged. "Even though it's been hotter than hell, Stet and I rode for miles through some of those wooded trails. It was actually cool…well, less hot in those woods than out in the open. He is quite a good conversationalist. We've just enjoyed each other's company, that's all."

She purposely left out the parts about the sex in the woods…the sex in his bedroom…the living room…in the shower. Mary had forgotten how young guys' libidos are insatiable. She had not had sex three or four times a day since…well, since never.

"Wait until Mary Anne hears about your escapades!" gasped Mary Pat with glee.

"What escapades? We've just gone riding and talking…and an occasional meal, that's all. Innocent as can be."

"Oh, bullshit, Mary! Nobody like you is going to hang around *that* guy for hours just for the chat. Get real. But…your business is your business. You just better not show up here pregnant one day!"

Mary laughed loudly. "Oh, for the love of Pete! Ladies, I've been on the pill for years…just on the off-chance that I'll get lucky sometime. And that hasn't happened for some time."

"Uh-huh. Until now, you mean," sighed Mary Pat. "Well, someday… just maybe someday…soon, you might like to fill little ol' me in on some juicy details. He looks good enough to eat." And she gave Mary a sly look, a wink and a grin. "Wow, this is a first for me."

"What do you mean?" asked Mary with a puzzled look.

"I've never known a cougar before," and she and Jessie laughed.

"Oh, go shit in your hat! I'm *not* a cougar…hate that term anyway."

Stet's talents had fascinated Mary. She admired the paintings that hung in his living room. Several of them were of racehorses, some wearing their riding silks. On one of the visits to his place, he had shown her his studio. It was a large, open expanse at the back of his house, with a very large skylight. A painting was currently "under construction" as he called it, on an easel in the center of the room. It was of a young blonde girl standing beside a gorgeous Arabian mare. A snapshot of the girl and a separate one of the horse were clipped to the side of the canvas. Both photos looked old. Obviously Stet was combining the images into one.

"I thought you said that your profession was farrier," she looked at Stet as she gestured around the room at all the works.

"Let's just say that as far as the IRS is concerned, that *is* my profession," was his response as he winked and arched an eyebrow.

SEPTEMBER

Welcome Thunder

"If there were no thunder, men would have little fear of lightning."

Jules Verne

The leaves had begun to change color earlier than normal. Perhaps it had been the lingering drought that robbed them of their moisture and nutrients. Dusty browns, faded yellows and an occasional cluster of orange dotted the landscape. The remaining dull green leaves looked tired and listless. The air had the aroma of autumn.

As she approached the stable, Mary Anne noticed that, for the first time in weeks, storm clouds appeared to be forming on the distant horizon. The Crepe Myrtles lining the driveway to the stable, still clinging to a smattering of their brilliant fuchsia blooms, were swaying in the gentle breeze. There was one car, parked at an odd angle, near the tack room. Mary Anne recognized it as Julia's car but was certain Julia had mentioned that she was going to be in California for the week on business. She parked, stepped out of her car and heard the tack room door slam shut.

"Oh, crap," she muttered to herself, as she saw Rance stumble in her direction. He was holding something in his hand, but it was hidden by the direction in which he moved. When he saw who had just arrived, he got a huge grin on his face. But Mary Anne did not like the look of that particular smile.

"Well, well, well…little Miss Priss, who's just *so* fuckin' friendly with the gendarmes," he said.

Damn, she thought, not only is he here, but he's drunk as well. She could smell the alcohol from where she stood, and Rance was having difficulty even standing. He swayed a bit, advanced straight towards her, slurring his words.

"What fate that you, you bitch, would be here today. Here. Now." And he pulled his hand from behind him.

"Sweet Mother of God!" Mary Anne exclaimed almost to herself, as she took half a step backwards. He was holding a gun. It was a little black pistol. She knew nothing about guns but she *did* know that it spells danger if a gun and the person holding it are both loaded.

He raised the gun and pointed it directly towards her face. A cloud hid the sun and the shadow advanced across the pasture. The wind was beginning to pick up and the tall grasses around the stable began to sway. A flock of crows suddenly flew up from the woods and started circling the treetops; their angry caws following their swoops up, down and around overhead.

"Don't you back away from me, you goddamn whore. Don't you *dare* back away."

"Where's Julia?" asked Mary Anne, trying to ease his temper and tension a bit. Wrong question.

"Ha! She's another goddamn whore. You're all sluts. I hate you all. She's out there in Cali-fuckin'-fornia servicing her goddamn boss!" He made air quotes when he said 'servicing', nearly dropping his gun, but he recovered quickly.

Suddenly he turned the gun away from Mary Anne and put the barrel into his mouth.

"NO!" she screamed, putting her hands to her ears in absolute fear and horror.

She was certain that he had pulled the trigger but nothing happened. The gun slowly withdrew from his mouth, but then it went right back being pointed directly at her. He started walking closer but she was frozen in disbelief that this was happening and she couldn't move. The gun was getting closer to her face; his finger was on the trigger.

"Please, sweet baby Jesus, do not let this horrid little man be the last living creature I see." She looked around and saw the horses lazily grazing in the pasture. She saw the grasses blowing in the wind. She saw Rance, even closer, with a vile grin on his face. This was it.

She closed her eyes and squeezed them tightly shut, waiting. She heard a loud crack, a dull thud and then a low moan. But she had felt nothing. Slowly, cautiously, she opened one eye. Then the other. Nothing. She looked down. Then she looked straight up.

The dead limb that Remy had promised to cut down had finally broken loose. Rance lay on the ground, the limb beside him, with a noticeable gash on his forehead. The pistol was still in his hand but with a relaxed grip. Mary Anne bent over to retrieve it and noticed what appeared to be a drop of liquid at the end of the barrel.

"What the…?"

She picked up the pistol and sniffed the barrel.

"Ha! You little twerp!" she squealed in delight. "You little weasely jackass!"

It was a water pistol. And it had been filled with tequila. Cheap tequila, of course. "So," she thought, "you *did* pull the trigger when you stuck the barrel in your mouth. What a loser!"

Mary Anne dragged the limb into the woods, out of sight. She would later convince Rance that he had passed out and hit his head on the side of the deck as he fell. She didn't want Remy and Zara to be the recipient of a lawsuit that Rance certainly would have issued. The little weasel started to awaken as the first few drops of welcome rain began to fall.

The playwright Chekhov once said, "If in the first act you have hung a pistol on the wall, then in the following one it should be fired. Otherwise don't put it there." That probably applies to dead tree limbs as well.

What little rain had fallen earlier in the day went unnoticed and had dried up by the time Marty and Jessie arrived at the stable to give their horses a little exercise and an early feeding. The horses were retrieved from the pasture and hooked up to lunge lines. They had just begun to do some groundwork with them in the riding ring when they heard a distant roll of thunder.

"Hey," Marty shouted to Jessie. "Now *there's* a sound we haven't heard in a long time."

They continued to work out the horses even as the sky darkened and the trees began to blow in the wind. The cooling breeze felt good after the energy-draining temperatures during the summer months. With the first flicker of lightening they decided to get the horses back to the safety of their stalls. The first drops of rain began to fall as they neared the riding ring gate. By the time the horses had been put up, they were dripping wet. Marty had hoped they could get the horses to their stalls before the approaching deluge. They weren't quite fast enough. After months of hot, dry, dusty days the sky opened up. The sound of the rain on the tin roof and in the surrounding woods was refreshing. The horses stuck their heads out of their stall doors and seemed to be enjoying its coolness. Even though there was an overhang protecting the stalls from getting rained in, the wind blew mists of wetness onto the horses' faces and they nickered. Marty and Jessica returned to the tack room to get the horses' dinners.

"Mmmm…I love the smell of rain, don't you?" Marty asked Jessie. She agreed. "I'll run down and dump their feed. No need for you to get wet too. Well, any wetter than you are now anyway. Just stay here and roll up the lunge lines…I'll take care of the babies."

He filled the feed buckets with grain and made a mad dash from the tack room, hanging close to the stalls as he went, towards their horses' stalls. Their two stalls were the furthest from the tack room, at the far end of the stable. A stand of tall trees next to the far wall swayed in the wind. The horses saw their dinner approaching and let out loud whinnies. Marty laughed.

Marty entered Gemmy's stall first and dumped the feed into the attached bucket on the wall. Closing the door, he then turned and went into Dan's stall to dump his feed. Even in the short time that the rain had been falling, the horse was soaked. As Marty leaned against the stall door, watching the rain, Dan stomped the ground firmly with one of his hind legs. Marty had seen a huge drop of water roll off the horse's back and down his leg. The horse, perhaps thinking that it was a fly, responded with a kick.

"Nothing there, big boy," Marty sighed. "You're just kicking at raindrops. Nothing there at all." Marty wondered how many times throughout his life *he* had merely kicked at raindrops.

Suddenly, there was a bright flash as lightning struck a nearby tree, followed immediately by the loudest crack of thunder that Marty had ever heard. There was a brief, pungent scent of ozone in the air. Strangely, the horses barely reacted as they continued eating. But the noise seemed to go right through Marty's head. He was knocked against the stall wall by the intensity of it and he was momentarily disoriented. Everything was spinning.

"Jesus H. Christ!" he exclaimed, trying to regain his bearings. His head buzzed and he soon realized that everything he heard sounded like his head was inside a wastebasket. His ears rang and sounds echoed.

"Holy shit. What the hell just happened there?" he questioned aloud as he put his fingers into his ears, shaking them, trying unsuccessfully to clear his hearing and to stop the ringing sensation.

"Marty!" Jessie called out as she ran from the tack room. She had seen the flash and heard the deafening crack of thunder. "Are you okay?"

Her voice was like a distant echo. The rain, pelting the tin roof, sounded like thousands of marbles hitting the metal. There was another distant rumble of thunder.

The rumbling thunder awakened Mary and Stet. They were lying, naked, in each other's arms, in his bedroom. An afternoon trail ride through the woods of Between, followed by a few glasses of wine had led to a rambunctious, sweaty romp between the sheets. Stet was always very inventive and energetic when it came to sexual activity. Each session brought new, unexpected pleasures to Mary.

"Hey, gorgeous," Stet said softly, as he looked into Mary's slowly opening eyes.

"Hey, gorgeous, yourself," she smiled back. "You know, Stet, there just might come a time when I can't keep up with you!"

"Aw, never...*never*!" he laughed. "You give me a run for my money, lady. You're awesome. You suit me to a T...*three* T's, for that matter."

"Three T's? And they would be...?" she asked quizzically.

"Trim, toned and tight." And he smiled.

They kissed and she felt...*saw* that he was getting aroused again.

Suddenly a bright flash of lightning and a crack of thunder broke the spell.

"Yikes!" Stet exclaimed as he hopped out of bed. "If *this* is what we're in for, I'd better get George and Gracie into their stalls."

Sudden storms in the south, especially after long periods of heat and humidity, can be violent. Tornado warnings are common. Damaging winds, along with pelting rain and hail go hand-in-hand.

Without bothering with his briefs, he pulled on his jeans, grabbed a t-shirt and yanked on his boots.

"Going commando, eh?" snickered Mary, as she watched his swift actions.

"Hehehehe...I expect to be right back and finish what I had in mind thirty seconds ago. And I don't want to waste any time doing it, either!" And he winked at Mary as she pulled the sheets up around her shoulders.

"Don't you want me to help you with the horses?" she asked as she started to get out of bed.

"Nope. Stay right where you are, gorgeous. It won't take me two minutes to get 'em in. They'll be ready to eat anyway, so I'll dump their feed, lock their stall doors and be half naked again by the time I get back into the house."

Mary liked that thought and pictured him running from the barn, naked except for his boots.

George and Gracie were half asleep in the paddock when the first bolt of lightning nearby startled them awake. Neither one was a nervous horse. Storms didn't really bother them. Stet just didn't like the idea of them being out in the open when lightning was so prevalent. Cattle often take shelter from rain under trees, then, if that tree is struck, the cattle are killed. Stet simply didn't want to take any chances. Although the rain would be a cooling, welcome relief from the enduring summer heat, Stet would be far more comfortable if his horses were under cover. George was really beginning to show his age and Stet was very protective of his equine friend.

The horses saw Stet run from the house and nickered softly, expecting, perhaps, an early supper. When they saw him bring their feed buckets from the tack room, they both pricked up their ears and followed his moves. Luger came running out to the stable with Stet, barking loudly and nipping at the horses' hooves. They, in turn, responded by bucking and kicking out at the frisky dog.

"Who's ready for supper?" Stet called out. This was his daily ritual. The horses understood it and responded accordingly by letting out loud whinnies. "Thanks, guys. I love it when you talk to me."

The rain began slowly at first, as he ran to the stalls. The horses followed him into their respective havens and waited patiently as Stet dumped, first George's feed, then going to Gracie's stall and dumping her feed.

"Be good horses. I love you. Good horses." He shut and latched each stall door.

Just as he left the paddock area and latched the gate, the rains came with force. He was drenched by the time he got back to the house.

"Stay out here on the porch, Luger. Shake off and get dry. Good boy."

He pulled his boots off and tossed them onto the floor of his back entryway. He yanked off his wet jeans and dropped them in a heap on the floor. He kept on his soaking t-shirt and walked back into the bedroom.

"Damn!" exclaimed Mary, her eyes widening when she saw him. "Adonis has returned! And he's wet...ooh, and he's getting horny."

He stood in the doorway to the bedroom. His wet t-shirt clinging to his chest, his large right nipple very evident. His erection grew larger as he walked towards the bed. Mary threw back the sheet; he pulled off his shirt, bent over and planted a kiss firmly on her lips as he slowly slid into her for the third time that afternoon.

A bolt of lightning flashed, followed by a large clap of thunder, but they paid no attention to it.

Zara was awakened from her afternoon nap by a loud clap of thunder. She bolted upright in her bed. At first, she thought she had been dreaming. But when she opened her eyes and looked out the window at the darkened sky she realized that the weather, finally, had changed. She glanced at the clock on her night table and saw that it was passed time to head to the stable. Remy was probably already there, she surmised, and if it's stormy, he would definitely need help with the horse. The incident with the mysterious notes from Kristine stuck in her memory and she had just been dreaming about another confrontation. The two of them had had a very brief one-on-one conversation prior to her daughter's departure for her vacation. It had gone fairly well, but there were so many issues yet to be addressed. Kristine *had* apologized for the "overly dramatic", her words, method of reproach. Zara and Remy were still very upset about the whole thing. It will pass…we *will* get through this, Zara had thought. She had tried calling several times since Kristine returned from Europe, but the calls always went directly to voice mail.

Zara's cell phone on the nightstand rang…the bugler calling the horses to the starting gate…but she was in the bathroom and didn't hear it. Kristine was calling in hopes of coming to see them both that evening. Back from Europe and into the new school year, her schedule had been beyond hectic. She had felt terrible about not returning her mother's many calls. She wanted to talk about the help that she desperately needed. Basically, she just wanted to talk.

Coming out of the bathroom, Zara grabbed her cell phone, without checking to see any missed calls, hurried through the kitchen, picked up her car keys and a can of soda to drink on the way. The wind was blowing and the trees were swaying wildly as she backed out onto the road and headed to the stable. The car radio wasn't loud enough to drown out the crashes of thunder that would follow one bolt of lightning after another.

"Damn!" she muttered out loud. "I know we need rain, but do we really need to get it all at once?"

She lifted the can of soda out of its holder just as a bolt of lightning struck nearby. She jumped because of the sudden flash and the can slipped from her grasp.

"Shit," she muttered, as she leaned over to retrieve the now-emptying can from the floor, one hand on the steering wheel. She had been admonished by Remy countless times for never using her seat belt. She then noticed a "Missed Call" message on her cell phone screen.

She failed to see that a young deer had bolted from the woods along the road and was running towards the street. Zara was only a few minutes away from the stable. She looked back up just in time to see the deer run directly into the path of a fast-approaching oncoming little red sports car.

"Oh, no!" she cried out.

The young woman driving the sports car swerved to avoid hitting the deer, but headed her car directly towards Zara. Everything was happening so quickly, yet felt as though everything was in slow motion. The young woman driving the sports car over-compensated and tried to correct her car by steering in the opposite direction. Zara, also, turned her car to avoid a collision but both cars ended up heading straight towards one another.

The very last word that Zara would ever utter was "Shit!"

The sound of metal crashing headlong into metal lasted a mere second. The impact, then sudden stop, tossed Zara forward, then abruptly backwards, snapping her neck instantly. The deathly silence that followed was broken by one sound: The Assembly of Buglers.

The young woman driving the little red sports car lay in a coma for two weeks, finally succumbing to massive internal injuries.

OCTOBER

Beggars On Horseback

"Destiny has two ways of crushing us – by refusing our wishes or by fulfilling them."

Henri Frederic Amiel

Gary Smart poured himself a third cup of coffee. He loved the aroma of coffee and even inhaled deeply as he walked down the supermarket aisle where it was sold. It was also his favorite flavor of ice cream. He walked back into the bedroom and sat down on the side of the bed. His sleeping wife, Linda, stirred, rolled over towards him and slowly began to awaken.

"Mmm, something smells good," she said groggily as she opened one eye then the other.

"It must be my manly scent," Gary responded playfully. "My new after-shave…eau de caffeine."

He leaned over and gave her an affectionate kiss. Then he patted her pregnant belly.

"Good morning, baby," he whispered as he leaned close.

It had been a little over two weeks since Zara's tragic death but the boarders were still reeling from the shock and disbelief. Although, as a rule, Remy eschewed such folderol, he had a memorial service for her at the church she attended often and him rarely. The church was overflowing and the floral arrangements overwhelming. Every boarder was in attendance and even Rance was there, uncharacteristically subdued, albeit in his usual black attire...this time a suit. Zara had been cremated and her cremains were placed in a beautiful silver urn adorned with a horse's head on the cap. The service was long on testimonials from friends, family and a few boarders. Kristine and Taylor stood side by side, expressing the love for their mother, each with such guilt in their hearts they ached. Tears flowed. Remy joined them at the front of the congregation. He started to speak but could not. Not one boarder expected to see such emotion from this man. His daughters hugged and kissed him. He thanked everyone for coming and wished them all a safe drive home.

The people filed out, shaking hands with the grief-stricken trio, hugging the girls and offering their heart-felt condolences. Some lingered in the parking lot for a while, chatting with each other before eventually heading home. Gary and Marty Howce, coworkers, chatted about work and about Gary's approaching fatherhood.

His coworkers would not recognize *this* Gary Smart. He was the best salesman among the eight others at the Compton Paperboard Packaging Company's southern office...and the youngest. He was a sly, crafty wheeler-dealer who could seduce customers away, with ease, from rival competitors. He knew all the angles, conducting business on the golf course as well as in the office; in a bar room as well as in a board room. A lot of work to sell empty boxes, one of his friends had teased him. Blond, blue-eyed and very handsome, he knew the name of every secretary and receptionist of his clients and of his prospects. He played the "charm card" very well. He knew his product and was proud of the service his company offered. True, he came across to some as arrogant, egotistical and manipulative, but he continually earned top sales bonuses for his territory. He was watched, with envy, by a few of the older salesmen who couldn't hold a candle to his abilities. Terrance Vance, the oldest salesman who, ironically, had used similar tactics decades earlier, vacillated between calling him "Gary Smarmy" or "Gary Smartass." Nevertheless, Gary was admired and popular at work.

Away from the business environment, Gary was pleasant and fun to be with. He and Linda had recently celebrated their tenth anniversary, having married just after each one turned twenty-two. They both loved children and were eager to become parents. They had been trying to enter parenthood for the past five years.

At first, they had attributed their lack of success on anxiety...or timing...a multitude of things. It didn't help the situation that both of their respective mothers were beginning to put the pressure on to become grandmothers.

"I'm not getting any younger, you know," said Libby, Gary's mother. "And neither are you. You don't want to be hobbling around with a walker when your kid's in high school"

"Well, thanks for your sweet sentiments, Mom," Gary answered sarcastically. "We'll have kids when we're damn good and ready, that's all." He never let on that they had been trying for years.

Gary remembered, with a tug at his heart, the night he and Linda helped celebrate his mother's birthday last year. His dad never questioned him about kids, figuring it wasn't really any of his business anyway. Gary appreciated that fact. One of his mother's loud-mouthed friends dominated the conversation that night. There were several other friends present, but they all had known Lucy Reilly for years and just let her yack away endlessly...Loose-Lips Lucy, they called her. She was genuinely funny and kept everyone laughing. Until she dropped the bomb.

"They're making a grandmother outta me!" she practically squealed as she helped cut the birthday cake.

Lucy's son, Freddie, had been Gary's classmate all through their grammar and high school years. Freddie and his wife, Glorianna, had been married for just over a year. Good Catholics. Gary and Freddie had drifted apart after high school and didn't keep in touch. Freddie never had the drive and ambition that Gary had.

"You mean...?" Libby started to ask.

"Yep, little Glory-girl ain't gonna be little for long!" Lucy let out a big, deep laugh. "They just found out this afternoon. Great, eh?"

Libby turned and looked at Gary. Gary turned and looked at Linda. Lucy turned and looked at Gary.

"Freddie has the recipe if you want it!" Lucy teased Gary, with another laugh and a slap on his back.

Gary tried to make his smile look genuine. "Thanks. That's okay...I have the recipe too. Sometimes it takes just a little practice in the kitchen, doesn't it, dear heart?" as he winked at Linda, who responded with a wan smile. "Congratulations, Mrs. R. I'm sure you're thrilled. Please give my best regards to Freddie and Glory."

No one there at the party had a clue about the anxiety, frustration, yearning, fertility testing and false alarms that Linda and Gary had experienced throughout the years. When they got back home later that evening, Linda collapsed into Gary's arms and sobbed.

"I'm sorry, Gary. I just wish *so* badly that we could have kids."

"Hey, hey, hey," he said in his most comforting tone, embracing her tenderly. "We will. It will happen when everything is right. I wish it would happen too. I wish we had a houseful right now! I wish I had a million bucks...I wish Zara hadn't been killed. I remember what someone told me once, when I was wishing to land a big new account. If wishes were horses, beggars would ride."

But that had all changed nearly nine months ago. Linda had her suspicions that something was happening but she didn't want to jinx it by saying anything to Gary. She waited a few more weeks before buying a pregnancy test. Then she made a doctor's appointment.

She heard Gary's car pull into the driveway and waited for him by the door. She had put on her party-best outfit and splashed on Gary's favorite perfume. He registered surprise to see her standing there when he stepped inside.

"Whoa, you scared me!" he exclaimed. "What's up? You look fabulous... and ready to go out. Oh, crap. Did we have plans that I forgot about?"

Linda had been holding something behind her back. She withdrew the pregnancy test and held it up.

"Hello, Daddy," she said softly.

They embraced. They kissed. They cried for joy. Then they went out to dinner to celebrate.

After the pregnancy was confirmed, neither one wanted the baby's gender to be revealed. They wanted to be surprised. Gary envisioned many scenarios: his son on a soccer field; his daughter in ballet recitals; his daughter on a soccer field; his son in ballet recitals. He didn't care. He remembered what *his* dad had told him when he was young. "I don't care what you are when you grow up, just don't be boring."

They waited until Linda had been pregnant for six weeks before breaking the news to their families, coworkers, friends and everyone at the stable. The response was overwhelming. Being an only child, Gary had been mercilessly spoiled while growing up. If she could have, his mother would have done cartwheels when she heard the news.

"Well, it's about damn time. My wish came true, then, didn't it?" she trumpeted into the phone when Gary called her. There was just the hint of a slur to her speech. "I was beginning to think you were sterile…or gay… or something like that."

"What the hell, Mom? Jesus. You scare me sometimes. What goes through that pickled head of yours?"

Libby loved her cocktails. She was almost never seen without a rye and soda in her hand. Should she be fighting some sort of depression, a vodka martini filled the bill even better. But she would never drink before 4 P.M. It was a rule she broke only if she might go out to lunch with some of her friends. Lunch and drinks would usually lead to a Bridge game afterwards, including more drinks until it was time for them all to go out for dinner. By the time they returned and continued their Bridge game, they were all too soused to remember who trumped whose ace on the previous round.

"Oh, hush, Gary. Don't be rude to your poor blue-haired old mother!"

Gary was certain he heard ice tinkling in a glass at the other end of the line. He glanced at his watch. 7:30 P.M.

"Where's Dad?"

"Bowling league tonight, sweetie. He'll be happy as a clam, whatever *that* means, to hear the news. I just may stay up to tell him about it when he gets home," she answered, followed by more ice tinkling.

"Nah, I'll just get him on his cell. I haven't had the chance to chat in a while. Perhaps I can catch him between frames."

"Well, perhaps you'd better wait for a while. It's a tournament tonight and he's hoping his team beats the crap outta the others. Hey, gotta go!"

chirped his happy mother. "I'm gonna call that old bitch Lucy and tell her the news. Tell her to tell Freddie to shove that recipe up his fat ass!" she laughed and dropped the phone. "Oops, sorry, sweet pea…hope I didn't bust your eardrum," she said swiftly into the receiver.

"I'm fine, Mom. And I have the feeling that you're fine too…*really* fine!" and he laughed too. "Pleasant dreams. Mom. And tell Lucy I said… oh, never mind. Just give her my warmest regards."

Gary sat up slowly in bed. The alarm hadn't gone off yet, but it was going to be a big, important day at the office and he couldn't sleep. He was on the agenda at the quarterly sales meeting. He had rehearsed his presentation until he knew every comma, period and dollar sign forwards, backwards and inside out. The divisional vice president was going to be in attendance and Gary hoped to knock his socks off with his ability. He felt a slight, dull throb in his right eye. He rubbed his eyes, thinking that he had been spending way too much time at the computer these days and eyestrain was the result. Still in his boxers and t-shirt, he ambled out to the kitchen to pour a cup of coffee from the automatic timed maker. A little sugar, a little cream, a little sip and he was awakening. He walked down the hallway to his home office and booted up the computer. Checking his e-mail, news and his portfolio was a daily ritual. He sat in front of the monitor and gently rubbed his right eye again. He glanced at the time. Linda wouldn't be awake for another thirty minutes.

He had twenty e-mails awaiting him, most of them stupid jokes that friends would send, urging him to forward them on to at least twenty other friends within twenty-four hours or his left nut would fall off. He deleted half of them without bothering to open them. He had to pee. He picked up his coffee mug and walked down the hall to the guest bathroom. He laid the mug on the marble counter, peed, scratched himself, flushed and turned to head back to the computer, picking up his coffee again on the way.

He casually glanced at his reflection in the wall-to-wall mirror as he walked out of the room. He stopped so abruptly that some coffee splashed out of his mug onto the floor. He looked into the mirror again, leaning so close to his reflection that his nose left an imprint on the glass.

"Holy crap! What the fuck?" he exclaimed loudly, almost in fear. Half of the white of his right eye was solid blood red.

He raced back to his computer, leaving his coffee mug behind, and immediately did a search for *blood in the eye*. He was relieved, in one respect, to learn that it was probably nothing serious and, in fact, can be fairly common: a broken blood vessel that could have been caused by something as simple as a sneeze. The only cure was time and patience. It should clear up, he read, in two to three weeks. *Two to three weeks?!*

"No, no…no! Shit, shit, shit! Fuck, fuck, fuck!" he bellowed, awakening and alarming Linda, who came running down the hall towards his frantic voice.

"Gary…where *are* you? What's wrong?" she called out. But then she saw him sitting at the computer, staring at the monitor and wringing his hands.

"What the hell is it?" she asked nervously. "Is the world coming to an end or what? Another terrorist attack? Another 9/11? What? You're freaking me out."

He slowly swiveled his chair around, facing her. She was looking at the monitor, expecting to see some horrible calamity unfolding on the screen. With both hands, he gestured towards his face.

"What?" she asked, somewhat confused. She squinted her eyes, then leaned forward and looked directly at him.

"Eew, yuck. What did you do to yourself?"

Gary took a deep breath, calmed himself for all of five seconds and then let loose again.

"Christ! I didn't do a fucking thing. This eye decided to pop a vessel on its own. Oh, God damn me! Fuck me! I have a major presentation to give in front of half the fucking world in less than three hours. *And*, I have to follow fucking Howce on top of everything. Damn. Damn. DAMN!"

"Oh, Gary," she tried to reassure him, but she was stifling a laugh at the same time. "It's not so bad. Maybe nobody will even notice it. Just keep your eyes sort of squinted."

He looked at her in disbelief.

"Nobody will notice? Are you *nuts*? I look like a fucking vampire. I'd spook the horses and frighten little children! Not notice?" he was almost crying.

"Honey," she continued sympathetically, "there's really nothing, at this point, that you can do. You'll just have to get on with it as though nothing happened. I mean, really...what else can you do?"

He was dejected. His big day...his big show and tell time...ruined by one half of one eye.

"Gary, really. It *isn't* the end of the world. Just explain to the group what happened and carry on. Hey, how would Marty handle this? He'd make a big deal out of it and put it to his advantage somehow. Why can't you do the same? Think about it."

Gary just stared at her.

"Or," she continued, almost choking back a laugh, "or, you could always get a patch and do the Pirate Pete thing." And *then* she giggled.

"Well just damn, Linda. That's not the least bit funny. I don't find a fucking thing about this fucking funny. Damn!"

"Well, Gary. You have two options. Get on with the day as though nothing has happened...or hop on the next plane to East Bumblefuck and run away."

He paused for a moment, then reached for the telephone. Picking up the receiver, he turned to her.

"Can you remember the number for Delta offhand?"

Being that Linda's due-date was less than two weeks away, she was working only half-days. She was a well-respected paralegal at an Atlanta law firm. All her coworkers got more nervous by the day, suggesting that she start her maternity leave immediately. But she wanted to remain as active and vital as possible, right up to the time of delivery. She worked until noon, and then spent the remainder of the afternoon at CedarView Stables, helping Remy. It had been nearly a month since Zara's tragic accident. Naturally, Remy had been in a state of shock for the worst first week. He then sank into a deeper depression and ill humor than anyone at the stable had ever seen. Linda and several of the other boarders had pitched in to feed and groom Zara's horses and help tend to the normal chores around the place. Surprisingly, Remy's and Zara's daughters had shown up to help too. Kristine had been particularly helpful.

Linda was talking with Mary and Mary Anne when her cell phone sounded with its new ring tone: a lullaby.

"Hey," Linda said when the two ladies responded with smiles when they heard it. "I'm prepared, aren't I?" and they all laughed.

She saw that it was Gary on the line. She looked at her two friends and shrugged. She had told everyone at the stable about the start to poor Gary's day and the mood he was in when he left for the office. They had laughed until tears rolled down their cheeks, especially the thought of "Pirate Pete" giving a major sales presentation.

"Uh-oh," she said with a wince before answering. "What will this bring? Do I dare answer it?"

"What the hell," said Mary. "Go for it, lady, and hope for the best. If he's loud, put it on speaker…we want to hear too!"

"Hey, honey," she answered cautiously. "How's your day going?"

"Sorry, babe, this was the first time I had a chance to call. Shoulda texted you but I wanted to hear that sweet voice of yours."

Linda held the phone out and stared at it. This is the same Gary who left the house in a tizzy hours ago?

"Hey, you were right…as always. Everybody laughed good-naturedly at my plight and didn't give a second thought about it. You know my vanity, and me though, right? I shouldn't have been such a jerk this morning. I'm so sorry, sweetie. And, again, you were right. Just before Marty finished his presentation, he turned to a blank page on his big flip chart. He drew a quick sketch of me as a pirate with a big honkin' parrot sitting on my shoulder. Loved it…brought down the house. Funny as shit!"

"Awesome, honey. Didn't know shit was funny, though. What about that V.P.? Was he there?"

"Oh, yeah. He was there. Thought my presentation was amazing. Came up to me at the break to congratulate me and talk for a little bit. He's a bit of a pompous asshole. But, ha! He had a huge booger hanging from his nose when we were talking, so I thought a bloody eye was better by far! And how are *you* doing, by the way?"

"Doing great. Just finishing up over at the stable. All the ladies say hi. We're worried about Remy. He was such an unhappy guy to begin with and this has made matters a zillion times worse. I can't even imagine what the poor guy is going through. OW!"

"What was that OW for?" Gary asked quickly.

Linda chuckled.

"Your little Smart-ass just kicked me. I tell ya, I love being pregnant but I'll feel *so* much better when this basketball or watermelon or whatever the hell it is is no longer inside me. Hey, gotta go finish helping the ladies get all the horses back out in the pasture. Have fun at your dinner tonight. Please don't drink too much and get home as soon as you can. Can't wait to see Pirate Pete get naked!" and she laughed and laughed.

"Hey, should you even be playing with little Petey in your delicate condition? I don't *think* so!" and he laughed so loudly that others around him turned to stare. "Oops, sorry, guys."

They said their goodbyes, sending kisses to each other. Linda turned to let the horses out of their stalls and Gary turned to head into the restaurant with the rest of his sales team. Both felt the day had turned out a hell of a lot better than it had started. Gary realized that the substance of his masterful presentation had trumped his vanity regarding his glaring right eye. Although questions had been asked, the rumors regarding the sale of Compton were not addressed. Gary stopped off in the men's room before heading into the private function hall with the rest of his buddies. He peed, scratched himself and washed his hands. He leaned in very close to the mirror and looked at his eye.

"Aaaaargghh!" growled Pirate Pete, and then he headed for his first beer of the evening.

Three weeks later, Alexander Garrison Smart was born. Everybody was fine and healthy. Gary didn't say anything to Linda, but he had secretly wished for a boy.

He called his mother. "Good morning, Mom," he said cheerily when she answered. We just wanted you to be the very first to know."

"Oh, tell me, tell me, tell me! I just *knew* it would be today! I felt it in my bones." Libby was so excited she was almost shaking.

"Well, Grandma, we have a little boy!"

"Thank God!" cried Libby. "I was so hoping and wishing that it would be a boy. Sorry. I would have loved a little girl too but, you know, I'm partial to boys. I'm thrilled! And you call him…what?"

After the fiasco at the 4th of July party at the stable, and Rance's rude remarks about names, Gary and Linda had decided to keep their name choices secret too, to avoid any uncalled-for and unwanted remarks.

"Alexander Garrison Smart."

"Wonnnnnderful name…so strong!" Her favorite adjective for just about anything is "wonderful" and she always drags it way out. Gary laughed.

"Alex Smart," she continued. "That will become Smart Aleck or Smart Ass before he's even in high school, you know that, don't you?"

"Always thinking, aren't you, Mom?"

They conversed for several more minutes, with Gary filling her in on all the details of the birth.

"Gotta go," he finally said. "I have to call Linda's folks now to tell them, too. Tell Dad for me. And tell him I love him. Love you, too, Mom!"

"Give everybody hugs and kisses for me," his mother responded. "We'll see you soon. I'm just so excited I may have to have a drink."

"It's eleven A.M., Mom."

"And your point is…?"

Gary just shook his head. "Love ya, Mom!" and he hung up.

He waited excitedly as the phone rang; ready to alert Linda's parents about the new arrival. Her mother answered.

"Good morning, Carla. We just wanted you to be the very first to know."

NOVEMBER

Head, Heart & Hooves

"We have no reason to believe that an animal can grasp the notion of extended life, let alone choose to trade current suffering for it."

Bernard Rollin

The crisp, clean air smelled of autumn. Brown, yellow and red fallen leaves crunched underfoot as Stet walked out to his little stable. Thanksgiving was still two weeks away but the chilly mornings seemed to have arrived earlier this year. He did not like the way old George had been acting. He was off his feed and the playful nature was no longer there. Gracie was being her bitchy self but she was being especially mean to George. She would back up towards him and look as though she was about to kick out. George would sway his head upwards but stand firm, letting out a sorrowful little nicker. Throughout the heat of the summer, no matter how strongly Stet had used the shedding blade, George had not lost his entire winter coat. Now that it was getting colder, his coat was blotchy and much coarser than when he was younger. He preferred to stand, for hours, in his favorite part of the little pasture behind the paddock. His head was drooped and his eyes barely open. He had not eaten in several days, even refusing carrots, his favorite treat.

"Mary," Stet said sadly into the phone. "Hey, would you be able to come out here for a while this afternoon…please?"

"What's the matter, big guy…feeling horny and have to phone out for some fun?" she giggled.

"Uh…no…sorry to say. It's something else, but I sure would like to have you around."

Mary sensed something about his voice that she didn't recognize. He was always chipper and playful. But now he sounded morose.

"Oh, I'm sorry I joked, Stet. What's the problem? Are you not feeling well?" she asked with genuine concern. This tone in his voice actually unsettled her.

"George is speaking to me. In his own way. He's letting me know."

Mary knew exactly what he meant and her heart sank. Horse owners know and comprehend the telepathic communication between their mounts and themselves.

"Oh, no. Is he down?"

"No. But he's…well, I think he's experiencing a lot of discomfort. I've called Doc Morrison, told him what George is doing. It's time, Mary. I just know it and I don't think I want to go through this alone. I'll be perfectly honest with you. I haven't cried over anything or anybody in years…but today might be different."

"Oh, honey, I am *so* sorry to hear this. Yes, of course I'll come out there. What time is the vet going to get there?"

"He has a couple other stops to make before he hits my place. He said a couple hours but, if it's the norm with him, it'll be like three or four hours before he gets here. I figure he'll get here around three-thirty or so. But you can come out here earlier to hold my hand, if you'd like. I can guarantee, Mary, this will be a Stet you haven't seen before." His voice almost cracked when he said that. Mary wanted to be there with him this very instant to hold him tightly.

The word euthanasia comes from two Greek terms. Eu, meaning "good" and thanatos, meaning "death". When administered properly, the methods for putting a horse "to sleep" are painless and peaceful…although not necessarily for the owner of the beloved animal. More often than not, the horse is sedated at first with a tranquilizer injected into the neck. This allows the owner, or handler, better control when the horse does go down. The horse may become wobbly at this point, as though he is about to fall into a normal, everyday sleep. The next injection is the barbiturate, usually Sodium Pentobarbitol, which will stop the horse's heart and breathing. At this point, the horse is actually unconscious, feeling nothing, and will drop to the ground.

Mary slowly drove down Stet's long driveway, parked in front of the house and stepped out of her truck. She looked towards the paddock and saw Gracie prancing around, tossing her head in the air as Arabians often do. George was standing off to the side with his head down. His lower lip was drooping, his ears were down and his eyes were half-closed. As she walked closer, she could tell that George's breathing was heavy, a possible sign of pain or discomfort. She also noticed that he appeared much thinner than when she last saw him, which was only a week or so before.

Stet heard the truck arrive and came out of the house, followed by Luger who ran up to Mary and started sniffing her jeans.

"Luger," Mary said, smiling. "Will you ever get used to my scent? Honestly, dog, that's rude."

Stet zipped up his Carhartt jacket and Mary put her arms around him, holding him tightly. She had never seen him this way. She just wanted to mother him and smother him with her love.

"I knew this was inevitable," he said, "but you just keep hoping, somehow, that they will live forever."

"He *will* live forever, Stet, in your heart. He will always be there, you know that."

"You know," he responded, "I've been with folks throughout the years, when I was with my dad, when they had to put their horses down. It was never easy for any of them. Especially if the horse had been a part of their lives for years. I'm sure you feel it with Thunder. I *know* you feel it with Thunder. There is such an incredible bond between folks and their horses. Quite often, when people put their horses down, they keep a clipping of the mane...or tail. God knows what for, but so many folks will do that. Maybe they hope that they'll be able to clone their beloved horse sometime in the future. Who knows?"

Stet paused for a moment and turned his head away from Mary. She gripped his hand and squeezed it tightly.

"You know, when the big, winning racehorses are put down they bury only their head, heart and hooves. The rest is cremated. Actually, there have been a couple big-name racehorses buried in their entirety. I've been to one of the gravesites. Secretariat. I felt his presence."

They opened the paddock gate and walked up to George. Mary gently stroked the horse's neck. He didn't move except for his labored breathing. Stet stoked George's muzzle and looked into his half-closed eyes; eyes which had been so bright and alert throughout the years. Stet was fascinated by the eyes of a horse…their depth, their beauty and their intelligence. George's eyes drooped even more, as if he simply wanted to go to sleep.

"I love you, big guy," he whispered into George's ear. "You've been the best friend ever. We've had some great adventures together, haven't we?"

The sound of a vehicle coming down the driveway broke the silence. Stet stiffened as he turned to watch the vet step out of his truck and walk towards the paddock. Luger went running towards the man, barking, and then sniffed at his pants as he walked. Doctor Morrison carried a big white metal case with him. Stet introduced Mary to the vet. He was younger than Mary had expected, probably in his mid-thirties, and slightly taller than Stet. He had sandy brown hair and deep blue eyes. When he spoke, Mary thought that he should be doing voice-overs. His voice was resonant yet very soothing. He had been one of Stet's friends who helped him build his house. Aside from his professional title, "Doc" had been his nickname since he was ten years old when he had announced to the world that he was going to be a veterinarian when he grew up. He hadn't gone by his name, Peyton, for decades.

"So," said the doctor, glancing at George, "how's our friend doing?"

"You tell me, Doc," answered Stet quietly.

The vet had a stethoscope around his neck. He looked at George, and walked around the horse. He listened to his heart and checked for any gut sounds. He looked into his eyes, and then into his mouth, looking at his gums. Instead of a healthy pink color, George's gums looked almost blue. A sure sign of distress. Blue gums were always a sign of poor oxygenation of the blood. Stet had checked that also, earlier, and had known what that indicated. The call to the vet was inevitable.

"I know you told me on the phone how he's been acting for the past few days. I think you're absolutely right about him being in discomfort now. Actually, I think this poor guy is in a lot of pain. He's not a happy horse, that's for sure." The vet paused for a moment, then put his hand on Stet's shoulder, squeezing it slightly. "Sorry to say, but this is a very telltale sign what I'm seeing here. I can also tell you, my friend, that he won't be getting any better. He'll go downhill in a hurry from this point on, I'm afraid. Yes. He's suffering."

"I want him to go out with dignity," Stet said, after taking a deep breath. "He's showing us the way to do it. We humans aren't allowed the same sort of dignity, are we?"

"Afraid not," answered the vet. "Afraid not."

Stet had decided that George would be buried in his favorite spot in the pasture behind the paddock. It was shady and cool there during the summer. George's halter and lead line were hanging over the paddock fence and Stet went to retrieve it.

"I'm going to put Gracie in her stall and close up the doors. I don't want her to watch what's going on," Stet said as he handed George's halter to Mary.

Gracie was wearing her halter already and Stet used the lead line from the fence to hook her up and direct her to the stable. She danced around, a bit confused as to why she was being lead in without a feed bucket around. Stet unhooked her and hurriedly closed the bottom, then the top part of the split-door. Gracie showed her displeasure at this by giving a swift, hard kick to the side of the stall. Stet walked back to George, hooked up the lead line and slowly led him to the little grazing area he had selected. At first, George resisted moving. Stet had to use a bit of force to get him to even take a step. He stumbled clumsily a couple times on his short, last walk. Mary and Doctor Morrison followed.

The vet opened his case.

"Have we said our goodbyes?" he asked.

Stet stroked George's cheek and then put his arms around the old horse's neck. He buried his face in the wooly coat and inhaled deeply, trying to hold on to the scent of his beloved friend.

"We've had some amazing times," he whispered very gently into the soft ear. "Will you be waiting for me, my friend, when it's my time? Please be there. Please." He leaned in and gave George a kiss on his muzzle. He held his lips there for a minute.

Stet unhooked the lead line and removed the halter. They would not be necessary with George. He stepped back and nodded to the vet.

In all her years around horses, Mary had never witnessed one being put down. She wasn't sure if she was ready now, but she was there for Stet.

The vet administered the tranquilizer, with no reaction from George, except that his head seemed to droop a bit more. Stet's heart was pounding. Wait, he wanted to yell. Wait. Maybe it's too soon. Maybe he'll get better. I've changed my mind. Stet nearly stopped breathing himself as the second, lethal needle entered the horse's neck and the liquid pumped into the vein. The reaction was swift. George's front legs went down, as simply as though he was lying down to rest. His hindquarters followed and he gently rolled over onto his side. Stet's chest heaved and Mary held him tightly as George surrendered to endless sleep.

The vet waited for a moment then bent down to the still horse's side. He held the stethoscope to the now not-breathing animal.

"He's gone," he said, matter-of-factly.

Stet thought that his chest would explode but he maintained his composure. He knelt down and gently, very gently ran his hand down the horse's side.

Stet had called a good friend who had a backhoe to bury George. He was due out later in the day, but he had called just before Mary arrived saying that it would have to be first thing in the morning. Some emergency at home would prevent him from being there today. George would lie in peace, in his favorite spot, for one more night before being buried. Stet explained that to the vet and asked what he should do about Gracie.

"Let her out. She'll probably go to him. She won't understand, of course, but it should be okay."

"Thanks, Doc. I appreciate all that you have done for George and me…and Gracie, too, the past couple of years. Hopefully I won't have to go through anything like this again for a very long time."

The vet nodded, smiled and patted Stet on the shoulder. Then the two men hugged. They had been good friends for years. Doctor Morrison never charged his clients for euthanizing their beloved pets. He had a great bedside manner and was very well liked. He picked up his gear, started to walk back to his truck and held out his hand to Mary.

"It was very nice meeting you, Mary. Sorry it had to be under these conditions but..." he turned to look back at Stet who was kneeling beside George. "Thanks for being here for your friend. Stet's a hell of a guy. He's a great friend to have. He's one of my favorite clients. Quote me to any of my *other* clients and I'll deny it, though!" and he smiled.

Mary smiled back at him and walked him to his truck.

"Thank *you*," she said sweetly. "I think Stet's a hell of a guy, too."

Stet had gotten up and headed back to the stable to set Gracie free. She bolted out of her stall and raced around the paddock, obviously looking for George. She sensed that something was different. When she located his lifeless body, she slowly approached him and sniffed his side.

"Sorry," said Stet, "I can't bear to watch this. Let's go back into the house.

Gracie stood by George for the entire night. She would shift her weight from side to side during her vigil, but she didn't leave his side. Every so often she would nudge him gently with her nose, as if to say, "Come on, old friend. Get up. Let's play."

Stet was awakened the next morning by Luger's loud barking. His friend with the backhoe had arrived and was ready for the grim task. The weather had turned chilly and gray. Mary had spent the night and was brewing coffee. Stet took a deep whiff as he pulled on his jeans, then his boots. He grabbed a bulky sweater out of his dresser and headed out towards the back door. "Thanks, Mary," he said as he passed through the kitchen.

"Thanks for what?" she asked.

"Thanks for being you," and he smiled. "Stay here Luger. You can't go out yet."

He greeted his friend, explained the ordeal and showed him George and the burial site. Gracie hadn't moved.

"I'm going to put her back in her stall. There's no way I want her to see what you're going to be doing. She's going to experience enough trauma over the next few days anyway," Stet said, and he knew, from past experience years ago, what would follow.

Stet got Gracie's feed bucket, filled it, hooked up her lead line and walked her back to her stall. After dumping her feed, he released her, stepped out of her stall and latched both of the doors, top and bottom.

"Here's your check," he said to his friend, as he pulled the payment from his pocket. They had agreed upon a price over the phone the day before. Stet wouldn't let his friend do this without payment for his time and equipment. "There's no way I'm going to watch this either. I can't stand this. Just do it. I don't mean to be rude, but just do it and go."

His friend understood and nodded.

Stet glanced down at George for the very last time. "Goodbye, old friend", he whispered, "I will always love you". He turned on his heels, waved to his friend over his shoulder and headed straight for the house… and a cup of coffee. He heard his friend's backhoe start up as he closed the back door.

Stet watched as his friend loaded the backhoe onto his trailer and drive away. He and Mary walked back out to the stable and opened Gracie's stall door. Again, she bolted out and started running, frantically looking for George. She ran to the spot where she had last seen him. He was gone. There was a mound of Georgia clay in his place. She started to call for him with the loudest, most piercing plaintive whinnies that Mary had ever heard. Then she started running from one end of the pasture area, through the paddock and back around again, calling all the time.

"This will go on for at least a day," Stet told Mary, "perhaps longer."

"Oh, my God, that's so sad," Mary responded. "I had no idea. The poor, sweet girl."

Mary had to leave for other obligations. She was going to help Remy with the sale of one of Zara's horses. Another painful experience lay ahead for her. She kissed Stet goodbye and sadly drove away.

All day, Gracie looked for and called for her missing friend. When Stet finally went to bed late that night, he lay back, his head sinking into the pillow, his eyes welled with tears as he listened to a lonely horse call… and call…and call.

DECEMBER

Happy Hollidays

"Departure of a year welcomes so many new memories"

Munia Khan

Like her namesake flower, Camellia Holliday bloomed in December. This was her favorite time of year. She and her husband, Max, took days to decorate the entire house for the season. They would always buy a tree that was much too tall to fit into their house and Max would have to cut off the top. When they put up the tree, it would appear as though it was going right through the ceiling into the floor above. They loved everything from the 1940s, from the way they dressed, to their home décor, to Max's vintage toy collection and, finally, to all the collectible Christmas tree ornaments. The centerpiece on a living room wall was a large oil painting of a young blonde lady standing beside a saddled racehorse. The Hollidays attended the symphony on a regular basis; attended every art gallery opening and were known in virtually every fine restaurant in Atlanta. Their collection of original artwork was the envy of all their friends. To say that their home was a showplace was an understatement. To receive an invitation to their annual New Year's Eve party was a sought-after accomplishment.

Camellia knew that she was a character and played it to the hilt. She was always "on". She stood 5'2" tall, spoke in a voice that sounded like Truman Capote on helium and weighed in at no less than two hundred pounds. But, as the cliché goes, she carried herself well. Her friends had absolutely no idea what color her hair was. For all they knew, she could be bald. She was never without a large, floppy hat of some sort. She was fifty-two years old. Max was sixty-two. They had decided before they wed not to have children. Camellia said that she was too selfish to be a mother and Max simply did not care for kids at all. And that was that. No debate. No further discussion. And no regrets.

Although she never developed an interest in her family's business, she came from horse-breeding country in California. Camellia Starr was the only daughter of Barratt Starr, founder of SouthWind Farms, one of the most prominent racehorse farms in the state. Several of his horses had been in contention at the Triple Crown events. As a young girl, Camellia had hosted the sons and daughters of diplomats, movie stars and royalty from around the globe as their fathers came to the stables to make their purchases. The role of hostess suited her very well and, as she grew older, her parties became more elaborate and more fun. She was invited to spend summers abroad at the homes and villas of her father's clients.

She had met Max at an art gallery opening during one of those summers. He was teaching a course in graphic design at an art school in Paris. Camellia bought a painting; Max stole her heart. She was remarkably grounded. Having money...and lots of it...did not make her spoiled or callous. She always did her own housework, never hiring help of any kind.

"I don't ever want to catch anybody poking through my panties," she would answer when questioned about not having a housekeeper or maid. "Besides, I can clean better and cook better than anyone I know or could hire. Why should I pay someone for mediocre work?"

She was also very outspoken. Demure, she wasn't.

Having started out in the advertising business on the west coast, she was now fashion coordinator for one of Atlanta's finest stores. She was on top of every trend although she deplored much of what the current designers were offering. She could never understand the concept of designer jeans. "Why would anyone pay $200 for a pair of cut-up, torn dungarees?" she would laugh. She, herself, never, ever wore slacks of any kind. Usually she wore dresses or suits that would have looked good on Joan Crawford. If Joan Crawford had been overweight. Her one vice was smoking. Despite warnings from friends, doctors and the surgeon general, both she and Max continually had a cigarette burning. They did honor the non-smoking rules at their respective work places and in the local restaurants, but thoroughly enjoyed their vacations to Europe where, it seemed, everybody was a smoker.

Max was slightly over six feet tall but slouched a bit. Camellia was always telling him to straighten up, which he did for a minute before resuming his slouch. He walked with a pronounced limp. He told everyone that it was due to a riding accident while trying to impress Camellia's father. In actuality, years ago he accidently shot off the three smallest toes on his right foot. He had always been fearful of home invasions and slept with a rifle under his bed. Late one night, after more than a few martinis, he was awakened by a strange sound. He feared the worst, leaped from his bed, grabbed the gun and stepped on the cat. The cat let out a screech; Max lost his footing and squeezed the trigger without thinking. The gun went off, as did his three toes. The carpet was ruined, Camellia was furious and the cat was missing for three days. Camellia had been the one making the noise that Max had heard. She had not gone to bed when Max had and was making herself another martini. In his stupor, the ice in the shaker had sounded like breaking glass. From that point on, all firearms were prohibited in their home. Max, still fearing home invasions, now slept with a Civil War saber under his bed. Camellia felt certain, considering that Max slept in the nude, any invasion that would bring a running naked senior citizen brandishing a rusty sword would render the attacker helpless with laughter and could be easily apprehended.

Aside from being tall, albeit with a slouch, Max always looked dapper. He still had a full head of blond, wavy hair and was proud of his handlebar moustache and goatee, which he stroked repeatedly. Businesses had long since gone to more casual attire, but Max always sported a necktie, vest and sports jacket or suit. At times, when the Hollidays hosted at home, he would wear an ascot, which always drew comments from their guests. He, like Camellia, was always "on". They both cultivated an air of sophistication without being pretentious. They were well read and well traveled. They could speak at length about current events, past history, art…or simply make stories up on the fly and make them appear authentic. In other words, one had to be on one's toes to keep up with the Hollidays.

Max and Camellia start planning their annual parties months in advance, always with a "surprise" guest who would entertain their friends in some way. Although they didn't associate with their neighbors very often, everyone from the neighborhood would be invited. The cars parked up and down both sides of the street on the night of the function, thought Max and Camellia, would be offensive if everyone wasn't included. Camellia knew that a couple of their neighbors were snobs, which she, herself, could not tolerate but she put up with them one night out of the year. Besides, everyone would be "polluted" early on and no one would care or notice.

The house glowed. Every room had Christmas décor of some sort, usually vintage artwork from the 1940s. The magnificent tree was another masterpiece this year. Guests would admire the ornaments for hours… and even more so after a few drinks. Their huge dining room was set for a lavish buffet. Camellia had made several trays of lasagna, one of her many signature dishes. The recipe, which she had refined over the years, rivaled that of any up-scale Italian restaurant. One of her dinner guests within the past few years had been a chef at one of those up-scale Italian restaurants and had requested…*pleaded* for the recipe. Camellia declined. Had the party been on a smaller scale, Camellia would have made one of her famous, fabulous desserts but this evening she had her favorite bakery design and prepare dozens of uniquely flavored and decorated petit-fours. Created from brightly colored icing, tiny animals of various species topped each pastry.

As was their custom, Max would greet the guests as they arrived. Camellia would always wait for the appropriate moment to make her grand entrance. She wanted to make sure she would have an audience. While Camellia did all the cooking for the meal, Max, as adept as he was at the bar, hired a bartender for the evening. This was one thing about which he and Camellia disagreed, but Max prevailed. Liquor would continue to flow as he and Camellia held court.

The first guests began to arrive. Show time! Max was the art director for a corrugated packaging company and his designers were, without fail, the first to arrive. Drinks were served and the conversations and laughter began. Pleasant chat and polite laughter would turn more raucous as the night progressed. Neighbors began to arrive, coats were collected and placed in a spare bedroom off the living room and more drinks were served. Camellia had placed trays of hors d'oeuvres throughout the house before she had departed to make herself ready. The house was beginning to fill. Closer friends of the Hollidays arrived, all of whom were greeted with much gusto by Max. The house was noisy.

Laughter, conversations and loud greetings as more friends joined the party sent the awaited signal upstairs. It was time for her entrance. Camellia started her descent down their grand staircase and made her appearance.

"Camellia!" shouted one of her dearest friends. "Happy New Year… and, oh, my god, you look divine!"

Other greetings were voiced and acknowledged. She always got the admiring reception she was seeking. She looked striking in a billowing, floor-length caftan of vivid colors. Multiple strands of long, dangling beads of all shapes and colors hung from her neck, cascading over her undulating breasts. A dozen jangling bracelets that clattered with each wave of her arms were on both wrists. She brandished a very long, jewel-encrusted cigarette holder. Her lips were fire engine red to match the color of her fingernails. She was topped off with a brilliantly colored turban.

"Camellia, darling," exclaimed one of her friends, looking her up and down, "you should be wearing plumes in your turban!"

"I considered it," Camellia responded, striking a pose," but I thought it would be too much."

Max and Camellia were gracious hosts. They both worked the room on opposite sides, drifting into one conversation after another and drifting out again to move on to the next little group. Max was bored easily by small talk. He would smile politely to the guests whose conversation he deemed to be superficial, beg to be excused and then he moved on. Camellia, on the other hand, found inane banter amusing. She would listen, laugh loudly, try to catch Max's eye from across the room, then wink at him and shake her head slowly. This was her signal that she had found some entertaining guests but perhaps he should keep his distance from this particular group. Camellia loved idle gossip about people in the entertainment world and especially those in the fashion industry. She landed in one conversation about the recent deplorable state of advertising in general and TV commercials in particular.

"I don't know," one guy was saying, "Maybe it's because I'm getting older. So many of those damn commercials leave me scratching my head. What the hell were they thinking? Whoever approved that crap? The concepts are terrible, the copy is terrible. But, hey, the special effects are great, though!"

Everybody laughed. And agreed.

"Not like back in your good old copywriting days, are they, Camellia? When folks knew what the hell the advertisers were selling. You sure knew how to turn a phrase. You certainly wrote some classic lines."

Camellia had to agree.

"Did you know," another guest was heard saying, "that there's a small town in Italy that has barred its residents from keeping goldfish in a curved bowl? Yes, that's true. Really! They say it's cruel to give the fish a distorted view of reality. Ha! I've had a distorted view of reality for years!"

"Well," laughed his wife, "that sure explains a lot of things, then!"

How many of *us* have a distorted view of reality? How many of us even recognize reality? But then, what do we actually see around us? Max pondered that thought for a moment. The mention of Italy triggered a memory. He had a quick flashback to the time he and Camellia were in Rome. They were riding the metro. He was always careful with his wallet when travelling abroad, especially in Italy, but on this particular day he had been careless. Max was observant. Max was standing. For some reason, he kept his eye on a young man seated just off to his side. The train stopped, Camellia stepped off onto the platform in front of Max. The young man stood, as if to get off, bumped slightly into Max, then looked as though this wasn't his stop after all and sat back down again, as Max got off the train. Max immediately realized that his wallet was gone. He turned to look at the train as it was slowly leaving the station. The young man was standing at the door and waved to Max as it disappeared into the tunnel. Realizing it was going to be a fruitless venture, they went to the police office at the metro station to report it. Max described the young man perfectly...so he thought. "He was about 5'9" or 10"...wearing a black t-shirt, black jeans and had a white iPod plugged into his ears." said Max to a very unsympathetic and bored-looking policeman. The policeman took notes, asked a few pointless questions, shook his head and offered an apology. Knowing that absolutely nothing would ever…*could* ever be done about it, they went about their business. Credit cards were immediately cancelled, a few euros were now missing, but Max's passport was elsewhere on his person and was safe. When they exited the police station Camellia said "That's funny. I could have sworn that young man was wearing beige." So who had a distorted view of reality?

The conversations and laughter grew louder as the drinks flowed. Camellia was in her glory. She had lost count regarding her favored martini and was feeling giddy. She held up her glass, peering through it to catch the sparkling Christmas tree lights.

"I hope whoever invented gin won a prize," she said to no one in particular. It was not the first time she had uttered this phrase, nor would it be the last. Guests who had overheard her laughed and raised their glasses in a toast to the various gods of booze.

As always with their parties, dinner would not be served until very late in the evening. An old friend caught Camellia's eye and she rushed to him.

"Marty!" she exclaimed, as she hugged him and gave her guest a big sloppy kiss on the cheek. Her bright red lip prints remained and she reached up to wipe them away. "Oh, look what I did," she said coyly.

"Don't you *dare* wipe them off," replied Marty. "That's a mark of honor tonight!" And they hugged each other again.

Camellia stepped back and then looked quizzically at his ears.

"Since when did you start wearing hearing aids, Marty?"

"Since I was nearly struck by lightning a couple months ago and the horrendous clap of thunder that followed did a little damage. Funny, though," he continued, "it mainly damaged my ability to hear or comprehend female voices."

"Gracious!" Camellia said, and then silently mouthed some words as though she were actually speaking to him.

"Ha, ha! Very funny," he said, shaking his head and rolling his eyes. They both laughed and hugged yet again.

"Does Maxwell know you're here?" asked Camellia, glancing around the room in search of her husband. Marty and Max worked together at the same company but in different divisions.

"I assume so," responded Marty, nodding in a direction. "He's over there hugging my wife half to death."

The Hollidays were city people, living in one of the toniest sections of Atlanta. The Howces lived in a fashionable suburb thirty-five miles out from the city. Marty remembered that when he had first invited the Hollidays out to their home for dinner years before, Max had commented about Camellia's aversion to anything remotely bucolic. They had arrived, nearly thirty minutes late, with Camellia looking somewhat frazzled. Although Marty had told them to dress casual, Max and his wife had dressed as though they had just stepped out of a Town & Country ad from the 1940s. Camellia then, as tonight, had left a bright red lip print on Marty's cheek when they first met. She was clutching a bouquet of fresh, but wilting, flowers, which she immediately handed to Jessie, Marty's wife.

"Here," she said, relinquishing the bouquet, "I hope they're not dead. Max told me you lived out in the country but I had no idea it was in Tennessee. I figured we must be getting close to your place when I spotted cows along the roadway."

They had all laughed about that first meeting for years afterwards. While they were a few years apart in ages, The Howces and the Hollidays hit it off right from the start and socialized often. But there were things that neither knew about the other.

Over the din, Camellia heard the doorbell and glanced at the wall clock. She smiled broadly and tried to get Max's attention. She did and mouthed the words "He's here," while pointing to the front door. Max loved to have little surprises for his guests and tonight would be a clever test. He and Camellia chuckled silently to themselves.

Camellia opened the door with a grand flourish. "Happy New Year, dear! You're right on time."

Stet Brandson and Mary Gordon stood together on the front porch. "Give me a big hug, dear," said Camellia. "Ooh, you're a tall one, aren't you?' she added, looking up at Mary.

"Mary," said Stet, "this is…"

"Camellia, dear…just Camellia. That's all you need to know," she said as she gave Stet a wink and a smile.

"Well, then," smiled Stet, "Camellia, this is Mary…just Mary. That's all you need to know." And they all laughed.

Camellia gave them each a hug, ushered them inside and took their coats. "We'll get a chance to chat in a while, dear," she said to Mary, "but your friend has a job to do and I want to introduce him. I'll have you meet Max in a minute and he can get a drink for you."

Stet had brought a large pack containing a stack of fine drawing paper, cut into 11" X 17" sheets. He also carried a new box of medium and fine-tipped black markers and a portable drawing board for stability. Camellia stood in the center of the living room, clutching the handle of an old school bell. She swung it and it rang loudly, jolting the nerves of everyone in the house. Conversations came to a halt. Drink glasses that had been heading towards lips stopped in their travels and held there.

"Ladies, gents…this young man," indicating Stet, "is our special guest tonight. He has a very fine talent. Well, one of several actually. He is a great caricaturist as well as a great artist. Max and I have several pieces of his work. He's going to spend a few hours here drawing anyone who might be interested. I can tell you, he is *very* good. Oh, his name is Stet, by the way."

"Well, I'll be damned!" Marty Howce exclaimed, as he poked his head in from another room. "Hey, Stet…Mary. I had no idea you were going to be here. When you said you were going to a party Jessie and I had no idea that it would ever be *this* one. Wow, Gary and Linda are here, too, somewhere. Small world, eh?"

Stet and Mary greeted the Howces. Max came over to them and introduced himself to Mary. "Well," he said as he shook her hand, "I may have fallen in love all over again."

"Oh, God, Mary," said Marty, laughing loudly, "watch out for him. He might look dapper, but he's a dirty old man!" Max shook his head, took Mary by the arm and led her to the bar. Stet was close behind.

"This is going to be so much fun, Camellia," said one of her guests. "You and Max are always *so* inventive with your parties."

Several other guests commented to Max and Camellia about this clever surprise.

Stet took a quick sip of his drink and gave Mary a kiss on the cheek. "It's show time," he whispered into her ear. "Remember what I told you about caricatures and women."

"Okay, folks," Stet said loudly. "I'm going to find a nice comfy chair in the sunroom. If anyone…and I sincerely hope that there will be a *lot* of you…is interested, come see me. I'll chat with you for a minute or so, to get to know a bit about you. Your interests, hobbies…whatever. Something to give me a clue about the *real* you…" at which point he laughed. "If you like, I can do husband and wife together, as a couple. Or not. Let's have some fun with this, gang!"

Stet found his place in a comfortable nook as the guests began to line up, eager for this artist to capture them. Camellia used this time to get the dinner in place, ready to be eaten after her guests had been charmed by Stet.

"Bring your drink and come chat with me, Mary," Camellia said as she grabbed Mary's elbow. Mary turned to glance in Stet's direction. The long line of guests waiting their turns amused her. She was eager to hear some of the reactions. As she turned back, the beautiful painting of a young woman with a horse caught her attention. Something about it looked familiar. I must remember to ask Camellia about it later, she thought to herself.

Mary followed Camellia back and forth between the kitchen and dining room, chatting excitedly the whole while. Camellia gave Mary a huge block of Parmigiano-Reggiano to grate and put into several little bowls, which were then placed around the table. Bowls of extra tomato sauce were placed near the trays of lasagna and an extremely large salad bowl contained leafy greens of various types. Cruets of salad dressing were moved from the refrigerator to the table as well. The entire house now smelled like the back alleys of Tuscany at dinnertime. The air was punctuated, from time to time, by loud guffaws and applause coming from the sunroom. Mary noticed that the loudest laughs were male. Then she realized that the *only* laughs she heard were male.

"I've got to sneak out there and see what's going on, do you mind?" she asked Camellia.

"No, no, dear, not at all…go ahead. I think you'll get a chuckle out of it. I know Max is. I'll be out there, too, in a minute or so to circulate."

Clusters of guests were comparing their caricatures. The men were laughing and slapping each other on their backs. The women, some of whom were amused, were not as vocal. Stet sat busily drawing and chatting with the guests. He would ask questions and sometimes the answers made him laugh. Mary could tell that he was having a very good time. She was amazed by how quickly he could capture the essence of a person from a few short bursts of information and observation. Stet had been drawing, non-stop, for an hour.

"Oh, God…this guy is so freakin' good!" "I haven't laughed so hard in years!" "How the hell does he do it…it's right on!" were some of the remarks that Mary overheard as she made her way towards Stet. "I'm framing this for my office.", "Yep, he's got my beer gut right!", "Damn, that is so funny!" "I *love* this guy!" Male voices. All male voices.

Female voices: "Do I really look like *that*?", "My nose isn't *that* big, is it?", "Oh, my God, I look like an alien!", "He made me look like a freak.", "Oh, I think *mine* is cute.", "Don't take yourself so seriously.", "I love it!."

Mary passed behind a group of ladies just at the moment one haughty-looking older woman huffed as she gazed at her caricature. She was dressed in a very tailored, buttoned-up-to-the-neck suit and sported a hairstyle that went out of fashion during the first Clinton administration.

"I'm a psychologist," she grunted, "and I can tell you that that young man does *not* like women."

Mary couldn't help but laugh out loud and nearly choked. "I'm so sorry for eavesdropping," she said, "but let *me* tell *you* from personal experience, he likes women. A lot!" She winked and kept walking.

Mary was able to glance at several of the sketches as she walked around the room, most of them being proudly displayed to everyone…proudly displayed by the men. There were characters on horseback, guys shooting hoops…swinging baseball bats…riding in sports cars…climbing the Great Pyramids of Egypt…surfing…women playing cards…shopping…taking yoga…and each one captured the person's face perfectly. Mary could recognize them all, especially one caricature of Gary and Linda Smart with a new baby in their arms.

Mary leaned against the doorjamb leading into the sunroom. Max came up beside her. "We need to get to know each other, young lady," he said with a warm smile. "Your young man has quite a gift, doesn't he?" As Stet finished each drawing, he signed it and gave the guest a plastic sleeve, so they could roll up their prize and transport it home without harm.

"His talent blows me away," replied Mary. "And, yes, I'd like to be able to chat with both you and your fabulous wife. It's been a little hectic here since we first walked through that front door. Goodness, you guys sure know how to throw a party!"

She was watching Stet as some of the men were actually returning to him, wanting another drawing with a different hobby as a theme.

"What made you decide about this gimmick for your party tonight, Max?"

"We've had psychics, poets, magicians and musicians of all types in past years. Ha! One year we had a hypnotist and that was hilarious. Had one of our guests tap dancing like she was five years old. Poor thing damn near fell into the Christmas tree. This was Camellia's idea, really. She hired Stet for one of her fashion events earlier this past year. Oh, the characters he had to deal with there, you can't imagine! He was a huge hit...with a few exceptions, as you *can* imagine," Max answered, as he tipped his head towards a group of gaggling ladies across the room. "You have *no* idea about the egos that abound in that profession. And the gender-bending scenarios add to the fun...and confusion. I'm a student of human behavior, as is your friend over there with the drawing pad. I love to laugh at their foibles and peccadilloes. Lord knows we all have them, that's for damn sure. Folks who can't laugh at themselves are obviously too self-indulgent...too preoccupied with their own importance. Whether it's real...or imagined...or desired. Who knows? We all wear masks of some kind. So many people try to be things they aren't. This certainly shouldn't come as a revelation to you, Mary. I have a feeling that you've been around the block. I don't mean that in a bad way, mind you. My beloved Camellia and I are certainly living, breathing caricatures, now, aren't we?" And with this he gave Mary a big wink and a nudge against her shoulder. "But, you know what? As flamboyant as you may think we are...and we *do* go over the top at times... we *are* genuine. This is who we are when there are a hundred people in the room, or whether it's just Camellia, the cat and me. As I said, there are so many nut cases out there trying to be things or someone they aren't. If your eyes have been open tonight, you've observed a lot of phoniness here. But, on the other hand, there are a lot of really, really nice, true folks here tonight. Fortunately, they outnumber the idiots in the house. Camellia and I both look forward to this feast of fools every year. It helps to remind us who *we* are...and how to appreciate each other even more. We're never disappointed."

Camellia mingled with her guests and chatted with one group after another. She was moving closer to one of the newer couples in their neighborhood. They were a middle-aged German couple who had recently moved from the New York area. Camellia found them rather snooty but, being they were new to the neighborhood, it might be a good way for others to meet them. The husband and wife were holding glasses of red wine. He leaned into his wife and said, none to quietly, *"Das ist sehr gewöhnlicher wein"*, ("This is very ordinary wine"). Camilla glanced at them, they both raised their glasses to her, as in a toast and each sipped as they smiled at her. She, too, smiled and raised her glass in return. She mingled for a few more minutes before heading off into the kitchen.

Shortly, Camellia announced that dinner was ready. She had carried steaming hot trays of lasagna from the kitchen and placed them on the dining room table. She also noted to everyone that midnight was a mere forty-five minutes away. Some of the guests made their way to the food while others lingered with Stet. The lasagna smelled delicious and was beautifully presented at opposite ends of the decorated table. Next to the stack of plates and silverware on a side table was a stack of papier-mâché masks. The masks were of various animals, wild and domestic, done in the design style reminiscent of the 1940s.

"Please get yourself a mask from the table," announced Camellia as she directed their attention to the assortment, "At midnight, put on your mask and let out the loudest sound you can make, just like the animal that you'll have on your face."

She eased close to Mary. "This was Max's idea," she said sotto voce.

Sometimes creativity overrides logic.

Guests located places throughout the house to sit and enjoy their meals. Mary walked towards Stet as he was finishing up another caricature. But no one was with him. This one he did from memory. He held it up as Mary approached. It was perfect. There, in vivid black and white, were Camellia, flowing robes, dangling necklaces, holding her glass to the heavens and Max, twirling his moustache and casting a loving eye at his wife. Mary's eyes glistened.

"That's just beautiful, Stet. God, you're so perfect, aren't you?" she said softly.

"Oh, hell, no!" laughed Stet. "I might be good but I'm not perfect." He stood up, took her in his arms and kissed her passionately.

"Sorry to disagree with you, Captain America, but I happen to think you're perfect," Mary whispered. "Come on, let's eat."

The dinner was done; the guests were talking and laughing…some still bragging about their treasured drawings…as Camellia announced that midnight was one minute away. "Make sure to get your champagne…and get your masks ready!"

The countdown was on. Max stood in the center of the living room, looking at his watch as the seconds ticked away.

"Five…four…three…two…one…Happy New Year! Up with your masks!"

Everyone took swigs of champagne, kissed their respective partners and put on their animal masks, laughing harder and harder as they glanced around the room. Then the zoo came alive. Squeals, squeaks, moos, barks, meows, roars, heehaws, whinnies and braying shattered the sound barrier. Cell phones came out of pockets and pictures were taken over and over again. Selfies to laugh at or be embarrassed by for years to come. Max simply watched, laughed and shook his head. Camellia went in search of another martini as all of the animals began singing auld lang syne.

Mary and Stet had found Gary, Linda, Marty and Jessie and sat with them. Mary wore a horse's mask. Stet had found a tiger; Marty, a zebra; Jessie was a giraffe; Linda, an elephant and Gary was a chimpanzee.

"What the hell does a giraffe sound like?" Marty asked Jessie.

"Damned if I know," answered his wife. "I faked it, just grunted and hoped for the best."

The cacophony died down within a couple minutes and slowly the masks came off…some guests simply pushing their masks back up onto their heads.

Clusters of conversation resumed. Camellia announced that coffee had been brewed and was ready and that the dessert was now in the dining room. The beautiful petit fours, with the tiny frosting animals atop each, related to the celebration perfectly. Camellia was the busiest hostess that Mary had ever known.

Camellia walked past a group of guests discussing their views on reincarnation. Max was involved with this one, too. Marty overheard the topic and slid himself into the group as well.

Camellia struck a regal pose and said, "I just know that in a former life I was a queen!"

"Big deal," remarked one of the guests in the group. "I have a brother who's one in *this* life!"

Everybody roared with laughter.

"You know," Marty interjected, "I have a theory about reincarnation and time travel."

His little group turned to listen intently. Perhaps it was the lateness of the evening combined with the alcohol.

"I just know that someday we'll break the time barrier. But what about when we die? Everybody thinks that time moves forward. That it's linear. Everybody who believes in reincarnation thinks that if, say, I died tonight that I'd be born again maybe next year…or the day after tomorrow. But who's to say that if I died tonight I wouldn't be born again back in 1857? Perhaps that's how all these prophets see the future. They have been reincarnated backwards in time. They aren't seeing the future at all. They are simply digging up some recessed, repressed memories from their previous past."

There was absolute silence.

Suddenly Max blurted out a loud, "Ha! That's the dumbest thing I ever heard."

"More dessert, anyone?" Camellia called out, and headed back to the dining room.

It was nearly three o'clock in the first morning of the new year. Most of the guests had sobered up enough to head to their respective homes.

The German couple thanked both Max and Camellia and headed towards the front door. Camellia, ever the gracious hostess, followed them smiling broadly. As the gentleman leaned in to kiss Camellia on the cheek, she whispered into his ear "Entschuldige den wein. Viel glück beim nächsten mal" (*"Sorry about the wine. Better luck next time"*). Camellia spoke fluent German. And French. And a smattering of Arabic. The man pulled back suddenly, staring at her. He turned crimson, then he laughed loudly, gave Camellia a very tight hug, kissed her on both cheeks and giggled foolishly as he and his wife hurried out the front door. Camellia shook her head and returned back to her remaining guests. "Arschloch", she muttered under her breath.

The small group from the stable hugged and kissed each other and wished each well in the coming year. It was sure to be a better one ahead. Those were the hopes that we all have every January first. Mary offered to help Camellia with the horrendous task of cleaning up but it was declined.

"Oh, thanks, dear, but I have my own system. I appreciate your offer but, frankly, you'd get in my way," she smiled broadly. "I mean that in a good way, though. Please don't be offended."

Mary laughed a tired laugh. "Nope. No offense taken. I understand perfectly. You have a fascinating place here. I'm sorry we didn't get more of an opportunity to talk tonight but, my goodness, you were *so* busy and your friends were so eager to trap me to hear more about Stet."

Camellia paused and smiled. "He *is* such a good boy, isn't he? We've been…ummm…friends for a long time."

Mary thought for a moment. "Camellia, are you…,"

Stet's voice interrupted her question.

"Hey, it's really time to say goodnight Gracie now, ladies," he said. "This guy's hand is about worn out. And, believe it or not, I think I'm going hoarse from all the talk tonight."

He approached Mary from behind, put his arms around her and squeezed, nestling his head on her shoulder.

"Camellia, as always, your parties will leave 'em talking for days," he said. "Thanks a bunch for the gig. I enjoyed every minute, if I do say so myself."

"Max has an envelope for you, dear," Camellia responded, "but I think he's passed out in the living room."

"I won't disturb his highness. I'll catch up with him sometime soon."

Stet leaned down and kissed the hostess on the cheek. She gave him a great big bear hug, burying her face in his chest.

"Damn! This place is a mess," Stet remarked as he and Mary walked toward the front door, putting on their coats as they walked.

"Only way to have a party, dear," Camellia retorted. "If the house is neat when they all leave, then it must have been a boring-as-hell party, that's all *I* can say. Now I'll have to go and count my silverware. Some of these folks tonight I wouldn't trust with a nickel," she said with a sly grin. "Mary, should I check *your* pockets before you get outta here?" Then she laughed loudly.

"You're a sweetheart, Camellia," Mary called as she and Stet walked down the sidewalk to their car. "I sure hope to see you both again sometime soon."

"You will, dear. I'm sure you will." And Camellia disappeared behind the closing door.

JANUARY...AGAIN

Major Changes

"If you don't like something, change it. If you can't change it, change your attitude."

Maya Angelou

The offer came out of the blue and took Remy Major totally by surprise. A developer had contacted Remy a few years earlier about buying the property on which CedarView stood. Remy had rejected the offer outright because, at that time, he was not interested in selling. Today's phone call left Remy shaken and conflicted. The prospect of the stable being demolished and replaced by thirty houses was presented to him in succinct terms. The price offered was impressive, though not as much as he thought the land was worth. Remy had hated the property for years but, with Zara now gone, he somehow felt more connected to it than ever before. It was where she "lived" every day. His torment was great. He missed her. As tragic as their past had been, he had reconciled with the demons that had torn their marriage apart. He and his daughters had resolved their respective issues. He mellowed. He changed. The telephone call was unsettling, to say the least. How could this be, he thought? He had actually grown closer to all the boarders. If he sold, obviously, the boarders would have to find other stables. They would be out of his life, probably forever. But what would his life be if he held on to the stable? Why would he even do that? He would have to give this turn of events some serious consideration.

Three hours later he was on the telephone again.

Marty Howce was being bombarded with questions from his designer, Peter Scott. Rumors had been circulating for weeks about a possible, imminent purchase of Compton Packaging by a holding company from New York City.

"Sorry, Peter," he told him, "I know about as much as you do. I'm out of the loop as far as that kind of information is concerned. In my book, no news is good news. People always seem to shudder in fear when they hear the word *change*. Change can be a good thing, too, you know. Or not. As soon as I hear anything, one way or the other, I'll let you know."

In fact, Marty knew exactly what was going to happen but was sworn to confidentiality. His close friendship with the upper management team allowed him access to very intimate details. Even the rumors on Wall Street were inaccurate. A rival packaging company was purchasing Compton. The very rival that Compton had mocked a mere five years earlier for inefficiency and shoddy product had, now, surpassed them in every way to become a very major player. A sharp, shrewd younger sales team had beaten out the "old guys" at Compton time and time again. Compton had been embarrassed over the past couple of years by quality issues, the news of which circulated throughout the industry like a plague. The sad truth was that Compton hadn't kept up with all the latest production technology. The economic downturn in the industry in general had made Compton far too conservative in capital investments for the needed improvements. Their rival had *not* been conservative. They had branched out from the standard offset and gravure printing into digital and wide-format printing, with sleek, new, jaw-dropping presses. Something that Compton had eschewed. It had now come back to bite them in the ass.

There was much duplication in departments, locations and responsibilities between the two companies. Marty was getting himself mentally prepared for being terminated and, perhaps, dedicating all of his time to his freelance accounts. He wasn't certain about the rest of his coworkers. One thing *definitely* certain, though, was that major changes lay ahead for everyone at Compton.

Stet had watched Gracie for weeks, as she still seemed to search for her lost friend. At least once a day she would let out a loud whinny as if calling to him. She waited for an answer in vain.

"Hey, gorgeous," he said into the telephone when Mary answered. "Whatcha up to this afternoon?"

"Oh, just trying to update my résumé," she said plaintively. "I think it's about time I re-enter the work force. Not the best of times for an old broad to go looking, I know, but it's worth a shot."

"What old broad are you talking about?" he shot back, "Your mother?"

"Funny," she laughed, "Funny."

"You have a marketing background, right?" he asked.

"Yeah…why? Do you know someone who's hiring?"

"Well…" he started, "I've been giving this a lot of thought lately and I want to run something by you. I've been pretty scatter-shot with my work over the years. You know, with my paintings and such. I've been in a few gallery shows and arts festival kinda shit. But…" he trailed off.

"But?" she questioned, wondering where this was going.

"I want to open my own gallery," he blurted out. "I want to show and sell *my* stuff, of course, but I want to introduce fresh, young talent to the market. I think the time is right for this. And, believe it or not, I think I've found a place. Actually, I have a couple of backers as well."

"And…?" she prodded.

"And…I need a manager. Somebody with marketing savvy and, frankly, I'm looking for sex appeal up front. And, guess what? You got it, babe!"

"Ha! Are you saying that you'll *hire* me?"

"Well, I *do* need to see some credentials, of course," he teased. "Meet me in my bedroom at six o'clock this afternoon…oh, and be naked."

"Jesus Christ! Sexual harassment and I haven't even been interviewed yet! I'll have to alert the media."

"Oh, lady. Just you wait to see what kind of sexual harassment I'm capable of." and they both laughed uncontrollably.

"Actually," Stet continued, turning serious for a moment. "I called with something else in mind as well…but you distracted me with your nakedness."

"Oh, please. I did no such thing," and she laughed again. "Okay, so what was the *real* reason for this intimidating call?"

"Well, poor Gracie gets lonelier and lonelier every day. It breaks my heart to see her…and hear her looking for George. She needs company and I was wondering if you'd be willing to move Thunder up here?"

"Oh, wow. Hmm…I don't know. That would be a bit further for me to drive every day to take care of him and ride him. CedarView is so much closer to where I live."

"Damn. I guess I was a bit too subtle in my question. Or maybe I better reconsider my offer about that manager position. I thought you were smart." And he laughed very loudly.

"Oh, shit," said Mary, with an embarrassed tone. "Wait. I missed something, didn't I? Were you asking *me* to move there too?"

"Well, duh. Hello in there!"

"Stet, I'm sorry. I guess you *were* a tad too subtle. Well…now I *really* have to think about this."

"Hey, no hurry with your answer. Really. I can wait thirty seconds or so."

And there was silence after their laughter.

"I have to go to a meeting that Remy has called for all of us boarders. We all have to be over at the stable around three this afternoon. He wants to talk to us in person, as a group. We are all speculating about some changes coming up. We don't know if he's sold the place…if he's *going* to sell the place…or what. It's anybody's guess. You know, he's not been the easiest of guys to get close to, but he's changed since Zara's accident. I'll call you after the big pow-wow."

"Don't call…just come up here. Oh, and I wasn't kidding about that naked comment."

"How do you feel about Chicago?" Gary asked Linda.

Gary had emerged from an hours-long meeting and immediately called home. The rumors had been correct, up to a point. Compton was being bought out. Changes, transfers and terminations were put into place. He had impressed all the right people with his performance over the years, especially at the most recent sales meeting. Pirate Pete was being rewarded with a promotion in the newly formed takeover. It did involve a move, however. He and Linda had discussed this possibility often throughout his career, knowing that moving from place to place was an inevitable part of the climb up the corporate ladder.

"Great city," she answered, "sure does get cold there during the winter, though."

"Yeah, colder than a stepmother's kiss for damn sure," he laughed, "and a hell of a lot more expensive than down here, too…but…"

"I know, I know. We need to really talk about this, Gary. It's something great for you and our future, but it *is* a big move. Alex will have to start rooting for different teams along with you, I guess. Hope your new company realizes it will be paying to move a horse as well. Poor thing will have to grow a thicker winter coat from now on."

"Hey, that reminds me. I know you have to head over to the stable soon for that meeting with Remy. Wonder what *that's* all about? Sorry I can't go too, but I'm heading out with a couple of the guys for a beer or two. I won't be late. He glanced at his watch. I'll be home before Mickey's big hand is on twelve and his little hand is on nine, I promise, and we'll talk when I get home. Let's really give this some serious consideration. I love ya, sweet girl. Give Alex a big kiss for me too."

"Love you too, Gary. I'm so proud of you."

"God damn!" said Max to Marty over lunch. They were dining at one of Buckhead's trendiest restaurants and figured the company could afford one last expensive fling. "I felt like I was hit over the head with a baseball bat. Turning me out to pasture. One day I'm Max Holliday, art director… the next day I'm Max Holliday, nobody."

"Tell me about it, my friend, I know exactly how you feel," answered Marty as he took a sip of his second gin and tonic. "Max, you'll *never* be a nobody, though. But let's be fair. We saw this coming. We're not too dumb to have missed the handwriting on the wall."

"True," said Max dejectedly, "but it still hurts the old ego, doesn't it? Oh, don't even bother to answer that. It was just a stupid rhetorical question."

"And I was about to give you a stupid rhetorical answer," responded an equally dejected Marty. "Here's to us!" He raised his gin and tonic and clinked glasses with Max's martini.

"You know," Marty started, as he glanced at his drink, "I think I read somewhere that drinking gin is a good prevention against colds during the winter. Something, I guess, having to do with the botanicals in it."

Max narrowed his eyes, then gave him the squinty-eyed "you've-got-to-be-shitting me" look. He rolled his eyes and shook his head.

"I'm not terribly sure that that's true, Marty. Really. Sounds kinda fishy to me. Something the gin association cooked up. But…" he shrugged, "if indeed that's accurate, you, me…and Camellia should be healthy as horses this winter!"

They laughed, downed their drinks and signaled their server for another round.

"I will say," Max continued, getting back to the subject of their job losses, "they are more than fair about this. I *did* get a pretty good put-you-out-to-pasture package out of this. And, actually…I had been thinking about perhaps taking an early retirement. This just seems to nail the decision for me…okay, a bit sooner than I had thought. But…what the hell. Life moves on." And he let out a big sigh.

"Yep, me too. The package will help while I get my freelance ducks in a row," Marty replied after taking another gulp of his drink. "Poor Peter Scott, though…the kid with two first names. He hasn't been onboard all that long. My designer…well, my soon to be ex-designer, got a week's vacation pay and a handshake along with his good-bye. He's good, with a terrific portfolio. He'll find something soon. The young bounce back quickly. Not terribly sure how to take what he said to me about the situation, though.

"Oh?" queried Max.

"Yeah. He thanked me profusely for helping to get his career off to a great start. Then he said he felt sad because *my* career was winding down. Winding *down*? That statement made me feel like I was a hundred and ten years old. The little twit. Oh, well…as you just said, life moves on."

"How's Jessie taking this?" Max asked Marty.

"Humph" Marty grunted. "As well as can be expected, I guess. She does *not* take well to change. Never has. Hell, she stopped shopping at Kroger months ago because they changed the layout of their damn store."

"Seriously?"

"Seriously…I kid you not. She'll get over it. Always has. Just takes time. She's stressed out. But she'll be fine. I assume Camellia has taken it in stride?"

"Oh, hell, yes," Max responded quickly and with a broad smile on his face. "Nothing rattles that old girl…except perhaps a couple of obnoxious German neighbors on rare occasion." He relayed the New Year's departure story to Marty and they both howled with laughter.

They both sipped their drinks and sat quietly for a few moments, reflecting on their respective pasts. And futures.

Marty pulled a large binder out of an old attaché case that he had brought with him to the restaurant. It had been put under the table to discuss after a few drinks. He set in on the table in front of Max, who looked at it questioningly.

"Hope you don't have a bomb in there and plan on blowing us both to kingdom come," Max said with a grin, "along with all these other fine folks enjoying their over-priced luncheons."

"I want you to do me a favor, Max. Well, actually more Camellia than you. She was the copywriter. I need a professional opinion."

"What the hell *is* that?" asked Max as he eyed a manuscript.

"Well," Marty started, a bit sheepishly, "I've been secretly writing a book. The ideas have been sloshing around in my brain for years. I finally concocted a sort-of novel out of the whole mess. I want you both to read it and tell me, honestly, truthfully what you think. Pull no punches."

Max opened the cover of the binder. The title caught his eye immediately: *"Stable Affairs"*.

"Damn," he said with a devilish glint in his eye. "My mind is racing already. Any juicy stuff in here? Any shades of gray? Any riding crops involved? Any girl-on-girl action?"

"Max! NO! Jesus. But really, please tell me what you think. Let me know what has to be fleshed out and what has to be flushed out."

"And then what?" Asked Max.

Marty shrugged. "I don't know," he responded. "I. Really. Don't. Know." Each word its own sentence. "I've had a lot of fun writing it. It's been good therapy. Maybe I'll try to self-publish. Maybe it'll hit the trash compactor. Hell, maybe I'll win a Pulitzer!"

Max chuckled. "Have another gin and tonic, Hemingway," he said, raising his glass. "Here's to fame and fortune."

Jessica hadn't spoken to either Mary Pat or Mary Anne since a few weeks after Zara's death. She had volunteered to help at the stable any way she could and did so for a week. Then she got involved in her own life and time passed before she realized it. Things were changing in the Howce household. Change…change of any kind, always frazzled her. She didn't know why. That was just part of her nature. She glanced at her watch and saw that it was getting close to the time she needed to be leaving for the stable…and Remy's strange meeting. She punched in Mary Anne's number on speed dial and caught her just as she, too, was about to leave for the stable.

"Hey, you. Where *have* you been?" asked Mary Anne. "Thought you must have dropped off the planet for a while. You okay?"

"Oh, yeah," answered Jessie, with a little sigh. "I'm so sorry. Just been sort of crazy around here lately. Changes are happening and, well, I sorta get stressed out with change. Any change. I know, it's no excuse for not helping Remy more. I know that you, Mary Pat and Mary have been big helps to him, and that's great. How's he doing? How's he holding up?"

"Strange. He's been sort of strange. I guess it's because we're spending more time with him. He's opening up to us like never before. I have no idea why he wants to meet with all of us, do you?"

"Honestly, I don't," replied Jessie.

"We all sort of suspect that he might have sold the place." Mary Anne continued. "He had been hinting about that and about developers in the past...but, hell, that'll be so sad, though. That'll mean we'll all have to find new places for our horses. We're all like a family...as you well know. Well, all except that asshole Rance. Remy's sold most of Zara's horses. And given a few away, too...to kids in the area. Hey, we both need to get going. You can fill me in on what's going on in *your* world when we get to the stable."

"Sure," Jessie replied, "and then we can...what the hell was that?" She was interrupted by the sound of breaking glass. "Shit, Mary Anne. Now I have to go and see what just happened. I think those damn cats must have broken something. Talk to you there. Bye!"

As much as she searched the house, she couldn't find broken glass anywhere. And the two cats were sleeping, side-by-side, on the recliner in the sunroom.

Rance's new year got off to a horrible start. An anonymous phone call to the police department, from a phone with caller ID blocked, had alerted the authorities about some possible marijuana dealings at a local bottle shop. The operator at the front desk who took the call was skeptical. Something about the call just didn't seem right, but she routed it along to someone who handles drug violations. At first the officer who then took the call was very dubious. The voice sounded like a young kid, of undetermined gender. Probably a prank he thought. He logged it in and thought about it. Although he didn't frequent that shop, he knew of the owner. The asshole who caused a disturbance a few months back by frightening some innocent kids at a party. On a whim, he decided to stop by the shop. He was accompanied by his drug-sniffing K-9 "partner". It was not a good day for Rance.

Remy arrived at the stable well ahead of the time he had requested, three o'clock. Uncharacteristically, he brought a thirty-cup coffee urn and had it brewing. He had stopped off on the way to CedarView and purchased three dozen fresh Krispy Kreme glazed donuts. The "HOT" sign was blinking and he couldn't resist. He was nervous about this meeting, but he had his little speech all prepared. He had given so much thought to this situation over the past couple of weeks, since his phone calls and meetings. He wanted to sell. He didn't want to sell. He wished he could move a million miles away and forget the tragedy. He wished he were young again. He wished Zara had not been killed. If wishes were horses, beggars would ride. Where had he heard that? The decision was made. Every decision we make leads to an alternate universe.

The boarders were curious when Remy had called all of them. He had never summoned them to the stable for a meeting before. They all felt this was a very mysterious thing and had them confused. Telephone calls flew from boarder to boarder. Whispering was done when they bumped into one another while at the stable. There were rampant rumors about an imminent sale. Maybe Remy had been harboring a dreaded illness all this time and hence his grumpy attitude for years. Rumors beget fears and fabricated scenarios.

Remy paced nervously in the dusty tack room. It smelled of leather, Neat's Foot Oil, horse feed and, now, fresh coffee. There were a few folding chairs that he had set up, but he thought most of the boarders would remain standing anyway. He heard the first car slowly ease its way down the gravel driveway and come to a stop. He recognized Amber's car. She parked and slowly headed toward the tack room. She had been particularly distraught by the accident. She had often confided in Zara about her relationships. Amber seemed so conflicted, at times, between her own goals and those of her boyfriends. Remy overheard many of those conversations. He remembered one in particular. "We need to take ownership of our own destiny, sweetie," Zara had told Amber.

Don't I know it, thought Remy.

The tack room was filling up, Remy greeting each arrival with a firm handshake and a smile. This made them very suspicious. Is this the Remy we've known all these years? It was a cold, bleak afternoon and the coffee was a welcome surprise. They remarked about the donuts also, each person licking the sweet sugary glaze from their fingers as they downed donut after donut. The mood got almost party-like. Almost. They were here for a yet-to-be determined reason. Was it good news? Bad news? No news? Jessie and Amber stood side-by-side talking about the weather; Mary, Mary Pat and Mary Anne were huddled together whispering and giggling about Stet's recent invitation this afternoon; Julia, without Rance, stood alone, arms folded; Linda Smart, holding baby Alex, leaned up against a wall, close to the space heater that was warming the chilly tack room.

"Okay, folks," Remy started, after clearing his throat once, then again. "I know this is a very strange situation, calling you all here like this. I simply wanted to talk to you face to face. I guess I should really start with a major apology. No pun intended. An apology for my behavior to all of you over the years. This has been a very rough year. Well, several years actually. I want to set the scene and get to the reasons why I've made the decision I've made."

Bryan Dennison and his wife Brandy came hurrying through the tack room door. "Sorry we're late, Remy," said Bryan, "hope we didn't miss anything." Bryan spotted the donuts and hastened in their direction.

Remy smiled at them, nodded and continued.

"They say...whoever 'they' may be...that confession is good for the soul. Some of you *might* know, but I doubt most of you know, that Zara was an alcoholic. She...*we* wrestled with it for years. When we lived up in Pennsylvania. When she drank, she became abusive. To me. To the girls. Especially to Kristine."

The boarders were getting a little uncomfortable hearing this. Some that were standing shifted their weight from side to side.

"We moved south. Zara had always loved horses, so I bought her one. To help keep her occupied and away from the bottle. Yes, she had been to rehab. A couple times. But nothing seemed to be permanent until she got a horse. Then another. And another. I bought the stable to *really* keep her busy. As you must have guessed, I hated it. Never was much for horse shit...literally." That brought a nervous laugh.

He paused a moment to collect his thoughts and cleared his throat again.

"Unfortunately, Zara and I never got the opportunity to resolve our issues. That regret I will take with me to my grave. But...as a result of

Zara's horrible tragedy and some wonderful, caring boarders, I made a discovery. You are all good friends. Despite the way I behaved in the past, you stuck with me…with this turmoil, with my torment. You were all good friends to Zara. She loved you. Oh, she may have talked about you behind your backs at times…but she cherished your friendships. She wanted to know all about you…your ups, your downs. Whatever. I missed years of opportunities with you. And years of opportunities to open up about the secret that Zara and I had been harboring. Another regret"

He took a quick sip of his now-cold coffee and cleared his throat for the big announcement. All eyes were on him. Here it comes.

"Okay, so we have arrived at a turning point. The reason why I called you here in the first place. Kiddingly or otherwise, I've threatened about selling this place to developers for years. Right? You've all heard my ranting, haven't you?"

There were nods all around. Nervous nods.

"Well, a couple weeks ago I *did* get a call…and an offer from a developer. It was a decent enough offer, too. They want to demolish this place and build about thirty or so homes here."

There was deathly silence and everyone seemed to stop breathing.

"You can't believe the number of times I've been on the telephone the past few days. You can't believe the number of meetings I've had. But… after much discussion and consideration…" he paused.

A horse whinnied in the distance, breaking the silence.

"I have decided to sell CedarView."

There were gasps and a couple of "oh, no's"…and at least one soft sob. Aside from the hum of the space heater, the room became deathly silent. Disappointed faces stared at Remy.

"However," continued Remy, putting his hands up, trying to calm his boarders, "I have *not* sold out to the developers. I couldn't bring myself to doing that. Not to you. Not to all these horses…and especially to this beautiful piece of property. Perhaps, sometime in the future that might happen. I guess we can't stop progress. With progress comes inconvenience, at times. But…that's *not* today!"

There were looks of confusion and relief as the boarders all looked at one another, then turned to face Remy once more as he continued with his remarks.

"As fate would have it, not too long after I had received that call from the developer, I got another call. From someone with whom I've been chatting in the past about wanting to sell and get the hell outta Dodge. Someone who is looking for a purpose in life. We had a very...*very* long conversation. Several of them, as a matter of fact. Obviously the offer wasn't nearly as large as the one to turn this place into rubble, but I didn't care. Money isn't the issue. Okay, I've kept you in suspense long enough. And I know your emotions have run the gamut from low to high and back down again within the past five minutes. I have accepted a very gracious and generous offer from that beautiful couple over there," and he pointed to Bryan and Brandy Dennison, "Bryan and his wife are now...or soon will be...the new owners of CedarView."

The tack room burst into cheers, applause and tears of joy and congratulations. Hugs all around for everyone. Bryan's hand was shaken so hard he winced and Brandy was hugged so hard she squealed with laughter. The barn cats, Spook and Shadow, ran to hide from the racket. Oedipus Pex, who had been scrounging around outside the tack room looking for bits of feed, stretched his head up as high as it would go and let out a loud crow. Mother Clucker was nowhere in sight.

"Bryan, by the way," interrupted Remy, "is a far better handy man with a hammer and nails than I ever was or wanted to be. He's already told me about all the improvements he wants to make around here. And I'm not going to disappear entirely. I'll pop in from time to time to say hello. And please remember to invite me to all the parties you guys have around here. Especially that Fourth of July shindig. Perhaps this year I'll even contribute to your drunken rambling and ranting."

Hardy laughter filled the air. Remy's back was slapped, his hand was shaken and hugs were given again. The boarders took their turns in congratulating Remy for his decision and then congratulating Bryan and Brandy for theirs. The coffee urn was drained...the donut cartons were empty but no one was eager to leave this now-happy event. Cue the soundtrack. Jazz. Always cool jazz. Perhaps Coltrane this time. Some things were resolved, others not. Well, that's life.

It was late in the afternoon and the horses were getting restless. The sky, that had been a milky white earlier in the day, was turning a darker gray and becoming heavy with the threat of rain. The horses could sense that it was nearing feeding time. They jostled for position at the battered metal gate leading from the pasture to the stable area and their awaiting stalls. Their only instincts now were hunger and impatience, with neither a thought about yesterday nor a care about tomorrow.

AUTHOR'S NOTES

I, personally, have been involved in the world of horses and graphic design for decades. The pleasures and rewards that I've derived from both are immeasurable. The people and horses I have met on my journey have left indelible marks on my heart and I am forever grateful.

This is my first book. Honestly, it's probably my one and only book. Hey, look…I said in the introduction that I've been working on *this* book for 15 years or so. I'm now almost 77. What are the odds?

By the way, did you happen to count the number of different "scents" I mentioned throughout the book? Including the various horse scents, there were 32. Seriously.

As I previously stated, I've taken some liberties with reality and logic. Here's another such departure. Should a potential blockbuster movie ever be made from this insightful book, following is my fantasy all-star cast for all my characters:

Jeremy (Remy) Major – Tommy Lee Jones
Zara Major – Laura Dern
Kristine (their younger daughter) – Jennifer Anniston
Taylor (their eldest daughter) – Courtney Cox
Marty Howce – Armie Hammer
Marty (at 15) – Timothée Chalamet

Jessica (Jessie) Howce – Evangeline Lilly

Carson Howce (Marty's father) – John Belushi

Seranda Howce (Marty's mother) – Melissa McCarthy

Garrett Howce (Marty's brother) – Jim Belushi

Peter Scott (Freelance Designer) – Ansel Elgort

Amber Givings – Sandra Dee

Roger Givings (Amber's father) – Jeff Foxworthy

Lacey Givings (Amber's mother) – Ellen Degeneres

Raymond Futtz – Andrew Rannells

Mary Anne Forde – Reese Witherspoon

Mary Pat Phillips – Jennifer Lawrence

Just Plain Mary Gordon – Gal Gadot

Stet Brandson – Henry Cavill

Don Edwards, an EMT – Philip Seymour Hoffman

Doctor Morrison, a veterinarian – Alexander Skarsgard

Veronika Snapp – Linda Hunt

Rance Hurakon – Adrien Brody

Julia Constance (Rance's wife) – Bryce Dallas Howard

Bryan Dennison – Kenneth Branagh

Brandy Dennison – Emma Thompson

Cliff Ambridge (Brandy's father) – Hume Cronyn

Sara Ambridge (Brandy's mother) – Jessica Tandy

Young Woman in Little Red Sports Car – Selena Gomez

Gary Smart – Ryan Gosling

Linda Smart – Emma Stone

Libby Smart (Gary's mother) – Stockard Channing

Max Holliday – Monty Wooley (GOOGLE him…he's perfect!)

Camellia Holliday – Shelley Winters

And Katharine Hepburn as Mrs. Critchley

ACKNOWLEDGEMENTS

This has been an extraordinary experience. This book might sell zero copies, but I've had a tremendous amount of fun writing it. It was great therapy, not that I needed therapy, mind you!

I have to thank and commend my loving wife, Gaylin, for putting up with my shenanigans for 55 years of marriage and 7 years of friendship prior to that. She will always be the absolute best friend I have ever had. Her patience is amazing. She's also quite an accomplished equestrian, by the way.

I may not have been the perfect father for our two sons, Gregory and Christopher, but I've tried my best. I certainly learned a new meaning of love when they both came along. Maybe *they* learned a thing or two along the way. They both turned out to be exemplary men and fathers, extremely successful in their respective careers. Maybe because of me or in spite of me. Whatever. And I hope that our grandchildren have learned some things from me along the way as well. Although I strongly doubt that any of them remember our very short French lesson.

Printed in the United States
By Bookmasters